W9-BRO-680

IF YOU'RE READING THIS

TRENT REEDY

ARTHUR A. LEVINE BOOKS
AN IMPRINT OF SCHOLASTIC INC.

Library of Congress Cataloging-in-Publication Data

Reedy, Trent, author.
If you're reading this / Trent Reedy. — First edition.
pages cm
Summary: For a responsible sixteen-year-old, Michael Wilson has a lot of problems — his father was killed in Afghanistan in 2005, his overworked and overprotective mother will not talk about their situation, and does not want him playing football, and he has suddenly started to receive letters that his father wrote before his death.
ISBN 978-0-545-43342-6
1. Last letters before death — Juvenile fiction. 2. Families — Iowa — Juvenile fiction. 3. Mothers and sons — Juvenile fiction. 4. Soldiers — Family relationships — Juvenile fiction. 5. High schools — Juvenile fiction. 6. Iowa — Juvenile fiction. [1. Letters — Fiction. 2. Family life — Iowa — Fiction. 3. Mothers and sons — Fiction. 4. Soldiers — Fiction. 5. High schools — Fiction. 6. Schools — Fiction. 7. Iowa — Fiction.] I. Title. II. Title: If you are reading this.
PZ7.R25423If 2014
813.6 — dc23
2013045430

10 9 8 7 6 5 4 3   15 16 17 18
Printed in the U.S.A.   23
First edition, September 2014
The text was set in Sabon,
with the display font set in Flyerfonts.
Book design by Chris Stengel

This book is dedicated to the memory and honor of
Sergeant Seth Garceau (1982–2005) of Alpha Company,
224th Engineer Battalion, in Davenport, Iowa . . .

to all those who never made it home . . .

and to all the children everywhere who have suffered
because of our long wars.

May all of you always be remembered.

May all of us find our way toward peace.

ONE

My father had been dead seven years the day his first letter arrived. But before I received the message that would change my life so much, tenth grade started out like any other.

At lunchtime, I sat down next to Ethan Jones. "Hey, Mike." He flicked a chicken nugget with his finger. "Can you believe they feed us this crap? There's no actual food in this food."

I picked up a nugget and took a bite, but chomped down on one of those tiny hard pieces and spat the gristle into a napkin. "I think they're supposed to be educational. Life is like a high school chicken nugget." I smiled. "It can be pretty good, but you have to learn how to deal with the tough bits."

Ethan laughed. "Dude, that's so gross. True, but gross. Do you think . . ." His words dropped off as his attention focused behind me. I turned to see Coach Carter marching up to our table.

"Hey, Coach," Ethan said.

Carter put his hands on his hips and nodded to him. "Mr. Jones." He fixed his gaze on me. "Wilson! Did you give any more thought to what we talked about this morning?"

The guy was persistent. "I thought about it, Coach."

"And?"

"I don't know. I . . ." It was hard to talk around him. "I have to work a lot. Plus, my mom doesn't think . . . you know . . . that I really should."

"Yeah, but I bet if you asked her really nicely, she'd say yes," Ethan said. "Mike's real good, Coach."

"I know that," said Carter. To me, he added, "I saw you play in junior high. You have some real talent, and we need you. Your biceps are about to split the sleeves of your T-shirt. You've been working at Derek Harris's farm, right?" I nodded. "Mr. Wilson, you have the rest of your life to work. You only have three more years to play football. Don't miss out on the best years of your life."

I did want to play football. It was just complicated for me. "I don't know, Coach."

"Look, I don't chase everybody down like this. The rest of the guys have been busting their butts for over a week in camp and two-a-day practices. I can get you caught up if you start this week. But Friday's the first game. If you're not on the team before then, you never will be. Think it over." He turned and marched away across the cafetorium, his fists held out from his sides and his arms cocked back a little like always.

"Wow," Ethan said. "I thought he was on his way over here to chew us out about something. You never can tell when the Volcano is going to erupt. But he's right, dude. You need to get back on the team. You were so good back in seventh grade. What did the junior high coach call you? 'Hands' Wilson or something?"

"Something like that," I said.

"Well, are you going to —"

"Did you not just hear me talking to Coach?"

"I know, but can you at least ask your mom again? You've been kind of a hermit or something these last couple years. All you do is go to school, work on the farm, and do homework. Playing football might help you fit in more. I don't know, maybe you could even score a date to the homecoming dance."

I snapped my fingers. "Hey, speaking of the dance. I have good news about your quest."

"The quest?" Ethan leaned forward. "What did you hear?"

"The quest" was Ethan's name for his unending efforts to regain the affection of Raelyn Latham, his freshman-year homecoming date. To hear him tell it, his night at the dance with her had been more romantic than *Cinderella*, the royal wedding, and *Romeo and Juliet* combined. But the guy never made his move, never asked Raelyn out again, and Chris Moore moved in as her boyfriend in the meantime.

"Well, it could be nothing. You know how Hailey and the rest of the gossip girls aren't always so accurate," I said. "But in first period geometry . . ."

"Dude, what?"

"Well, they were saying Chris cheated on Raelyn, and the two of them are breaking up."

Ethan swore. "He never did treat her right."

I ate another spongy nugget. "Yeah, because you're *so* hoping they have a nice, happy relationship." He sat back in his chair, trying to look casual as he sneaked glances at Raelyn across the cafetorium. She was one of those pretty pale girls with white-blond hair who seemed perpetually sunburned all summer. "Anyway, as soon as you're sure she and Moore have broken up, you should ask her to homecoming," I said. "Get your second chance."

"Homecoming is weeks away," Ethan said.

"The quest is the quest," I reminded him. "Don't give them time to make up."

"How could they make up after he did that to her? I'd *never* cheat on her."

"I know you wouldn't," I said. "Not even while she's going out with someone else."

Ethan didn't get the joke. He never looked so happy as when he had some reason to hope that things might be improving between him and Raelyn. "Thanks for telling me this. I hope you're right."

We ate in silence for a while. "Hey, the Hawkeyes play this weekend," I said. "Should be on ESPN. Want to get together and watch it?"

Ethan looked down at the table. "Yeah, well, see, my dad is actually taking me to the game."

"It's in Chicago," I said.

"Yeah, we're borrowing my grandpa's RV and everything."

"Wow. That's cool." I'd give anything to be able to see the Hawks play live.

"My dad had a couple extra tickets. Gabe and his dad are going with us."

"Oh." I took a drink of my milk that had somehow already warmed up.

"Sorry," said Ethan. "But he had the two tickets, and he's friends with Gabe's dad. Plus Gabe and I are on the football team together and stuff."

"You have nothing to apologize for," I said. "All that driving time. I have to work, and anyway, I started the first book in this cool new series last night, and I've already checked out the second one. Should be great."

Ethan frowned.

"What?"

"I feel like we're leaving you out."

I shrugged. "Don't worry about it. I probably couldn't have gone even if you had a ticket for me." I made myself smile. "I'm pretty busy with everything."

* * *

When I stopped at home to drop off my books and change into work clothes, Mom was there, done with the Gas & Sip and getting ready to go to her night job at the nursing home. She was sitting at the dining room table with the usual clutter shoved to one side, and a calculator and papers spread all over the space she'd made. It was bills day, and that could put her in a rotten mood.

"Hey, Mom," I said with all the cheer I could muster. "What's up?"

"Ugh, boring old bills." She rubbed her eyes. "But never mind that. How was the big first day of sophomore year?"

"Fine," I said. "Pretty much same as last year."

"I got you something today when I was at work."

"The three wolf heads or the wizard fighting the dragon?" Mom and I always joked about these cheaply made but expensive ceramic sculpture things that they sold at the Gas & Sip, alongside the cigarette lighters and power adapters and windshield scrapers.

"Close!" She laughed. "I bought you the two-foot eagle with the sword in its beak."

"Oh, you shouldn't have," I said. "No, really. You shouldn't have."

Mom got up from the table and hugged me. "What, doesn't every nearly sixteen-year-old boy want a giant eagle knickknack in his room?" She handed me a small paper sack. "Here you go, hon."

I pulled out a cold PowerSlam energy drink and a little pack of beef jerky. "My favorite. Thanks, Mom. I swear, if I could have just this to eat and drink for the rest of my life, I'd be happy."

"Yeah, I'm always looking out for your health."

She was in a good mood. Maybe this was my chance. "Hey, Coach Carter talked to me today."

"Who?"

"The football coach."

"What did *he* want?"

"Well, he wanted to know if I would go out for football this year."

Mom frowned. "It's too late, isn't it?"

"He says I have until Friday to sign up," I said.

She started messing with her purse.

After a long silence, I asked, "So, can I?"

"Can you what?"

I pulled out the parental permission form. "Will you sign this so I can play football?"

"Oh, Michael, I don't know. You're doing so great with your schoolwork, and I don't want to see you get hurt again."

I used to have a ton of fun playing football in the backyard with my dad, and in fifth and sixth grade with the guys. But the best was the one and only year I'd been allowed to go out for the team. Our seventh-grade squad went four and one, and I was the second-leading scorer, two dinky points behind Clint Stewart. In my last game, I jumped up to grab this way-out-there pass, but landed wrong, spraining my ankle. The other team's safety launched himself at me for the tackle, but we landed in the end zone, so I still managed to score the touchdown.

Then Mom went crazy over seeing her "little boy" hurt. She had never been too happy about me playing football, and she blamed my sprain on the hit I'd taken, not on a simple, stupid accident. She then refused to sign the football permission slip for eighth grade and last year.

"I'm not going to get hurt, Mom. It wasn't even the —"

"Just, just —" Mom held her hands up. "Can we not talk about this right now? I bring you . . ." She pointed to my PowerSlam and jerky. "Those things are expensive, and nothing's ever good enough. I . . . I gotta go. Maybe next year, Mikey." She kissed me on top of my head as she walked out the door, leaving me alone with the unsigned form.

People who say Iowa is flat never had to bike up the steep slope to the Harris farm. I pedaled hard, pumping my bike up the big hill. I'd built Scrappy using parts from half a dozen junked bikes. Some of the guys at school used to give me crap about her, but I didn't care. With the money I'd saved on her and all that I'd earned at Derek's, pretty soon I'd have a car, and one day that car would take me out of this tiny town.

Derek Harris lived in a big box of a white farmhouse. It really belonged to his parents, but they'd retired to a condo in town a couple years ago, leaving him to run the farm. Beside the house was a huge gravel lot that connected up with the big metal machine shed, an old red barn with a silo, and the feedlot for the cattle.

Music beckoned me toward the machine shed. Derek usually left the radio on KRRP, Riverside's local classic rock station. His ancient Chevy pickup sat in the center of the building. It had a great old-style body and was painted this cool sky blue with just a little rust around the wheel wells and at the bottom of the doors. He called it the Falcon, after Han Solo's old but reliable ship in *Star Wars*.

Derek was down on the floor, welding the bottom beneath the passenger side of the cab. When he stopped for a moment, I cleared my throat.

He took off his mask, stood up, switched off his welding machine, and leaned over the hood. "Oh, hey," he said. "You're here. Everything okay?"

"Yeah," I said. "Same as always."

Derek frowned. "What's wrong?"

"Nothing." I usually did a better job at faking like everything was fine.

He rubbed his chin. "Something's obviously got you down."

"It's just . . ." I wasn't the kind of guy who whined about his problems. But Derek was a stand-up guy. He was grown-up, but still cool. Today was a perfect example of what was wrong. Like just about every other day, I came home from school and then went straight to work. Later, I'd go home, knock out some homework, and then go to bed. "I feel like I want to do . . . something more."

"I've got plenty for you to do tonight," Derek said.

"I mean, yeah, I'm ready for whatever work you have. Thank you, by the way. I need it." He started to say something, but I held up a hand. "But I finished with something like a hundred and five percent in English last year."

"That's good. It'll help you get into a nice college like you're always talking about," Derek said.

"But I want something else too, you know?" I shrugged. "Not just work and school. I've wanted to play football since forever. Coach keeps asking me to join the team."

Derek laughed a little. "I thought you were just focusing on your reading and your studies, like you'd given up on football."

"I don't think the two things have to be mutually exclusive."

"Well, if you're reading and not paying attention on the football field, you're going to get hurt."

"You know what I mean."

"Yeah. So why don't you go out for the team?"

"Are you kidding?" I asked. He knew my problems with Mom on this issue.

Derek pulled his gold chain out from under his shirt and ran his thumb over his small cross pendant. "She knows how good you were in junior high, how much you love the Hawkeyes and the Bears. Maybe if you tell her what you just told me, she'd —"

"She never listens. Never wants to talk about anything that matters, anything that might mean change." Mom had worked the same job, driven the same car, and even worn the same hairstyle nearly every day for as long as I could remember. "Anyway, now really isn't a good time to talk to her about much of anything."

"Why is that?"

"Tomorrow is D-Day, when my dad was killed in Afghanistan. August 28, 2005."

"Tomorrow's the twenty-eighth already," Derek said quietly. An old song by the Eagles played softly on the radio. "That's tough, buddy. Hey, uh . . ." He looked at me. "You've used the chain saw before, right?"

I nodded. Derek's house had a wood-burning furnace, so without a chain saw I would have had to cut about a million branches with an ax.

"Big old tree branch fell on the fence. You can start cutting it up. Just be careful not to slip in the wet grass when you're running the saw."

"No problem," I said.

"And I think it's time I paid you for last week." He pulled a bunch of cash out of his wallet and handed it over.

I counted the money. I suppose most kids were paid on a certain day of the week or month. Derek was never that organized, but he always paid fairly. More than fairly — he'd given me the money I had coming, plus an extra two twenties and a ten. "Whoa. I think you miscounted."

"No, no." Derek picked up his welding mask. "All that wood you split last time was way more than your hourly rate really comps for, so it's like a tip. You know, fair is fair."

I held up the bills. "It's an extra fifty. I can't take this."

"You will take that if you want to keep working here." He waved me toward the door. "Now go get that branch cut. I'll be down with the truck in a little bit to haul the pieces back up here to the woodpile."

I checked the chain saw to make sure it was fueled, then pulled the heavy thing off the workbench. I'd seen the branch he was talking about from the road on my ride up, and it was a good hike away.

The cutting, loading the wood into the truck, and stacking it on the woodpile took hours. We knocked off at about eight thirty and I rolled out on Scrappy, leaning forward on the handlebars, enjoying my flight down the huge hill.

At the bottom, just as Old Highway 218 crossed the English River, it started to rain. It wasn't the usual Iowa thunderstorm that starts with a few warning drops and then gradually builds up. Lightning flashed and thunder cracked across the sky, then I might as well have jumped into the river.

Two miles later, I put Scrappy to bed in our leaning shed, then slogged through the muddy yard around front. I struggled to pull my soaked T-shirt off, tripping over the crooked board that I still had to replace on the porch. I wrung my shirt out, almost afraid the old thing would shred apart in my hands, and went inside.

"What happened to you?" my sister, Mary, called from the couch in front of the TV.

"I went swimming."

She stood up. "Um . . . there's, like . . . a leaky thingy."

I sighed. "Mom at work?"

"Yeah."

"What kind of leaky thingy?"

"Like it's coming down into my room." She fidgeted with her fingers up in front of her chest. "Through the ceiling."

I let out a breath through my nose. "Great. Just —"

"It's dripping down all over this pink T-shirt I was going to wear tomorrow. Now there's this brownish stain. . . ." I shot her a look that said I really didn't care about her fashion problems. She flopped back down on the couch. "Can you fix it?"

Fix it? What did I know about fixing the roof? Why was it always up to me to fix everything anyway?

"I'll take care of it," I said. I grabbed a bucket from the bathroom closet and went up to my attic bedroom, where the rain tapped the roof like a thousand little snare drums. A few years ago, I finally moved out of the bedroom I'd been sharing with Mary to come up here. My fortress took its natural light through the single windows in the two vertical walls. Otherwise the steep underside of the roof sloped down all the way to the floor, the rafters arching above me like some huge animal's ribs, with pink insulation stuffed between them. A barrier made of pinned-together bedsheets divided the bedroom side of the attic from the storage side, where I hid my gym from my mother.

I could hear the water running from somewhere on the gym side, like someone had turned on a faucet. Past the curtain, I had to stop to let my eyes adjust to the dimness. The only overhead light was from a bulb hanging from a wire, and that was on the bedroom side of the attic.

There it was, back near the corner — a big, stupid, steady trickle coming down from the ceiling, ruining one of my best Iowa Hawkeyes football posters and making a dark puddle on the floor, which I guess ran down into Mary's room. I plunked the bucket down to catch the water. Hopefully the rain would stop before tomorrow and the weather would stay dry until I could figure out how to fix this.

The repairs needed to be cheap. Even with Mom's two jobs and some of my cash from Derek's, we never had enough money to take care of everything. I shivered in my wet clothes and sat down on my homemade weight bench, putting my head in my hands.

"Hey, Michael?" Mary called from over by the stairs.

"Go away," I said.

"Letter or something for you."

Weird. Nobody ever wrote to me. "Who from?"

"Don't know. Don't care."

I went to the bedroom side of my attic to find the envelope on the floor next to the stairwell. Mary had gone back downstairs. I picked the letter up and sat down in the metal folding chair at my desk. The letter was addressed to me in wobbly handwriting with no return address.

I opened the envelope and found some slightly yellowed sheets of lined notebook paper with the spiral fringe still on them. Who would be mailing me old paper? The clean white envelope looked much newer. The pages had been folded in thirds, and I carefully flattened them out.

Saturday, May 29, 2004 (365 Days Left)

Dear Michael,

If you're reading this, then I'm very sorry, but I didn't make it home. I ~~will die~~ was killed here in the war in Afghanistan.

I put the letter down in my lap for a moment. What was this? A letter from my dad? I skipped to the end to see it signed *Love, Dad*. But this couldn't be from my father, could it? He had been killed in 2005. Who would have kept this letter for so many years? The Iowa City postmark offered no clue. I didn't know anyone from Iowa City, but a ton of people here in Riverside worked there. I checked the envelope to see if the person who mailed the letter had also sent a note. Nothing. Maybe this was some prank.

As I write this, I miss you very much, and I've only been away for four months. I miss playing games with you in the backyard, teaching you to kick and pass with that little Hawkeye football. You had a pretty good spiral pass going before I left. We watched Iowa play in the Outback Bowl, and

*you wore that toy football helmet you got for Christmas
through the whole game. That was a great day.*

I remembered that day! Mom and Dad had made popcorn and we
had salami and cheese on a platter, like a sort of picnic in the living
room. That old helmet was in one of the boxes up here somewhere. It
had been a great day.

Only our family had been there that night. Nobody else would
know about it. This letter really was from Dad.

*This is the first day of what is supposed to be a one-year
boots-on-the-ground mission in Afghanistan. If you have this
letter now, then the day count doesn't matter much, since
I guess I'll never see the end of this tour. Right now, though, I
have to live as though I'm going to make it home, and that day
count helps keep me going.*

Wait. This didn't make sense. I flipped back to the first page of the
letter. It was dated May 29, 2004, but I knew for certain that Dad
died August 28, 2005. That was the date on his tombstone, which I'd
visited often enough. How could Dad die in the war three months
after his tour in Afghanistan was over?

*If you have this letter, that means I've been ~~gone~~ dead for
seven or eight years. I'm sorry I wasn't able to be more of a dad
to you. I know I've missed a lot of great moments — all the
Christmases and birthdays. More than that, I haven't been
able to tell you much about me or about life. A father is supposed to provide his son with some guidance. I didn't have
that advice growing up, so I intend to write you a couple of
letters to make sure you have some help from your old man.*

My plan is for you to be given my letters in order, one at a time, early in your sophomore year of high school, so that you'll have read them all by your sixteenth birthday.

Little Mikey doesn't know much about what I do in the Army National Guard, so now that you're grown up, Michael, I thought I'd tell you a little about it. I'm a combat engineer, which is like a soldier in the infantry. We are trained in battle tactics with the M16, as well as various machine guns and other weapons systems. Combat engineers are also trained to work with land mines, TNT, and C4 plastic explosives.

I'm a sergeant E-5 and a team leader in third squad. Each squad has nine soldiers, and one of those is the squad leader, an E-6 staff sergeant. There are two teams in each squad. I'm the A-team (or alpha team) leader, in charge of three guys. By now, you've already met one of those men, my friend Specialist Marcelo Ortiz, who has promised to deliver these letters to you.

Marcelo Ortiz? Who was that? He sure hadn't delivered the letter. The stamp and postmark proved it came through the mail, and Mary would have mentioned some guy showing up to drop off the envelope. What was going on here? Maybe the letter would explain.

Before I was in the National Guard, though, I grew up in a small town in western Missouri, less than an hour south of Kansas City. My parents were both teachers — Dad was a history teacher and Mom taught English. When I was in eighth grade, they were killed in a car accident while driving home on icy roads. I was sent to live with your grandmother in Riverside,

and I was pretty miserable that summer and through my fresh-
man year of high school.

Dad hadn't been born here. How had I never known that? I'd always assumed that, like me, he had been born at the hospital up in Iowa City and then spent his whole life here in Riverside.

For me, everything changed at sixteen. I got my first car, my grandma's old 1980 Chrysler LeBaron wagon. White, a little rusty, and butt ugly, but with it, I could go places on my own, without my grandma looking over my shoulder.

I also started hanging out with Taylor Ramsey and Todd Nelson, two of the best friends a guy could ask for. Wow, did we used to have fun. One night after we won a football game, I think against Kalona, I actually drove the wagon down the railroad tracks all the way out to the party at Nature Spot. Your mom scooted close to me on the bench seat, and when we went over the Runaway Bridge, she was freaking-out scared, but I acted like it was just a normal drive. Taylor and Todd laughed the whole way as we bumped down the tracks. Then I backed the wagon up by the fire and put the hatch up in back. We all sat there, listening to the music and talking and laugh-ing. I'd give almost anything to live those days over again.

I couldn't believe my parents dated back in high school. The idea probably shouldn't have been a surprise, since they both graduated from here. I guess I'd just never pictured my parents young. I'd only known them as Mom and Dad. But Dad was gone, and Mom never talked about life before she was Mom. And they'd partied at Nature Spot? It seemed impossible. All the best parties were supposed to be out there, just off the railroad tracks outside of town. People never just showed up to Nature Spot. You had to be invited. You had to be popular.

A couple of the guys I serve with just asked what I was writing about. I told them, and they immediately laughed at me. (If you ever end up serving in the Army, remember to never share anything personal with your fellow soldiers. In the Army there's no such thing as a personal secret, and everything is fair game to be made fun of.) The guys said I was being stupid and that high school is pointless and meaningless, but I know I'm right.

Your freshman year is a trial run, a chance to check out high school and what it's all about. But your sophomore year is the time to start to experience it all. I felt like I came alive at sixteen, and those really were the glory days. Adults say that the problems high school kids face are no big deal, or that they're just a phase. But those adults only say that because they've already made it. They have already worked through their issues, one way or another. You haven't yet. Your problems are real, and you don't know how it will all work out. You must think of real solutions, and your decisions will affect the years to come.

I want to remind you about the importance of school, about one day going to college. I didn't have enough money to go, so I enlisted in the National Guard partly because it offered great tuition assistance, and I thought I might become a history teacher and football coach, like my dad. One thing he did have time to pass along to me was his love of history. I especially loved reading about old sea explorers and naval battles on sailing ships. I love visiting historical sites. That's why we took that vacation down to Hannibal, Missouri, to the boyhood home of Mark Twain and the Mark Twain Cave. I remember watching your little eyes light up when we entered the cave and when we went on the riverboat cruise.

The cave! I sometimes thought about that trip, but couldn't remember where we had been or why. We'd walked through these really boring, old-fashioned buildings where Mom and Dad kept saying "Don't touch." That must have been a museum or something, maybe where Mark Twain was born. But the cave had been amazing, like a whole other world. And on the riverboat Dad and I had acted like pirates.

I had hoped that I could make history come alive for my own students in the classroom, but I never quite found the time and money to make that happen. That's why I've made sure that you and Mary both have college money set aside. Whatever else happens, I want my children to get college educations, so you can get good jobs where you work with your brains and not with your backs. Trust me. I've worked at a meatpacking plant and then as a construction laborer for this guy Ed Hughes since I graduated from high school. That kind of work can drain the soul.

I guess what I'm saying is that I hope you can find a balance between high school fun and success with school. You're a good kid, really a man now. Just be yourself and go for something great. Don't let your fear of failing prevent you from doing good things.

I don't know how involved you are with sports and other activities at school, but if you aren't, I want you to challenge yourself by getting out there. Maybe there's a club or a sport you've been wanting to participate in, but you've held yourself back so far. Well, I'm giving you a mission, just like the ones we have in the Army: Go for it! Whatever it is you've been wanting to do, give it your best. I know you can do it.

I did a lot of growing up without a father, and I would have liked to know if he approved of the choices I made. Ortiz is my very best friend over here, and if you have questions, you want some advice, or you want to know how I would have felt about something, feel free to ask him. He'll help you out.

How could I ask Ortiz for help if I'd never met him? Who was this guy? I made it my goal to find out.

I want you to know that I'm willing to do this, to fight these terrorist scumbags, if it means that you and Mary and everybody else back home can grow up without war and with the freedom to live your lives and chase your dreams. As long as you get the chance to live your glory days and start a good life for yourself, then all this will be worth it.

I wanted to be there for you. I tried. I swear to God nothing is was more important to me than getting back home to you and your mom and sister. I know you'll be good to them, help take care of them. I'll never get to know the man you're becoming, but I hope you'll take your time with my letters to get to know me.

They're calling me to formation. I have to stop for now. I miss you, buddy.

Love,

Dad

I held the letter up in the dim light. Besides Marcelo Ortiz, my father was probably the very last person to touch this piece of paper. It had gone from his hands to mine almost as if he were with me in my attic right then. It was amazing to hear from him. When he was in the war, we'd tried talking a few times on Skype, but the picture and sound were real jerky and kept freezing up. The phone connection had this weird delay so that one person had to make sure the other had finished talking before he said anything. As a little kid, I couldn't do it right and ended a lot of phone conversations in tears, frustrated that I couldn't figure out how to talk to my dad.

I wished I had more from him to read now. All my life I'd wanted to know about what Dad had done in the Army, especially how he died. Looking him up online only told me he'd been killed in action in Afghanistan's Farah Province. I'd learned so much about him just in this one letter. Had Dad written other letters? It sounded like he'd planned to. And if I could talk to this Marcelo Ortiz, maybe I could learn a lot more.

Dad's hopes that Mary and I wouldn't have to grow up with this stupid war hadn't come true. This thing in Afghanistan had been going on for almost my whole life, as long as I could remember, anyway. I'd read about it, but I couldn't seem to find a good explanation of what all this sacrifice was for, of what had happened to my father, or why he had to be over there in the first place. People sometimes said crap like, "He died fighting for freedom." Even Dad had used language like that. What was that supposed to mean? Freedom from what? On those rare occasions when people talked about my father, they called him a hero. But what did that mean? How did marching off to a useless, endless war make someone a hero?

His hopes for a fast end to the war had been in vain, but he had other hopes for me too, a mission. *Go for it!* he had written. *Whatever it is you've been wanting to do, give it your best. I know you can do it.*

I laid out the sports physical and parental permission forms on my desk. The physical part had been easy. I'd paid for the doctor visit myself at the clinic here in town, back when I naively thought that maybe Mom would let me play football this year.

The hard part was the "Parent's or Guardian's Permission and Release" section. One of my parents might not have given me permission, but years ago, my father had. He'd practically ordered me to play football. That was all the approval I needed.

I printed and then signed *Allison Wilson* exactly the way my mother would have.

TWO

The next morning, I lay on my homemade wooden weight bench, my biceps flexing and burning. My chest muscles trembled as I tightened my core and pushed the bar up. One hundred ninety pounds. Nine reps going on — I locked out my shaking arms — ten. I lowered the bar onto its cradle above me.

"Yeah!" I whispered to myself as I rolled up off the bench to pace around my secret gym. I'd achieved my new record working weight. I loved feeling the aching tension in my back relax, the way my muscles seemed to uncoil after a heavy lift.

I stepped up to my punching bag. Today was going to be the start of a new life. *One-two.* I threw a low right and left, turning my whole body into each punch. "Give it my best?" I whispered. "You got it, Dad." *One-two, one-two.* "Hundred ninety pounds!" I swung my right shoulder and upper body into a high right jab. Some days, a lot of days, it felt good to beat the heck out of this thing. While rich kids went to psychiatrists for help sorting out their emotions, I tore into a punching bag. That's the way it was.

I went down to the bathroom on the second floor to shower and dress, then came back upstairs to read.

"Mike?" Mary said.

I jumped in my seat. "Ever hear of knocking?"

She was just head and shoulders out of the opening in the floor for the stairs. "On that curtain you put up as a door to the hallway downstairs? Yeah, I knocked." She leaned her elbows on the attic floor and rested her head in her hands. "Funny, nobody answered. What are you doing, anyway?"

I snapped my Edgar Allan Poe book closed. "None of your business."

"I so don't care about your dorky books," Mary said. "I need some money."

My chair scraped on the wooden floorboards as I pushed it back from my desk. "How could you possibly think it's a good idea to come ask me for money this early in the morning?"

"It's seven o'clock," Mary said, in a tone she might use to say, *Duh! You're an idiot!* Since she turned thirteen this last July, she answered most people's questions that way. "Tara and I are putting up campaign posters. On Friday, I'll be seventh-grade class president."

"I've seen your posters everywhere already, even in the high school wing. You don't need to make more."

"The money's not for posters! Seriously. We have all that totally covered. I need it 'cause me and Tara and Crystal are going to —"

"Tara, Crystal, and *I*," I corrected her.

She rolled her eyes. "*Me* and Tara and Crystal are going to Piggly's Friday after school to celebrate our win."

Piggly's was this crazy barbecue restaurant out on the highway. "How are you getting there?"

"Crystal's brother has to drive us. His mom's making him."

The last thing I wanted to hear about was my little sister going anywhere with a guy like Nick Rhodes, even with all her horrible friends and even just for the mile-and-a-half ride out to Piggly's. "Does Mom know about this?"

"What? Are you kidding? No! Come on, Mike." She came up out

of the stairwell, dragging her feet as though they were chained together and weighted down, her hands folded in front of her chest almost as if she were praying. "Please? Please. I've already told the girls I'll be there, and if I back out now they'll think I'm a total loser."

"You don't even know if you've won yet," I said. "Besides, even if you do, I have more important things to spend my money on than —"

"I'll pay you back," she said. I looked at her. "I promise."

"Yeah," I said. "I don't think so."

"Mike, come *on*. You're totally my favorite brother, best in the world."

"I'm trying to save to buy a car someday, and we probably need the money to fix the roof. I'm sorry."

"You're so pathetic." She started down the stairs. I shook my head.

Then the music started, the same terrible song Mom played every year.

Mary leaned back against the stairs with a groan. "Oh no, is it today?"

The song was "From a Distance," sung (badly) by Bette Midler. Mom only played it once a year, on the anniversary of the day Dad was killed in Afghanistan. I'd been hoping this time would be different, that maybe she wouldn't be so sad.

"Great," Mary said. "Now she'll be in her zombie mood all day. No chance she'll give me a little money for Friday."

"Have some respect," I said. "This is the day that —"

"That a man I barely knew and hardly remember died. Gosh. Sorry if I can't make myself cry all day, sitting in the dark with candles, old photos, and crappy music." She rolled her eyes and went down the stairs.

I wanted to yell at my stuck-up, spoiled sister, in part because she needed to think about someone besides herself, and in part to drown out the music. Instead I let out a long sigh.

By the time I gathered my books and went downstairs, Mary had already caught a ride to school. I entered the dark living room to find the blankets we used as curtains drawn over the windows. Mom sat on the couch with tears in her eyes, picking at a bit of stuffing that had wriggled out of the armrest, staring past the flames from three candles on the coffee table. She had made this CD mix years ago when Dad was in Afghanistan. She must have skipped it back, because that stupid "From a Distance" screeched from the battered speakers again.

"Hey, Mom," I said quietly. I rested my hand on her shoulder.

She started a little at my touch, then pressed her wet cheek against my forearm. "Seven years. Seven years since . . ." She leaned forward and cried so hard that her body shook.

I patted her back with my other hand. What else could I do? Tell her it was all right? That everything would be okay? Everything *was* okay, kind of, every day of the year except this one. On D-Day it was as if someone flipped a switch, and all her memories and sadness came flooding back.

And that was the problem. She talked about Dad's death on D-Day, but that didn't mean she allowed anyone else to do it.

"Mom?" I could at least try. "Did you ever meet a guy named Marcelo Ortiz? Served with Dad?"

She waved away my question. "I don't know. It was so long ago. I can't remember."

At least she hadn't shut me down altogether. "About Dad. Nobody's ever told me much. You know, about what happened?"

She looked at me as if I were crazy. "What do you mean 'what happened'? They killed him. He died a hero."

But what did that actually mean? Why had he died months after he was supposed to be home? Maybe telling her about the letter would focus her on my questions. "I know, but you see, last night —"

"And it's just not *fair*." Mom took a sip of her coffee. "Everything should have been better."

"You're right, Mom, but I'm just wondering if Dad ever told you about any plans he had to —"

"Mikey, today's hard enough without you asking me all these questions. Can we just . . . Can we not do this right now?"

I checked my watch. Ten to eight. If I didn't get going soon, I'd be late.

"Will you be home after school?"

"I'll probably go straight to work."

She bit her lip. "I worry about you out on that farm, Michael. Please, please be careful. If anything happened to you . . ."

I took a deep breath and forced myself to stay calm. "I know, Mom. You've told me. I won't get hurt."

Bette Midler's song ended. Mom aimed the remote at the stereo, but even with fresh batteries, the cheap little thing hardly ever worked. She tossed it aside and went across the room to play the track again.

This had to be my cue. I couldn't take another helping of "From a Distance."

"I know it's a rough day," I said. "Um . . . try to hang in there."

The words sounded stupid as soon as they left my lips, but Mom nodded. She threw her arms around me, hugging me so close that I almost struggled to breathe.

"Mom . . ." I said, gently pulling away. "Mom, you're kind of smothering me. I gotta go."

With none of my questions answered, I left her there, crying in the dark.

I rode Scrappy to school, past the houses on Railroad Street that were actually more run-down than our place. The view of so many overgrown bushes, ancient hulks of cars on blocks, and rotting wood fences with bright orange NO TRESPASSING signs normally dared me to live better, to study hard so that I could get out of this town and move on to become a college professor, a doctor, a lawyer — anything but trapped here. But today, passing this scene of poverty, failure, and decay reminded me of my dad's wishes, and all his other dreams that never came true.

My memory of his funeral had faded with the years, like one of those old scratchy movies. It had happened in early September. A flag was draped over a coffin. I stared at it until the colors blurred together in my tears. Guns cracked in the air and I jumped.

Later, soldiers in dark green dress uniforms lifted the flag from the coffin. Folded it. Brought it to my crying mother.

After that . . . I don't know. We walked somewhere, to a car maybe. I kept thinking about how impossible it seemed that my brave, strong father had died. I'd never fetch his tools to help him with Saturday-afternoon projects around the house anymore. We'd never again watch Hawkeye football on TV or play catch in the backyard. The war had taken all of that away.

A crow had cawed from somewhere. That was a stupid thing to remember. . . .

One of the soldiers approached. He gripped my shoulder. I looked up at him, fixating for some reason on the depth of the blue sky above him. "Your father died a hero, so you're the man of the house now," he said. "Take care of your mother and sister. Be tough."

Who was that soldier who spoke to me at the funeral? Had he served with my father? Could it have been Sergeant Ortiz? That didn't seem likely. The guys my father had served with in Afghanistan were still over there at the time. He'd said my father had been a hero. But when everyone who wore the uniform earned hero status, the line "Your father died a hero" told me nothing.

Now this letter had come. Dad was reaching out to me across the years, and maybe he would tell me what I needed to know.

THREE

I hurried to the library during fifth-hour study hall to look up Sergeant Marcelo Ortiz online. He'd been in Dad's National Guard squad, so he was probably still here in Iowa. But a search for Marcelo Ortiz in Iowa City turned up nothing. Searching the whole state of Iowa didn't work either. Weird. He wouldn't have come from out of state to mail the letter from Iowa City.

Maybe the National Guard had information on him. I Googled *Sergeant Marcelo Ortiz Iowa Army National Guard* and found my answer. I should have recognized his name, but I hadn't looked this stuff up in a long time.

Sergeant Ortiz was dead, killed in action on August 28, 2005, in Farah Province, Afghanistan. He died the same day as my dad.

What was going on here? Frustrated, I took refuge in the back corner of the library, where wooden partitions divided a table into four study carrels. I had spent many fine hours in this corner reading *Treasure Island*, *The Catcher in the Rye*, *The Hunger Games*, and *Romeo and Juliet*. I'd also read the poems of Edgar Allan Poe, Emily Dickinson, and Robert Frost, along with dozens of other books.

Today, though, I knew I couldn't concentrate on reading if I tried. Instead, I distracted myself from the infuriating mystery by looking at the football forms. After American History II with Coach Carter seventh hour, I would turn them in, hope he wouldn't spot the faked signature, and join Ethan and the rest of the guys on the football team.

"Hiding back here?" Isma Rafee dragged a chair around to the back of the cubicle table.

Isma was the only girl I talked to at this school beyond the basic casual necessities, the only one who ever sought me out. Her parents had come from Iran to America shortly before she was born. Her father taught mathematics at the University of Iowa, twelve miles to the north in Iowa City, and her family had moved to Riverside last year. We'd been partners on a couple of school projects since then. Her long, almost black hair framed the tan, smooth skin of her warm face, and her faded jeans and her pink shirt looked nice without being super tight, like something Hailey Green might wear. It was a different style than what she'd been wearing the year before, and I saw her notice me noticing.

She pressed her lips together and raised her eyebrows like, *What do you think?* "Last year I won the battle to come to school without wearing a head scarf, and now I finally talked Dad into convincing Mom that I should be able to wear normal clothes instead of the superconservative stuff, the long-sleeve kameezes and all that." She sat down.

"I like them," I said, adding quickly, "the clothes, I mean. Really cool." I poked my finger through one of the little holes in my faded Pink Floyd *Dark Side of the Moon* T-shirt. "I could use some new clothes myself." This shirt had been old when I bought it at the second-hand store.

"So you don't have the newest stuff," she said. "That shirt is cool. It shows off your muscles."

"Whatever." I felt the heat building in my cheeks.

"You look tougher than a lot of the guys who are always in the weight room. Don't act like you haven't noticed."

I had noticed, but I wasn't going to talk about it, like I was bragging. "Yeah," I said. "Well, you look" — she looked really pretty — "cool too. Now can we stop talking about clothes and stuff? I'm boring myself into a coma." I leaned my head down toward the table with my eyes half closed like I was fighting against passing out. "So . . . bored . . . clothes . . . boring . . ."

She laughed. "Knock it off."

"Can't . . . stay awake . . . much . . . longer." My head hit the cover of *The Complete Poems of Robert Frost* with a thud.

Isma laughed again. "I'll save you." She grabbed me by the shoulders and pulled me upright. When her hands slid off me, a little shiver-tingle went up my neck. "What's this?" She snatched the papers from the table.

"Nothing." I made a grab for them, but she held them behind her head so I'd have to reach around her to get them. When I stood up, she brought them to her lap. "Football permission form?" She flipped to the next sheet, saw what it was, and returned it. "Oh, sorry. This medical stuff is none of my business."

"Neither is the rest of it. Now will you give that back?"

She handed the papers to me. "Are you trying to go out for football? It's a little late, isn't it? They've already started practicing."

I shrugged.

"Well?"

"Well what?"

"Your mom finally came around, huh? Is this really something you're interested in?"

"Yeah," I said, not ready to tell her the whole truth. "I used to be pretty good. It was fun, anyway. Coach keeps asking me to join. I figure —"

"Yeah, but you're always talking about college. Is football really going to help you with that?"

"My grades will be just fine. And football is fun, Isma. It's just something I've always wanted to do. Normal guys go out for football."

Riverside High was a small school with just over forty people in each graduating class. Most of the guys played football. Why was it so hard to believe that I would too?

She leaned forward a little. "You are *not* a normal guy."

"Wow . . ." I slumped in my seat. "Thanks a lot."

"That's a good thing. Why would you want to be just another sports-worshipping moron?"

"Hey," I said. "They're not morons."

Someone made a fart noise somewhere up near the front of the library. Some people laughed. Isma and I peeked up over the top of the table's walls. At the other end of the library, Clint Stewart, one of the football team's wide receivers, sat in an armchair by the magazine shelves. One of the linemen, Robby Dozer (seriously, that was his real name), sat in the other chair. Nick Rhodes, a tight end, stood in front of them, swinging one of the newspaper sticks like a sword and jabbing it at Denny Dinsler, who was a smaller kid in my class. I didn't know exactly what Rhodes was saying, but he looked like he was making fun of Dinsler's stuttering problem. The guys laughed again. I shook my head. Why couldn't they leave people alone?

"Yeah," said Isma. "They're real geniuses."

"They're not all like that. Look at Ethan. A bunch of the football guys usually make the honor roll. It's not like playing football will melt my brain."

"Well, that's good." She did not sound convinced.

"I just want to have some fun. What's wrong with that?"

"If it were just about having fun, it would be okay, but think about the ridiculous amount of money spent on sports and all the hoopla leading up to events like homecoming. They take us out of our classes to bring us into the gym, where cheerleaders lead the worship of the sports teams. All of this time, money, and effort for what? For games that don't really mean anything! We lost the game?" She snapped her fingers, pretending to be sad. "Who cares? We'll just play again next year."

"Okay, okay. I've heard this all before. Will you hate me if I join the team?"

"Of course I won't hate you," she said. "I'll just think you look really silly running around yelling and grunting with the rest of the football guys."

"It's not like that. Coach Carter —"

"Speaking of *Mister* Carter, I was wondering if we could talk about our Civil War project."

"Yeah, I can't believe he nailed us with such a huge review assignment yesterday. I thought the first day of school was supposed to be about reading the rules and procedures."

"I can believe it." Isma opened her binder. "He's busy coaching football, so he assigns group papers and presentations. And it's all stuff we went over at the end of last year, so he won't have to work to teach us anything new for a long time." She stared at me as if daring me to argue with her. I wouldn't take the bait. "I drew this map," she said.

She pulled out a big piece of paper on which she'd drawn the Civil War map for our presentation. The Confederate states had been shaded a light gray, and she'd used a sort of tan for the Union, with colored lines for borders. Symbols for different battles had all been labeled with her super-neat writing. This map belonged in a museum.

"You know this isn't due for another two weeks or something," I said.

"You don't like it."

"No! I mean, yeah, I love it. It's just . . . Wow."

She looked at me with this cool half-amused expression, excitement in her eyes. "How's your report coming?"

D-Day and Dad's letter had distracted me, so I hadn't started right away like I usually would. "Well, I've done some reading for it. You know, some prep work."

"I don't think you've really started."

"Don't worry. It's the second day of school! We have plenty of time."

"Yeah, and in that time we have to figure out what we're going to do for our presentation. You know Mr. Carter. If we don't —"

"Whoa, whoa, whoa. Take it easy. I'll get going on the report, and as far as the rest —"

"I was thinking we could work on the presentation at my house sometime. You know, after school or whatever." She rolled her eyes. "Plus, my brother has a ton of video games. If you wanted . . ."

What was this all about? We were friends, I guess, but just at school. We met here in study hall and talked a little between classes sometimes, but I'd never spent time with Isma elsewhere. "I'd have to —"

"Unless you're busy or whatever." She reached down and picked up her books. "I know you have a lot going on."

"No, but —"

"You don't have to answer now." She tucked her hair back behind her ear.

My cheeks felt warm. I must have looked so red. " 'Cause I'd have to figure out my work schedule."

"Yeah." Isma pressed her lips together.

"And I —"

Her words burst out of her as if she'd been holding her breath. "Just let me know." She hurried away, her hair swishing in the wake of her movement.

In other classrooms students bunched up by the door during the last few minutes of class. I rarely stood with them, preferring to spend the extra time reading. But today I joined the crowd, thinking again about the situation with Dad's letter. If Ortiz hadn't sent it, who did? How would I contact this person with questions about Dad? If this new guy had sent one letter, would he send more? How many more could I expect?

Nick Rhodes sat on the edge of Mrs. Potter's desk next to Dozer and Hailey Green. "Hey, Wilson, what were you and Isma doing in the corner?"

I glared at him. "Just leave me alone." Isma was flipping through a copy of *Time* over at the magazine rack, but I could tell she'd heard what Nick said.

"You back there feeling up Ass-ma?" Rhodes said.

Ass-ma was about as clever as guys like Nick ever got. He acted clever a lot.

"And what is she wearing today?" Hailey said. "Shouldn't she be wearing, like, her tribal clothes?"

"You're never going to impress her with that ratty old rainbow T-shirt." Nick flicked a paper clip at me. "Maybe wrap a towel around your head."

Clint laughed. I balled my fists and took a step toward them.

"Is there a problem here?" Mrs. Potter emerged from the storage room. Rhodes jumped off her desk and everybody went quiet. She watched us in silence for a few moments.

Then the bell rang, and I slammed into the door and took off down the hall, trying not to listen to the comments and laughter from the people behind me.

I lingered in the American History II room after the others had rushed out. "Excuse me, Coach Carter?" I said just as he reached the door and shut off the lights.

A rod from a back surgery years ago kept Coach's posture

completely straight, and he also lacked flexibility in his neck, so he turned his whole body to face me. "Wilson." He always addressed students by nearly shouting their last names. "You need to hustle."

"I was hoping to talk to you for a minute."

"What's on your mind?"

"I'd like to join the football team." I held out the papers.

Coach snatched the forms from me and looked them over. He said nothing for a long time. "I thought you said your mom didn't want you to play."

"I know," I said. "But she . . . Last night I convinced her to sign." I tried to look him in the eye, like a man.

After another long silence, he nodded. "Like I said yesterday, I can see you've been working out a lot. Bulking up. I think you might eventually really help the team." His mouth stretched into a half smile, half pained grimace. "It'll be hard work, and you might not get much playing time right away this year."

"I know," I said.

"Then come with me." He led me down the hall to the musty equipment room, where he issued me football pads and a helmet. Then he found me a larger locker to store it all. Coach whipped his pen over his pass book and then snapped off the top sheet. "This will get you into your next class, so you won't have a tardy on your record. Before you go to class, you need to stop by the fountain and drink a lot of water. See you at practice after school."

I smiled, glad to have football gear again. Glad to have my chance. "Thank you, Coach."

He narrowed his eyes. "You might not be thanking me after practice tonight."

FOUR

One summer a few years ago, when Grandma was still alive, Mom marooned Mary and me on her farm for two whole weeks. Once I finished the two books I'd brought along, all I had to read was a stack of old *National Geographic* magazines with articles about people in jungle villages beating drums and honoring their warriors.

Entering the locker room to be among my school's warriors reminded me of those stories. The place was full of a similar sort of primal energy. I loved it. It felt so good to be back that I hardly noticed the stench from all the sweaty clothes and gear. I hurried to my locker, eager to get started.

Cody Arnath stared at me as I started suiting up. He pushed his long hair out of his eyes. "Uh, what are you doing?"

"Just getting ready." I pulled my shoulder pads out.

"You got to be kidding me," Cody said. "You're just starting now?" He shook his head and walked off.

That happy-to-be-back feeling quickly faded. After hurrying to dress, I moved toward the door to the practice field, carrying my shoes, shoulder pads, and helmet like everyone else. I tried to ignore all the looks and quiet comments from the guys that made a twisted, hollow, vomitous feeling deep in my gut. My heart thumped nervously.

"Wilson!" Coach Carter shouted. "Get in here!"

I ran to his office. He closed the door behind me. Like the locker room, Coach's space was drowned in a dusty-salty smell, made only marginally better by a bunch of hanging pine-tree air fresheners. "Coach?" I said.

Carter motioned at a younger man with a goatee sitting on a stool. "This is Coach Brown. He's our defensive coordinator, and he'll be working with the linemen."

"Hello," I said.

Coach Brown stared at me as if he hadn't heard me at all. Carter went on, "Pay attention to what I'm about to say. We're bending the state athletic association rules a little by putting you in full pads tonight. The team already did their three required no-contact days. Someone might complain that you didn't get yours." He held up one finger. "So number one, if anyone complains about you practicing tonight, you will tell me about it after practice. I'll sort them out." He held up a second finger. "Two, if you're injured, you will tell me immediately. Got it?"

"Yes, Coach. I'll tell you if I'm hurt."

"No!" Coach Brown looked like he'd just bit into an extra-sour lemon. "You are only going to tell us if you are injured, if your body is broken. You *will* be hurting tonight. I promise you that."

"Three," said Coach Carter, holding up three fingers for a moment before making a fist. "Coach Brown is going to put you through some extra workouts. Some extra drills. He's going to add enough work to make up for all the practices you've missed. You won't be ready to play in our first game this Friday, but you can suit up with the team. Depending on how practice goes, you might earn a little time in the game after that. You need to mentally prepare yourself. We're going to work you hard."

Coach Brown flexed the muscles in his arms. "Got that?"

I flexed my own biceps and stared back. If I was going to do this, complete Dad's mission and play football like I always wanted to, then I would have to fight for it. "Got it."

"Got it, *Coach*!" Carter yelled.

"Got it, Coach."

Carter opened his door. "Get out of here."

I rushed out of the locker room, now one of the last people. Outside on the sidewalk, I got into my shoulder pads and crushed the helmet down over my head, strapping my mouth guard to my face mask. Then I bolted for the practice field.

The other guys were all in five lines starting on the fifty, with the next player back every five yards. Matt Karn, Jay McKay, and Tony Sullivan, the senior captains, were out in front, facing everybody else. "Hurry up!" someone yelled. Unsure where to go, I hurried to the back of one of the long lines.

Finally, McKay took a step forward, leaned back, and shouted "Get in line! It's football time!" so loudly that it echoed against the woods behind the game field. Everybody stopped talking and joking around.

"The head-and-neck stretch!" he called out. Everyone who knew what was going on answered with the same call. We rolled our heads clockwise for a while, and then switched to counterclockwise.

The three seniors took turns leading us through the warm-up like this. We worked our arms and legs. We did jumping jacks. Finally, the coaches marched out onto the field.

"Give me a lap!" Coach Carter yelled.

"Wilson!" said Coach Brown. "You better finish two laps before the slowest man finishes his one. Sullivan, make sure he does it!"

"Move it!" said Carter.

The entire herd took off running. They all seemed to know that they had to go around the back side of a certain light pole on the practice field. Tony Sullivan ran up right behind me and tapped his face mask on the back of my helmet. "Run faster or I will kill you," he said in a low growl. I sped up, but he stayed with me. "You better be five yards ahead of me all the time, Wilson."

I looked back and saw him still too close. I picked my pace up to a near sprint. We ran the length of the practice area, up a path that had been mowed in the grass on the steep hill toward the woods, a hundred yards along the ridge, down the slope, around the back of the softball diamond, another hundred yards, and around the outside of the practice field to the pole where we started. My chest felt like fire.

"That's one lap, Wilson!" Sullivan shouted. "Speed up!"

Faster? I couldn't go any faster! We were already ahead of over half the guys. Still, Sullivan gained on me. My thighs burned on the way up the hill for my second lap. I risked a look back. Sullivan followed a few paces behind me.

"If I catch up to you on this hill where the coaches can't see us, I'm going to smash you into the ground," he said. "Run!"

I kept snapping my feet down, one in front of the other, gasping for air, trying to ignore the stabbing pain in my side. By the time I reached the far side of the softball field, I had begun to lap some of the larger, slower linemen. I could get two laps before some of those guys finished, but how could I get through the rest of practice after that?

"Sprint out the rest, Wilson! Go! Go! Go!" Sullivan gasped from behind me. "You're dead if I catch you!"

I didn't think. I just ran until everything hurt. When I reached the pole where a bunch of guys had finished their one lap, I trotted out to a stop. Someone slapped me on the back of my shoulder pads. I leaned over, my stomach clenched, and acidy sick-sweet vomit burst out.

Sullivan ducked down to talk to me. "This is only the beginning."

"Puke it up!" someone said.

"Puke is weakness leaving the body," said someone else. "Good work."

I spat to try to get rid of the taste. If vomiting counted as a badge of honor out here, something told me I would be very well decorated by the end of practice.

Carter sent the linemen to one end of the field and took the receivers to run pass routes. Coach Brown grabbed me by my practice jersey. "Come with me." He picked up a football and led me to our own corner. He pointed downfield. "Go!"

I took off running again, a little unprepared. Was this punishment running? Conditioning? Coach Brown launched the football like a rocket, straight at me. I caught the movement out of the corner of my eye. I did a sort of half turn to catch it, but somehow my feet tangled while running. The ball would sail right past me as I fell unless I stretched out for it.

I snagged the football in my fingertips just before I hit the ground. When I opened my eyes, I still had it in my hands! It had been a long time since I last played, but I could still do this.

"Get up, Wilson!" Coach Brown shouted. "Don't just lay there!" I scrambled to my feet and made as if to throw the football back. Coach pointed at the ground next to him. "No! Run!"

I sprinted back to the coach's side, and he snapped the football from my hands without even looking at me. "I'm going to overthrow the football. You better catch it. Go!"

I darted off again as fast as I could move, looking a couple times over my shoulder. Twenty yards. Twenty-five. Then he threw it. He'd told the truth. This would go over me, but not by too much. I pushed my legs harder. Looked up quick to check the ball. Ran harder. Checked again. I had one chance. I dove for it with my arms stretched out and my hands like a basket, praying to get hold of the ball. I caught it!

That is, until I hit the ground and lost it. The ball went roll-ing away.

We must have run about fifteen passes. I caught all but two of them. After a while I couldn't count. Couldn't think. Just tried to breathe. Run. Find the ball. Try to grab it. Run more. Finally, when I reached Brown's side, he waited. I stood ready to run again.

"Wilson."

"Y-yes, Coach."

"Looks like you can catch. I'm going to walk over to the linemen. You will run over to the drinking fountain and get as much water as you can before you run to the linemen. You will get over there before I do. Go!"

I ran to the long tube and found the switch that sent six streams of water out in big arches. I put my mouth over one stream and drank and drank. Nothing had ever tasted so good in my life.

The moment ended almost before the water could hit my stom-ach. I ran off again to beat Brown to the linemen, who waited in seven lines in front of pads on a huge steel rack. Jay McKay stood on the back of the thing. He gave the "go" call and seven linemen launched out of a three-point stance to slam shoulder-first into the pad and push the whole sled back.

I took my place behind four other guys. Finally, a little rest. Coach Brown replaced McKay on the sled. "Wilson! You're up. Move to the front of the line!"

I heard a few chuckles and felt some hard elbows as I took my position. Coach blew his whistle and I ran into the pad, pumping my feet against the ground after he yelled at me.

It went on like that all night. The seven-man sled. The single-man tackling sled. The chutes where we just practiced running out low so we wouldn't hit our heads on a bar. Then we ran the starting offense against a defense of tackling dummies. I had to hold one across the line from offensive tackle Robby Dozer, who stood just over six feet tall and weighed over two hundred twenty pounds. When he dropped into his three-point stance across from me, he actually growled. McKay snapped the ball, and I barely saw Dozer. A blur hit the bag, I hit the ground, and the fullback Drew Hamilton blew right past me.

"You got to hold it!" Dozer said, glaring down at me.

Nick Rhodes messed me up even worse. As starting tight end, he sometimes lined up next to Dozer on the line. When the play called for Rhodes to block down on my dummy, he came full blast. The first time he hit a lot more of me than the dummy, and he crushed me into the ground again.

"Get up, Wilson!" Rhodes yelled.

Coach made them run the same play again. This time, I didn't care how tired I was. The bag didn't weigh nearly as much as the hay bales I'd been throwing on Derek's farm. I lifted that tackling dummy, bringing it up to slam right into Rhodes's chest, stopping him dead and even knocking him back a little.

A while later, we switched and the starting defense ran against a scrub offense. Coach mostly left me out of this, since I didn't know any of the plays. I had no problem with that. I needed the rest.

After defense practice, Coach sent us all to the end of the field, where we were grouped by class. The freshmen stood shoulder-to-shoulder across the goal line first. The rest of us fell in behind. The conditioning drill called for us to sprint ten yards, dive to the ground, get back up and sprint ten yards, dive again, and repeat all the way to the other goal line. If Coach saw anyone running too slowly, he'd call out that we had earned another run.

By the fourth, fifth, or sixth rotation, I can't remember which, I threw up as soon as I crossed the finish line. Then I readied myself for the next rotation.

Finally, Coach brought us all to the center. We took our helmets off, went down on one knee, and gasped for air while he talked about what had gone well at practice versus what we needed to improve. When he finished and sent the team inside to clean up, most everyone took off their shoulder pads and walked back to the locker room. I, on the other hand, was surrounded by the three senior captains.

"Wilson, for missing two-a-day practices, plus camp, plus Monday's practice, we're going to make you hurt for an extra fifteen minutes after practice every day!" Matthew Karn sent a football spiraling straight up above his head and then caught it. He led us to the bottom of Bleacher Hill. "Sprint up. Jog down. Go!"

I ran the five yards to the hill fast, but as soon as I hit it, I felt like someone had tied weights behind me. It was as if I were climbing the straight-up steep stairs to my attic, only at the top I found no bed, no rest, but more running.

"Faster, Wilson!" McKay yelled.

"Keep it up," said Sullivan when I ran around behind the three captains at the bottom of the hill. I stopped and rested with my hands on my knees.

"Who told you to stop, you lazy turd? Go!" Karn shouted.

McKay laughed. "Dude, you're gonna kill him."

"That's okay," said Karn. "We don't need him."

I glared at him. He flashed a sick grin and pointed to the top of the hill.

Finally, after many more laps and after I heaved up nothing a couple times, Sullivan stopped it. "That's enough, Wilson. You're done for the night."

"What?" Karn said. "He's got like five minutes left. Coach told us to work him for fifteen minutes extra."

"Fine," Sullivan said. "But he's still got to do a cool-down lap. I'll run it with him. You guys can go."

"You got guts putting yourself through this, Wilson," said McKay. "I'm glad I don't have to do all this extra stuff."

"You already did. We've been working all summer and in practice for days," Karn said. "This idiot just showed up today." He led McKay away.

"Come on," said Sullivan. He started for the hill again. I couldn't do any more. I wanted to drop to the ground. "Move it, Wilson!" he shouted. That got a laugh from the other two.

After we reached the top of the hill, Sullivan led us back farther toward the woods. When we had moved out of sight of the practice field, he dropped the pace down to a walk.

I didn't say anything. I'd had a pretty good practice, and it felt great to be back, but obviously a lot of the guys didn't think it was fair for me to start late. When Sullivan and I ran together earlier, he had threatened to kill me. Well, he could go ahead. I couldn't stop him.

But he didn't attack me. He didn't even say anything until we had walked at least the length of the nearby game field. "Matt Karn's a jerk. So is Rhodes." I looked at him to see if he was serious. "I saw the crap Rhodes pulled in practice today. I know what Karn was doing. Don't pay any attention to those guys."

We walked the rest of the lap in silence. As we neared the practice field, where someone might see us, Sullivan kicked it up into a pathetically slow jog. I matched him. "You really worked hard today. And you look tough enough. We need all the strength we can get if we're going to make the playoffs this year." He stopped and hit me in the shoulder. "Stick with it, okay?"

"I won't quit," I said, as much to my father as to him.

Neither of us said anything more for the whole walk back to the locker room. It seemed like every muscle in my body ached individually. Sweat ran in tiny rivulets through the dust on my legs, which were so tired I couldn't stop them from shaking. So far, football had been physical misery, but a lot of fun. I'd never quit.

The ride to work always challenged me, but that night, I think I might have walked about as much as I rode my bike, especially up the last hill. After petting Annie and throwing her rope toy a few times, I found Derek in the shop.

He saw me and frowned. "What happened?"

"Nothing."

"Scraped elbow. Bruise on your bicep. You're even later tonight than last night. Come on."

"Sorry." I thought about coming up with some story to tell him, but why bother? "I was at football practice."

"You don't play football."

"I'm on the team. Coach is sort of giving me a trial run, I think."

Derek looked surprised. "Really? So you finally get to play, huh? It's about time." He slapped his hand on the Falcon. "How was it?"

I stretched my sore arms. "Well, it would probably be more fun if they didn't stick me with extra drills to make up for missed practice."

"Rough on you, huh?" he said.

"Oh yeah."

Derek put his hands on his hips. "So how did you get your mom to change her mind?"

"See, that's the problem. She doesn't really know about it." I saw the skepticism in his expression. "She works all the time, so I don't really get to see her much. And she doesn't like to be bothered with this kind of thing anyway. So I just filled out the forms for her."

"Including her signature?"

"Yeah," I said quietly after a moment. The old rusted windmill squeaked in the breeze. "Please don't tell."

"I don't know, Mike."

"Come on. If she finds out what I've done, she'll tell Coach and I'll be off the team before I've even had the chance to become part of it."

"That bad, huh?" Derek said. "Have you two been fighting or something?"

"It's not that," I said. "We get along fine, as long as we're going along through our routines. Anything outside of that and she shuts down or, worse, gets all upset."

"And playing football is outside of your routine."

"For the last two years, anyway."

He sighed. "I don't like keeping secrets, but I guess I could go along with you on this one. Now come on. I need your help with the tractor." Derek's ancient John Deere 3010 narrow-front tractor seemed to spend more time in the shop than in the field. He already had the cover off to get started. He bent over the engine and held out his other hand to me. "Can you get me the nine-sixteenth?"

I gave him the right size socket wrench. Of all the work I did on the farm, helping like this — just waiting around to hand Derek different tools — bored me the most. Today, though, I was grateful for the chance to stand still. Would Dad have been proud of me? I wished I could write back to him to ask.

"Hey, you awake?"

"What? Sorry. What do you need?"

"Pliers." Derek grabbed the tool himself and went back to the engine. "What's the matter?"

"Nothing." I sat down on one of the small front wheels. "Only . . ." Derek was probably the only adult I could truly trust, the only one with whom I could talk about stuff that mattered. "You knew my dad, right?"

"Yeah." He reached deep into the machinery, twisting hard on something. "But not that well. He was a couple years ahead of me in school."

46

"Yesterday I got a letter in the mail that my father wrote when he was in Afghanistan. Someone mailed it to me."

"Oh." Derek wiped his oily hands on his jeans. "Are you serious? Are you sure it was from your dad?"

"Yeah, I'm serious." I told him all about the letter, including the memory of my family watching that Hawkeye football game, which only my father would have known. Then I filled him in on the mystery with Ortiz. "You don't know who might be sending them, do you? Like maybe it's someone else he served with?"

"I guess it could be," Derek said. "Gosh, buddy. That's a tough one. Still, it must be pretty cool to be able to hear from your father, right?"

"Oh yeah." I smiled. "He basically told me to go out for football. I just wish I could find the sender."

"Is that so important?" He picked up a crescent wrench and went back to work on the tractor.

"Maybe not, I guess. But if there are more letters, what gives this guy the right to hold on to them? They're mine. And if the sender was really close to my dad, he could maybe tell me more about him, like how he died."

"You already know that, though. He was killed in action, right? He was a soldier. He died a hero."

"Yeah, but that's what they say about all soldiers, at least the ones who die in war." Derek looked like he was about to object, so I continued quickly, "And they all are. Absolutely. But what does that even mean, 'He was a hero'? I mean, did he die in like a sniper attack, or from a rocket-propelled grenade or something? Was he standing in the street, or did he take out a whole bunch of Taliban on the way?"

"Kind of morbid, isn't it? What difference would it make to know that?"

"I don't know," I said. "I just *need* to know." I couldn't explain why certain girls were pretty or why I liked my favorite foods. Some feelings just existed. But maybe it was more than that. "I didn't get a lot of time with my father. He devoted his life to my mother, sister, and me, and he gave his life in this war that doesn't make much sense. I'd like to know if his death counted for something, if it made any difference."

Derek shook his head. "Well, I wish you luck. Those letters sound like a really neat second chance."

I hoped more letters would come. I'd hate for the one letter I'd received to be my last chance.

FIVE

My body ached all through the next day's classes, and I only suffered worse through Wednesday's practice, so that by Thursday morning I walked down to the kitchen as stiff as a mannequin. Mom's shift at the nursing home didn't end until eleven p.m., so I was surprised to find her awake and sitting at the kitchen table in her faded pink robe, her hands around a cup of coffee. She offered me a half smile, the lines creasing in the corners of her eyes. "What are you doing up so early?" she said.

"I was about to ask you the same question." I poured myself a big glass of water from the tap. Not only did my body ache, but I thought I might fall asleep standing up. I'd reread Dad's letter a few times last night, which kept me up half the night thinking about who he was and wondering what had happened to him.

"Mom, did Dad ever send us any letters home from the war?" I asked. Surely he must have, but I had never seen them. Except for D-Day each year, Mom had kind of put away all memories of Dad.

"What?" She wrinkled her nose like she smelled something awful. "Why do you want to bring up all that old painful stuff?" She rested her head in her hands. "As if the anniversary of your father's death wasn't hard enough, Mrs. Dinsler died last night. She had some grandchildren. Some granddaughters, and I think a boy in your grade?"

Denny and his cousin Alyssa were in my grade, but while I was sorry to hear about their loss, I didn't want to let Mom steer us off topic like she usually did. "Yeah, but, see, I got this letter from —"

"I was just talking to her while I helped her get her medication." Mom wiped a tear from her eye. "She was looking forward to her grandkids visiting this weekend. Eighty-seven. Stroke. Died in her sleep."

"Mom, do you think Dad —"

"Michael, please! Not today, okay?" She took a drink of her coffee. "You're dressed with your bag and everything. You never get ready this early."

I should have known I'd never get her to talk about Dad. About anything, really. "I have to go in to type up my 'What I Did During My Summer Vacation' paper for English class."

"I'm sorry I can't afford a computer. It would help both of you kids so much with your schoolwork. They're just so expensive." She closed her eyes and rubbed the back of her neck.

"It's okay, Mom. The computers at school work fine. No big deal." I took a spotted banana from the counter.

"Mikey, what happened?" She stood up with a look of horror on her face.

"What?"

"Those bruises!"

I held the banana up. "It's still good. The peel always looks worse than the —"

"I'm talking about your arms." She moved closer to examine me. When I tried to back away, she put her hand behind me and held me there as she peered at my arm. If she figured out where those bruises really came from, I'd have suffered them for nothing.

"Um, just got a little banged up on the farm yesterday. Cutting wood."

"You've never been this hurt from farmwork before." She pointed to my raw elbow. "And this. Don't try to tell me that was from an ax."

"It's just a scrape, Mom."

"Michael, what happened?"

"Okay." I sighed. This was my last chance to throw her off. "I was . . . roughhousing with Ethan after school. We both wanted, you know" — I did not know, and hoped something would come to mind — "the last Mountain Dew in the box. He tried to grab it from me, and I made a run for it. Then I dropped it, and we both kind of scrambled after it, trying to keep the other guy from getting it. Kind of a dumb game. Sort of, you know, wrestling."

Mom shook her head and smiled. "You boys. How is Ethan, anyway?"

"Good," I said. "He's really good."

"Well, be more careful from now on. I don't think one pop is worth all these cuts and stuff."

"Mom, I'm fine, really. It looks worse than it is."

She reached out to squeeze my hand, pulling me closer to kiss it. "You're such a good boy, Mikey." She let me go.

"I know, Mom," I said, at once relieved and disgusted with myself.

I tried to act normal as I entered seventh-hour American History II, but I couldn't help groaning a little when I sat down at my desk.

"Wilson! Have you been drinking water like I told you to?"

"Yes, Coach."

He held out his drinking-fountain pass. "Listen up, football men. All of you, starting with Wilson, will go drink water for a full minute. I mean it. A minute. Count it off. Then count off two minutes without drinking. After that, drink for another minute. Then come back to class so the next man can go. Move it, Wilson!"

I left my desk, took the pass, and went to drink from the cruddy old fountain where the water tasted like our rank locker room smelled. When I came back to class, everybody had moved into groups to work on their Civil War projects. Isma had two desks pulled up to our usual corner in the back.

"What was that all about?" she asked when I sat down.

"He's big on hydration."

"Okaaaay . . ." She stretched out the word as if she thought he'd acted crazy. "All that running around. The hitting and yelling. It doesn't seem like you." She leaned closer to me and spoke quietly. "You're smarter than that."

"Believe me, sometimes that's exactly me." I thought of Dad's letter. "I used to watch and play football all the time with my dad. Just because I love reading and care about my grades and future doesn't mean I have to hate sports. Why do so many people think that it has to be one or the other?"

Isma shrugged. "It just seems like that's how it usually goes."

As if on cue, Coach Carter appeared beside our desks. "Wilson." He smacked a small red three-ring binder on my desk. "I forgot to get you this yesterday. Here is your playbook. You will memorize every play. Pay close attention to the tight end position. I will quiz you at random times in the coming days. Be ready."

"Yes, Coach," I said.

After he left, Isma shook her head. "So I guess we won't be getting together to work on the presentation." She kept her eyes focused on the doodle she was making in her notebook.

I pinched the bridge of my nose. With football and Dad's letter, I'd forgotten all about Isma's invitation.

"It's okay if you don't want to," she said.

"What? No, it's just that with practice, I can't meet up after school. But . . . maybe Saturday?"

"No," she said sharply.

"Whoa. Sorry for the suggestion. Okay, what about —"

"It's no problem about Saturday, but my parents are really busy and I have . . . It's just . . . I'll probably get stuck with chores or something." She sighed. "I guess just forget it."

We went to work on our project.

In the locker room after school, I hurried to get my gear on so that I wouldn't be last again. I slipped into my football pants, pulling them up and then tying the laces in front.

"Idiot! What are you doing?" Matt Karn said on his way out the door. He was wearing just shorts and carrying his helmet and shoulder pads with his practice jersey.

Ethan leaned over on the bench next to me. "Didn't you hear Coach yesterday when he talked about a light practice tonight?" he said. "We don't go full contact on Thursdays. We're resting up a little, getting ready for tomorrow's game."

Compared to the day before, that night's practice did feel like a rest. We stretched out and ran our lap. I ran two once again with Tony Sullivan chasing me. After that, the first string walked through our starting defense, while the other second-stringers and I did our best to run the other team's offense.

Since I was playing scout tight end, I sometimes lined up across from Nick Rhodes. Every time my play called for me to block down on him, he pulled some cheap shot, like an elbow to the ribs or a quick tripping move that dumped me to the ground.

When the next play called for me to run an in-route, I'd had enough. I was supposed to run out about ten yards and then cut in behind the outside linebacker toward the middle of the field for the pass. Instead, when the center hiked the ball, I shot out straight for Rhodes, planting my hands on his chest under his shoulder pads and driving him right back into the cornerback, Noah "Monty" Monteray. As they both fell, I spun around off them and cut in across the middle of the field. Karn, the quarterback, frowned and whipped the ball hard toward the ground five yards ahead of me. I ran faster, dipped down to scoop up the ball before it could hit the dirt, and kept running, only to be stopped by one of our safeties, Chris Moore.

"Nice catch," Moore said.

"Wilson!" Coach Carter shouted. "This is a walk-through. You don't want to walk? You can run! Give me a lap!"

Rhodes glared at me as I took off, but Monty nodded. I poured on a lot of speed, empowered by my sweet, if temporary, victory. When we switched sides and Coach put me on the scrub defense against the starting offense, I was the outside linebacker, with Rhodes lining up across from me as the starting tight end. For a light practice, I still ended up getting knocked around quite a lot.

After a few forty-yard sprints, Coach brought us all in for his end-of-practice talk. We knelt down on one knee with our helmets off as he slowly looked us all over. "We've been talking about HIT for months now — *Hard Work*, *Integrity*, and *Team*. The Big Three!" He held up one finger. "Hard work! You've been working hard all summer in the weight room and in practice since we started this year. Integrity! Tomorrow you will play some good, hard-hitting, clean football, respecting the officials, playing with honor, by the rules. Team! We have all been helping each other get ready for this game. Every man here knows that every other man has his back!

Tomorrow is your chance to show that you live the Big Three when we play Dysart. Our first game. A home opener. I'd say we're ready!"

All around me the guys erupted in shouts and whoops. McKay put his fists in the air above his head and screamed "Roughriders!" He held out the end of the word for a while.

"Mount up!" the rest of the guys called out at once.

"Rip out their esophaguses!" Dozer punched the ground.

"Yeah! Our house, baby!" shouted Karn.

These guys seemed like they'd lost their minds, but it was cool. I looked across the mob and spotted Sullivan. Unlike the others, he kept his calm, but his shoulders rose and fell as he breathed deeply with a satisfied look on his face.

Coach quieted everyone down. "Dysart's a tough team. The Trojans went undefeated last year. They topped us by two touchdowns."

"Let me at 'em, Coach!" Cody Arnath called out.

"We *are* coming at them!" Coach shouted. "With everything we got!"

Again, the team erupted. A shiver went up my spine, like I wanted to punch something. Rip something apart. I clenched my hands into fists and flexed the muscles in my arms and chest. This intense, violent camaraderie had to have been part of what Dad wanted for me. And even if Isma would probably have laughed at it, I liked it. I wanted more.

Coach went on with his talk, ordering us to drink a lot of water and to get plenty of rest that night. "Believe. Achieve," he finished. "Now, tonight's team supper is where?"

"Piggly's, Coach. Six thirty," said Dozer.

I couldn't hold back a smile. For years, I'd watched the football team completely take over Piggly's a few nights a season for supper the night before game day. They always laughed and seemed to have a great time. Tonight, I would finally be able to join them.

"Right," Carter said. "Piggly's at six thirty. It's not a requirement, but it's good to be there. Helps build Team. So shower up and get your game jerseys from Laura and Kelsey in the equipment room. Hopefully I'll see you all tonight."

After Coach dismissed the team, I wondered for a moment if maybe I'd get lucky and not have to run extra.

"Captains, make sure you give Wilson his fifteen minutes of work tonight," Coach Brown added as he walked off the practice field with Carter.

So much for luck. McKay, Karn, and Sullivan put me through brutal running and bear-crawl drills for the full fifteen minutes. Karn was extra cruel. He kept complaining that my extra workout would make him late to see Maria Vasquez. If the rumors about them were true, Karn only wanted to meet up with her for one thing.

Finally, as I crawled with just my feet and hands on the ground, I reached someone's feet at the goal line. I looked up and saw Sullivan. "That's it. You're done." As I stood, I noticed McKay and Karn had left. "They wanted to get out of here. McKay had to gas up his car before tonight. Karn . . . well . . ."

We started walking back toward the school.

"A lot of the guys are pretty mad that Coach let you on the team so late," Sullivan said. "Some of them want us to work you hard enough after practice that you'll quit."

It didn't take too much careful thought to guess who the angry players were. Their little conspiracy made me angry too. "I won't give up."

"I hope not," Sullivan said. "I think you could really help us, and we need all the help we can get. We have to do well this year. I have a shot at some football scholarship money, and without it, I might not be able to go to college."

"I'll do my best not to let you down," I said.

He looked at me as if sizing me up. Then he nodded. "Good. Now come on. Hopefully the girls are still in the equipment room."

"What took you guys so long?" said Laura Tammerin, the team's assistant. She wore her brown hair pulled back in a ponytail like always, with a game jersey that said ROUGHRIDERS over her large chest and the number 17 below that.

The other team assistant, Kelsey Hughes, tossed a red jersey to Sullivan. "Here you go, stud." She blew a bubble with her pink gum.

"Thanks." Tony caught his shirt.

Laura rolled her eyes at Kelsey and then smiled at me. "You must be" — she checked a list on a clipboard — "Mike Wilson, the last guy to get his jersey." She turned around and bent over to reach into a cardboard box. I could tell that Sullivan noticed the view. Kelsey must have noticed him noticing, because she stepped to the side to block it.

"Here." A jersey came flying over Kelsey's head. I caught it and held it up in front of me, a big, bright white 42 on the red shirt with ROUGHRIDERS in white letters.

"I didn't know you were out for football," Kelsey said, wrinkling her nose a little.

"This is only my third day."

She chomped her gum. "They let you do that?"

"I think it's cool," said Laura. "I saw them working you extra out there." She led us all out of the room, switched off the light, and closed and locked the door. Then she gave me a light punch to the shoulder. "You got guts giving this a shot. You ever have any equipment problems or need any help, let me know."

"Thanks, girls," Sullivan said as we headed to the locker room.

"So we wear this to school tomorrow?" I asked him.

"Yeah," said Sullivan. "And to supper tonight, if you're going."

A few hours later, I leaned Scrappy against a tree at the edge of the gravel lot in front of Piggly's and straightened my jersey with a quick tug on the bottom. For a moment, I thought about getting back on the bike and returning to the farm. Derek hadn't seemed entirely happy about letting me out of work tonight, and I didn't want to have to put up with Rhodes or Karn if they decided to give me crap.

But right then, an older couple came out of Piggly's. The gray-haired man waved at me. "Good luck tomorrow," he said. I smiled and nodded at him like an official representative of the team, a Riverside Roughrider. Up on the roof, Mr. Piggly, a giant pink pig balloon with a huge grin and big wide eyes, beckoned me in.

Inside, before the door even finished its opening *Oink, Oink! Oink, Oink!* sound, Mr. Pineeda started his usual greeting. "Another proud warrior comes for his meal before tomorrow's battle! Welcome, young Mr. Wilson!"

I laughed. He straightened his dancing-pig apron over his enormous belly and his happy face became serious. "It's that time of year, isn't it? Sometime in late August? Early September?"

"Huh?" I said. What was he talking about?

"I remember your father." The enthusiasm had dropped out of Mr. Pineeda and he spoke in a completely different voice. "He was a good man."

Except on Veterans Day and Memorial Day, it seemed nobody remembered or spoke of my dad. How could he possibly have remembered the anniversary of my father's death? The thought flashed through my mind that maybe he could be the guy who got my father's letters after Sergeant Ortiz died. The Mystery Mailer, as crazy as that sounded.

I locked eyes with him. "Did you know my father well, Mr. Pineeda?"

He looked sad. "Not as well as I would have liked to. He came into the restaurant a few times. He was great in football, kind of a legend in his day." No, he couldn't have sent the letter. It just didn't make sense. The big man patted my shoulder. "Good to see you on the team. You make your father proud tomorrow, no?"

"I doubt I'll even play," I said.

"Well, you never know what will happen," he said, recharging like he'd just knocked back an energy drink. "You eat a couple sandwiches tonight, and Piggly's Super Secret Special Barbecue Sauce will give you all the strength you need to go out there and win the big game! Aaron?" The man's son jogged over from the other room. Pineeda gave him a double-chinned nod. "Escort this fine young man, this proud Roughrider, over to his teammates!"

The kid led me to the other room in the restaurant. Roughriders pennants and photos of Riverside sports teams decorated the walls. A row of shiny plaques proudly showed off how many times Piggly's had won "Best Riverside Restaurant" and even "Best Iowa Barbecue." Old bowling league and Little League baseball trophies stood on a shelf.

All the football guys looked up from different tables in a roped-off area.

Pineeda's son unclipped the rope and held it aside for me to go through. "Good luck tomorrow."

"Thanks," I said. Then I entered our section and stood there like an idiot. I had no idea where to sit. I knew everyone here by name, but I hadn't hung out with many people for a few years.

"Hey, Wilson!" Ethan called out. He sat at a booth back by the wall with Gabe Hauser and Monty. They had a pitcher of dark soda, and Ethan slapped an empty plastic cup down in front of the place beside him. I tried to look casual as I sat down. This kind of supper might feel normal for these guys, or even for my sister, but I never did things like this.

"It's great you decided to go out for football," Ethan said. "Coach got you backing up Rhodes at end?"

"I guess so."

"Cool," said Monty. He laughed. "That shot you put on him today totally ambushed me."

"Yeah, sorry about that," I said.

"No big deal." He poured me some soda.

Kendra Hanson, a freshman at school, stood nearby with a scowl on her face and a little notebook in hand. As a waitress here at Piggly's, she had to wear a plastic pig snout on her nose and a pink bow in her hair. When some of the guys started making grunting and squealing noises, she looked like she wanted to kill them.

Just then, Mr. Pineeda entered the room with his heavy arms spread wide and a big grin on his face. "Good evening, mighty Roughriders! Welcome, all of you! Tonight is a very special night. Tomorrow, you play against the Dysart Trojans —"

"Tomorrow we crush Dysart!" McKay shouted.

"Yeah, dude!" Karn yelled.

Mr. Pineeda laughed and waved for them to be quiet. "That's the spirit, men! But to win an important game like this, a man must build up his power and stamina. That's why it's important, on the eve of battle, to eat a big meal. Piggly's SSSBS will put the *fire* in you!" Some of the guys laughed. Others cheered or pounded the table. Mr. Pineeda nodded toward Kendra, who did not share the enthusiasm. "Miss Kendra Hanson and I will be around to take your order. Oh! And don't be shy, men. Tonight, for the Roughriders, everything is half price!"

The room erupted into loud whoops and cheers. Cody growled as he bit down on the middle of his fork. I could have sworn he actually bent it. The rest of the supper went like that. I mostly sat back and watched, enjoying the Piglet Dinner, a regular-size barbecue pork sandwich that came with an order of curly fries called Pigtails. Some of the upperclassmen made toasts, and we all raised our glasses. Otherwise, we joked and talked at our tables. It was the kind of fun high school stuff Dad had written about, it was all completely stupid, and I loved every moment of it.

Just when I thought the night couldn't get any better, when I returned home, I found another letter addressed to me, waiting in the stack of mail on the dining room table. I hurried up to my attic to read it. As I'd hoped, it was from Dad.

Saturday, June 12, 2004 (351 Days Left)

Dear Michael,

A lot has happened in the last couple weeks!

Since our base in Farah Province is only in the beginning phases of construction, there were rumors that me and my guys would be spending most of our year at Bagram Airfield, the main base in Afghanistan. We were hoping that would be true, since our only real duty there was ~~PT~~ physical training, and since Bagram has a coffee shop, a computer lab with Internet, a great chow hall, and even a Burger King.

But this last week, the leadership told us we'd be moving out to Farah. So we readied our gear and our weapons for leaving the main base — what they call "going outside the wire." I'm a team leader, so I've been issued an M203 grenade launcher, a short round tube beneath my M16 barrel. Each of us with an M16 was issued six magazines with thirty rounds in each one. On top of that, they handed me eight M203 grenade rounds. Plus, in our squad alone, two soldiers each carry an M249 Squad Automatic Weapon, the SAW. One of those guys always acts half crazy and the other is basically just a kid, and now both of them are walking around with loaded, fully automatic machine guns. Everybody is trained and retrained with their weapons, and I trust them. It's still nuts to think how much firepower we're all packing, and nobody seems to notice or care. With all these weapons, I wonder what kind of a fight command is expecting for us down the road.

Me and my guys were flown to the city of Herat, which is north of Farah. As soon as we stepped off the C-130, there were hajjis everywhere! ("Hajji" is what we call a person from Afghanistan.) Some of them had guns. AK-47s. Right away a couple of our guys yanked the charging handles on their M16s to chamber rounds.

I rushed over to them and told them to lower their weapons, because these hajjis didn't look like they were about to shoot us or anything. It turned out the ones with guns at the airport were on our side.

After a crazy ride down streets crowded with cars, motorcycles, and even donkeys, we made it to our base at Herat. It's kind of like an Afghan mansion, this huge building with a basement and two floors above that. It's really nice, finished off with fancy tiles and woodwork and all. There's a motor shop and another building for temporary soldiers.

Right now, I'm sitting in this weird room in our transient housing building. It's like a dining room back in America, with a big wooden table with padded wood chairs on top of an Afghan rug. When I first came in, I thought it would be a perfect place to write you a letter.

Then I noticed the big, tall windows. Looking out, I could see the tops of the buildings across the street. That meant it was also the perfect place for a sniper to take a shot at me. So I closed the heavy curtains. I know, I'm probably overreacting, but when I'm writing these letters to you — letters you won't get unless I'm dead — I can't help thinking that way. So I'm writing to you with my fully loaded M16 assault rifle sitting on the table next to me, just in case I have to return fire. I've been through training, but this still seems crazy. I'm just a Midwestern working man. How could I have wound up in a situation like this?

Another nice thing about this base is that they have a couple laptop computers to use. Tonight I got an email from my old friend Taylor Ramsey. He asked how the war was going, and said he hoped I'd catch Osama bin Laden. He told me to be safe. It was great to hear from him. The thing is, I haven't really talked to that guy much the last several years.

You need to understand that friends come and go. In high school, your whole life, your whole idea of who you are, is based on the people you are growing up with. If you're an outcast, you're an outcast because you are rejected by the people at school. If you're popular, it's because a lot of them like you. The friends you make in school are closer to you than the friends you'll make at just about any other time, but one day a lot of them will drift away from you.

This is sad, and it might make you wonder if the friendships are even worth much in the first place. But Taylor and some of the other guys helped keep my spirits up in school when I missed my parents, and they celebrated the good times with me too. I cannot imagine how much less full and meaningful my life would be without the memory of them.

Of course, my most important friendship from high school is also the love of my life, the girl I married — your mother. We started going out sophomore year, and except for a short breakup right after I graduated high school, we've been together ever since.

But I have to tell you a secret, Michael. She isn't the only woman I've had feelings for.

Early in my freshman year, soon after I'd lost my parents and moved to Riverside, my life took a nosedive for a while. I was pretty lonely and miserable, but there was one bright spot, this beautiful blonde, Hillary Bently. People said she liked me. I even kind of knew she liked me, since we talked all the time between classes, and she smiled a lot and laughed at my jokes. We got along great, but I'd never been so nervous or unable to talk to her as I was during our freshman-year homecoming dance. Every time a slow song came on, I'd start to walk over to ask her to dance, but then chicken out at the last second, telling myself, "Next song. I'll ask her when they play the next slow song."

On and on it went like that, until finally I just stopped worrying about it and walked right up to where she was standing with her friends. She seemed to sparkle in the colored lights from the stage as she smiled. I asked her to dance, and she said yes.

I froze in horror. I didn't actually know what to do next. I'd never slow-danced before. Yeah, at the high school level, it's mostly swaying back and forth while spinning in a circle, but I was nervous for my first go at it.

Then I learned there's something magic about a school dance. Hillary took my hand and led me to an open spot on the floor. Somehow my hands found her waist and she slid her arms up on my shoulders. As we stood there, moving to the music, my heart beat heavy as I felt her warmth, and she moved closer to put her head on my shoulder. In that moment, I forgot about everybody else at that dance, in the school, in the whole world. Hillary and I were the center of the universe, with little specks of white light spinning around us on the gym floor like a galaxy of stars. When the song ended, the lights in the gym came back on and the dance was over.

After that, since the night was warm, we went for a walk and somehow ended up heading just out of town, down the abandoned railroad tracks to the Runaway Bridge. With a big bright moon shining above and the English River gurgling below, and without saying anything or thinking about it much, I kissed that girl. My very first kiss. And none of that would have happened if I hadn't finally worked up the courage to ask her to dance.

Life is like a high school dance, Michael. You have to take a risk and take the opportunities as they come. You don't always get another chance. You never know when it's the last song.

Maybe you've kissed a girl. Maybe a couple. Maybe not. Either way, it's okay. I remember Valentine's Day during seventh grade. It seemed like every guy in the whole middle school except me had a girlfriend he could buy flowers or candy or balloons for. I was all alone, figuring no girl would ever like me.

I was helping my old man organize the tool room in the basement that night when he asked me why I was so down. After I told him, you know what he did? He laughed! He actually laughed. Then he apologized right away and told me what I want to tell you in case you ever feel like I did. He said, "Listen. I know it doesn't seem like it now, but one day, you'll work it out with the girls and you'll have more dates than you can handle." He grinned and punched me in the arm. "And one day, one of those girls will break your heart."

Wise words from your grandfather. They turned out to be true, because six months after our kiss, Hillary dumped me.

I'm very happy with the way things turned out with your mother and our family, but when Hillary ditched me I couldn't eat, couldn't sleep, and didn't feel like leaving my room for over a week. And even though she moved away before senior year, and I haven't seen or heard from her in ages, I still think about her once in a while.

Adults tend to belittle teenage love. They say it's not really love, or it's just hormones. And sure, some relationships are mostly just physical, but that doesn't mean that young love can't be real, and it doesn't mean young relationships don't matter.

I was lucky to find the love of my life when I met your mother sophomore year, but you might not marry the girl you date in high school. By the numbers, the odds are against the two of you working out. But even if it doesn't last, that doesn't mean you didn't love her. And you will remember her forever.

So that's your mission for this letter, Michael: Make your move with a girl. If there's someone you'd like to get to know more, find a way to spend time with her. Talk to her. Ask her to dance. Take her roller-skating. Make your memories with the girl or girls you date good ones. Make her happy.

And when you finally encounter the Heartbreaker — someone who by ending your relationship makes you so sad that you wonder if maybe you never should have dated anyone to begin with — let her go gracefully. When that day comes, and it will come, it will be one of the most painful experiences of your life. And I'm sorry, but even if I were still alive to talk to you about it, there would be nothing I could do to make it hurt less.

Just try to hold on to the idea that the pain will fade in time, and because of her, you'll have the gift of good memories *to take with you as you go forward in life. I wish you luck and joy with your mission.*

I have so much more to tell you, Michael, and I wish I had more time, both in life with you, and for writing more letters like this.

I love you very much.

Love,

Dad

I rolled onto my back on my bed and looked up at the ceiling. My collection of scrapes and bruises proved that completing my first mission wasn't easy, but this second one seemed just about impossible. Make a move with a girl? Ask someone to dance? Now Dad sounded like Ethan. I didn't care what Dad or my grandfather said, there was no way I'd ever have more dates than I knew what to do with. Girls were not into me.

About the only girl I ever talked to was Isma. Yeah, she was pretty and smart, but what was I supposed to do, go up to her in the library and tell her that I had to ask her out because this letter said so? Even if she said yes, then would I be going out with her because I wanted to, or because of this letter? And if I asked her to homecoming or something, and she said no, wouldn't that completely mess up the way we worked well together on projects?

I carefully folded my father's letter and slipped it back in the envelope. I didn't know the answers to any of my questions, but I was sure mission number two wouldn't be easy to complete.

SIX

On Friday morning, I hid my jersey from Mom and Mary in my backpack until I could slip it on over my shirt at school. When I went down the freshman and sophomore hallway toward my locker, some people looked surprised to see me in the red and white. Clint rolled his eyes. A couple girls in a group of freshmen smiled and waved. Between classes, a few people nodded and wished me luck.

"I can't get used to you wearing that," Isma said as soon as we moved into groups in seventh-hour history.

"Yeah, well . . ."

She smiled. "I guess I'll be cheering you on, then."

"Don't make a special trip on my account. I'm not even going to play, since I started so late."

"I'm in the marching band, remember? I have to help paint the backdrop for the set of the musical after school, but then I'll be at the game whether you play or not."

"Oh yeah," I said. I should have remembered she'd be playing her clarinet tonight.

"So, this project is due in a week. Have you made any progress on the report?"

"I've done some research, but not much else." I sunk my face in my hands. "I'm sorry. I've been buried in football practice and everything. But I swear, I'll get it done soon."

Isma sighed. "When? We need that report to make our presentation."

"I'll write it tonight!"

"The game is tonight."

"After the game," I said.

"You're really going to work that late?"

I often stayed up late, alone in my attic, reading. "It's not like I'm playing anyway. I'll have plenty of energy left for the paper. I'll knock it out, no problem."

She folded her arms and stared at me.

"I promise," I said.

She narrowed her eyes.

"Stop looking at me like that." I laughed a little, but Isma held her stare. "It'll be done tomorrow morning." I continued without thinking, "Come over to my house in the afternoon. The report will be finished and we can work on the speech."

"Really?"

Wait, had I actually just invited her to my house? Was that all there was to Dad's second challenge? No way. Dad had been talking about romance, and there was nothing romantic about this Civil War project. Anyway, if Isma came over, Mary would do everything she could to annoy us. Mom would ground me until forever if she found out, since she was ashamed of the condition of our house. I hadn't had anyone over since sixth grade, and even Mary's horde of giggling friends always met up somewhere else. But I couldn't back out now, and Mom would be working anyway. "I haven't had a Saturday off in forever," I heard myself saying. "Derek keeps telling me I should take a weekend off. How about four o'clock?"

Isma tipped her head to the side just a little. Her eyes kind of sparkled as she smiled. "That's perfect."

"Great," I said. "Sounds like a plan."

★ ★ ★

After school I felt like an idiot because I couldn't find the assignment sheet Coach Carter had given us for the history paper. His requirements were always very strict, and without those instructions, I would probably mess it all up. I hated to ask Isma for her copy because she already seemed to have her doubts about me, but it had to be better to suffer a little embarrassment up front than a lot after I'd screwed up the paper. I went down the hall to find Isma.

Riverside High School was too small for an auditorium, so our stage was at one end of the lunchroom, which we called the cafetorium. From what I'd heard, the lights were ancient and there was hardly any room backstage, but our English teacher, Ms. Burke, had directed some great shows.

When I entered the cafetorium, it didn't look like anyone was directing anything. Two freshmen almost knocked me down when they ran past, laughing and chasing each other. A group sat talking on the edge of the stage while others worked with saws and electric screwdrivers, building fake walls. I recognized the end of "Come Sail Away" by Styx from listening to my dad's old CDs, and watched as Denny Dinsler picked up the needle on an old record player to start the song over.

"Can't you guys find an iPod?" I asked Denny.

"M-Ms. Burke won't let us p-play music unless it's on v-vinyl," he said.

"Why?"

He shrugged. "No one knows."

"She's not even here," I said.

Denny nodded. "She's d-down the hall m-making copies, but the r-rule is vinyl or nothing."

"Are you in the musical?"

"I have a s-small part, but it's f-fun," Denny said. "I'm working on saying my lines w-without my stutter."

"Cool, man." In addition to his stutter, Denny was cursed with bad skin and asthma. People never gave him a break, but he had guts being in the musical.

"Mike, I'm so glad you're here." Raelyn ran up to me and grabbed my arm. "You *have* to help us."

I didn't know much about the musical, but I'd heard Raelyn had a big part. Ethan said she was taking it very seriously. "What's up?"

"We need a guy to play a random customer in the first act and a businessman in the second. There are just a few lines and a short song. Ms. Burke said I should try to find someone. Will you help us, *please*?"

I laughed. Ethan wasn't kidding. This girl looked like her whole life depended on this show. "I can't. I have football practice and —"

"We rehearse after sports p-practice, so it's n-no problem," Denny said.

"Yeah, I have to work after football," I said. Raelyn's smile faded. "But Ethan doesn't. I bet I could get him to join you."

She gasped. "Really? Do you think he would?"

If Ethan's total devotion to Raelyn this last summer hadn't convinced her that he'd do anything for her, the guy was going to have to work a lot harder to prove that he cared. "I bet I could talk him into it," I said.

When I finally broke away from those two, I found Isma standing on a ladder, painting an urban-wasteland scene on a canvas large enough to dominate the entire wall at the back of the stage.

"It's looking good," I said.

She turned on the ladder to face me. She wore old jeans and an oversize white button-down shirt, both peppered with paint splotches. "Hey, what are you doing here?"

My cheeks felt hot. "I lost the stupid assignment sheet for the paper. Can I borrow your copy?"

"Not off to the best start." She laughed, pointed to her black backpack with her brush, and went back to work on her canvas. "In my purple binder."

I quickly found the paper, then took the time to really look at her mural. "How do you know how to paint such a huge painting? Like, I could never do something like that."

"I've never done anything like this," she said. "Good thing Skid Row is supposed to look run-down."

"Well, you're great at painting something that looks run-down."

She looked at me with an amused frown. "I'll just assume that was a compliment." I shrugged, and she laughed. "Will you get out of here and let me paint? Besides, don't you have a game to get ready for?"

"Hmm. I have time. Maybe I'll stay here and bother you until then."

Isma dipped her brush in fresh paint and held it up, threatening to flick paint all over me. "You better watch it!" She grinned.

I put my hands up. "Okay. Okay. I'm going." I smiled as I headed for the door.

"Good luck tonight," Isma called after me.

I went home to drop off my books and check the mail, then was back at the school in time to prep for the game. The cheerleaders, dressed in their short-skirted red-and-white uniforms, ran through their routine in the front lobby by the trophy case.

"Good luck, Mike," Sarah Carnahan said as she shook her pom-poms. Despite sitting behind me in English, she hadn't talked to me at all so far this school year, and maybe only a couple times last year. Maria Vasquez tossed a lock of her black hair back and laughed before whispering something to Sarah.

Nicky Dinsler, Denny's sister and the only senior on the squad, elbowed Maria. "Yeah, good luck," she said. Nicky had never spoken to me in my entire life. This football thing was changing everything. I smiled and nodded at the girls and moved on.

In the gym, Clint, Rhodes, and Chris Moore were playing catch. Dozer burst through the doorway from the short hall that led to the locker room just as I reached for the handle. He stepped up in my face so close I could smell garlic on his breath. "Get. Ready. To. Kill." He grabbed my shoulders and yanked me around, then stepped past me.

I passed the training room off the little hall on the way to the locker room. Laura waved to me before returning to her work taping up Monty's ankle. Kelsey worked with a screwdriver to fix something on a helmet. Monty held up his fist, and I answered the same way.

The dusty-sweat smell hit me as soon as I entered the locker room. The guys were in various stages of suiting up, yelling at each other to be heard over the metal blasting from the stereo. I went to my locker to change.

Coach Brown poked his head out from the coaches' room. "Hamilton, get in here! I want to go over the read for that reverse Dysart likes to run." Hamilton ran to see what Coach had to say.

Cody Arnath shadowboxed and lightly punched the lockers. "I want to break something! Let's do this right now!"

"You'll get your chance!" Eddie Bracken hit Cody hard in the shoulder pads. Cody shoved back. They both laughed.

As I opened my locker, someone grabbed me from behind and pressed a rag or something to my face. The stench from the cloth was like a cross between burned fish and that ammonia stuff I sometimes used to clean the toilet. I struggled to break free, but the guy had me in a tight hold. The toxic gas filled my whole world.

When my attacker released me, I gasped for air. The locker room smelled fresh and clean for once. I spun around to see Karn shake his T-shirt at me. "Yeah," he sort of growled. "My game shirt. Worn in every game since I took over the quarterback position last year. Never washed. Breathe in that luck!" Then he slipped the filthy shirt on and went to his locker.

I'd been assigned the locker next to Tony Sullivan's. He was suited up in everything but his helmet, sitting on the bench in front of his locker, his eyes narrowed to slits and head rocking in time with the music. I dressed quickly and then took a seat next to him. I thought about saying something, but he didn't seem interested in conversation. He breathed deeply, and tension, not quite a tremble, rippled all through his body. McKay moved around the room playing air guitar. Drew Hamilton had folded his hands and bowed his head, mumbling prayers. Ethan studied the playbook.

I knew I could never explain it to Isma or anyone else, but the ritual of it, the energy coursing through everyone in the room, it charged me. I could face the nerves and anxiety about tonight's game as long as I would be facing them with these guys.

Eventually Coach Carter shut the music off and sent us out to the game field to run through our stretches. The sun hung low in the west and a few bugs circled the lights high above the field. The crowd began to fill the bleachers. I could hear the band warming up in the parking lot over by the school. After we stretched and did a walk-through of our offense, we returned to the locker room.

"Men." Coach spoke loudly as he walked the room. "Tonight is our first football game of the season. For some of you, it is your first varsity game. For the seniors, it is their last first game of their high school careers. Those ideas might make you excited. They might get you thinking about the time you have left to make a lasting difference to Riverside football." He stopped pacing and put his hands on his hips. "But I'm telling you right now that all of those considerations should matter to *none* of you! The only thing that is important is this moment. All that should be on your mind is that first kickoff or kick return. When we've crushed the Dysart Trojans on that play, all you will focus on is the next play, the enemy player you must block or tackle, the moves you must make. Each of you men is a model of Hard Work, Integrity, and Team, and now it is time to go out there and put the HIT to Dysart! Let's go!"

With an intense war cry, the team rushed to the field, and soon enough we kicked off. The Trojans were tough to stop on their kick return, and they brought the ball up to their forty-yard line.

"Okay!" Karn shouted from the sidelines. "Shake that off, and let's go, defense!"

But the defense couldn't halt Dysart's pass for a gain of nine yards. It also couldn't stop a dive for six more yards and the first down. Finally, McKay shot through the line to sack Dysart's quarterback, but on the next play, the Trojan fullback broke loose and ran the ball into the end zone. The point-after-touchdown kick set the score at seven to nothing.

When our offense took over after receiving the kick, Sullivan had a couple gains for ten, then fourteen yards. Our crowd roared back to life, and the guys gained a new energy to get back into the fight. We were still in the game. I just wished I could do something to help. Then Karn threw to Clint out in the flat, but a Trojan picked off the pass.

Dysart didn't slow down, with three large gains and a quick pass to score again. Another kick set the score at fourteen to zero.

Coach Carter called a time-out, pulling the kickoff-return team and the starting offense into a huddle. I couldn't get close enough to hear him, but whatever he said couldn't have worked too well. A near-frantic anger showed in just about all the guys. Dozer kicked at the ground.

"Let's go, guys! This is pathetic!" Rhodes yelled.

The Roughriders tried to return the kick, but the Trojans blew through the blockers and leveled Clint, who was lucky just to hold on to the ball at Riverside's twenty-five-yard line. I would never have admitted it to anyone, but a small part of me enjoyed watching that jerk stagger around a little after taking the hit.

Our offense didn't do much better than the return. A dive play was stopped at the line of scrimmage. Then, on second down, Karn took the snap, but before he could hand it off, one of Dysart's outside linebackers pushed Rhodes's block aside and throttled Karn. It was an ugly play. The whistle blew and the celebrating Trojan linebacker jogged back to his huddle.

Rhodes ran up behind him and shoved him in the back, knocking him to the ground. "How do you like *that* cheap shot!" he shouted. The ref immediately threw the flag for unsportsmanlike conduct and moved us back fifteen yards.

Coach Carter threw down his clipboard. "Wilson! Get in there for Rhodes, right now!"

"Coach?" I'd only had three practices. There had to have been someone else. Maybe I'd heard him wrong.

"Move it, Wilson!" he shouted, his face red. "Rhodes, get over here!"

My heart thumped hard as I sprinted out onto the field to take my place in the huddle. Karn called for a pass play. "Let's go, guys!" He looked at me. "Your first play. Try not to screw it up."

I ran out to the line, dropping into a three-point stance. The linebacker who had just sacked Karn looked at me and laughed. I bit down hard on my mouth guard and breathed heavy through my nose. McKay hiked the ball. I shot off the line, low and fast, straight for the linebacker. He came at me, but I ran lower, coming up hard into his numbers and running through him.

The linebacker fell. *Now what?* I tried to find the ball. Karn had launched a pass toward Clint, but a cornerback was sweeping in. He'd intercept it before Clint could catch it. I ran for it and reached out until my fingertips brushed the football. It fell into my hands. I had it. I had the ball, and I bolted fast, ducking the cornerback's out-stretched arm and heading upfield.

A safety closed in on me. He had a good angle, and I'd never get away. If I couldn't lose him, at least I'd give him a good shot before he took me down. I lowered my upper body to ram him in the chest, but at the last second he moved just slightly so I speared his shoulder. He spun and fell, but reached out to snag my ankle, leaving me stagger-ing for a few steps before I could run again. The other safety rocketed toward me. He was bigger than the first, and I'd never break his tackle.

Then Sullivan flew through in a blur and slammed him aside. "Go! Go! Go!" he shouted at me. "Don't turn around, idiot! Run!"

I threw one foot down, then the other, as hard and fast as I could. My arm ached from clenching the ball so tightly. Ten yards to go. Five. Touchdown! That was it. I'd scored! I wasn't even supposed to play tonight, wasn't supposed to have the ball, and I'd put our first six on the board!

Someone crashed into me from the side — Sullivan, who head-butted me with his face mask. "Yeah, baby! Touchdown! Awesome moves!"

He let me go and for a moment I just sort of stood there. Our crowd clapped and stomped their feet in the bleachers. The guys on the team jumped up and down and shouted. I didn't know what to do with the football.

"Come on," Sullivan said. "We gotta kick!"

"Here you go, son," the ref said, holding out his hands.

I tossed the ball to him and went back to the huddle. The guys slapped me on the shoulder pads and punched me in the helmet, laughing and cheering. When we settled into the huddle, even Karn leaned over so he could see me. "Nice catch," he said.

Our kick sailed wide, but I couldn't hold back a stupid grin even when I reached the sidelines.

"Sloppy play, Wilson," Coach Carter said when I ran up near him. "But good work."

We kicked off and our defense took over. The Trojans made a series of short gains, allowing them to keep earning first downs. Eventually they scored again, leaving the score at halftime twenty-one to six.

The team was pretty furious on the way to the locker room, but I couldn't help feeling a little pumped. Then Rhodes checked me in the shoulder, almost knocking me down. He ran on by without saying a word.

The coaches went over plays in the locker room, trying to point out adjustments to our strategy. Laura crouched down in front of me as she handed me a water bottle. She smiled and whispered, "Nice play, Mike."

"Thanks," I said, and smiled back.

That was the last nice moment of the game. Coach didn't let Rhodes play for the rest of the time, so I had to cover his spot at tight end. The linebacker I'd knocked down on that first play took his revenge again and again, laying tough hits on me. I never gave up a sack like Rhodes had, but I never pulled off another great play. Nobody else did either. We ended up beat, beaten down, forty-one to six.

After the game, Coach gave us a consolation talk in the locker room, throwing around words like *discipline* and *execution* and *determination*. Then we cleaned up. Nobody said much. Cody punched his locker. Karn showered and dressed and then sat on the bench with his head in his hands, looking down at his pile of sweat-soaked clothes as if he wondered what had happened to all their smelly luck. I walked past him on my way out of the room.

"Wilson," he said without looking up.

I stopped. "Yeah?"

"You kept us from being shut out. Nice play."

"Thanks," I said. I waited a moment longer. "Thanks for the good pass."

He sort of snorted. I went out to the gym, where the air smelled sweet and felt cool compared to the warm, damp stench of the locker room. Only two dim service lights held back the quiet dark, and my footfalls echoed on the wood floor.

I should have been all upset like the other guys, and I did wish we had won, or at least not been beaten so badly. I knew I'd have several new bruises too. But my mind kept running back to the lights on the field, the sense of power I felt when I knocked that linebacker down, the terror and exhilaration of my frantic touchdown run. The guy on the loudspeaker announcing my name. The crowd on Bleacher Hill cheering.

So far, all high school had ever meant to me was an opportunity for a better future. I'd viewed Riverside High as nothing more than a stepping stone on my way to college and a way out of this tiny town. Tonight, for the first time, school had meaning beyond the future. Tonight felt like it mattered on its own.

I wished I could tell Dad about it.

On my way toward the front of the school, I entered the dimly lit cafetorium to find my sister waiting for me with her arms folded.

"You are in so much trouble," Mary said. "Mom will *freak* when she finds out you were playing football." She put her palms against her cheeks and spoke in a high-pitched voice. "Oh, my sweet baby boy! You'll be hurt if you play football! You'll be hurt if you leave the house or have a life!"

"Knock it off!" I checked to make sure nobody else was around.

Mary laughed. "You are going to be grounded for the rest of your *life* when Mom hears about this. But then, you never had a life before, so what would be the difference?" She tapped her foot on the floor.

"On the other hand, you know, I had to borrow money from Tara and Crystal when we celebrated our victory at Piggly's. I'm supposed to buy for the girls next time. As the new seventh-grade class president, I'd say if you forked over fifty bucks, I might be persuaded not to tell Mom about this."

"Fifty!"

Mary shrugged. "Yeah, because there's also this shirt at the mall that I kind of want."

Why couldn't I have had a brother instead of a sister? A brother I could've punched in the arm for being such a jerk. But as smart as Mary thought she was, she could be a real idiot sometimes. "Does Mom know you're here tonight?"

Her smug grin faded a little. "What?"

"You're right. Mom doesn't let us do anything, so I'm wondering if you have permission to be here."

She remained silent.

"Hmm," I said. "I'm thinking Mom expects you're at home right now and you just went out anyway. She'd probably ground you if she discovered you'd sneaked out. She's even more protective of her little baby girl than she is of me." I took a step toward her. "If I had to stop playing football, I'd be home all the time to make sure you never went out with your friends, and I wouldn't give you any money for shopping trips or dinners at Piggly's." She wouldn't even look at me now, and I had to laugh. "I'll keep your secret if you keep mine."

She blew out a frustrated huff, like a five-year-old having a tantrum. "I hate you," she said, spinning away from me so fast that her hair whipped up in the air. She walked off toward the lobby but stopped near the trophy case and faced me. "I never pay any attention to the game, but Brandon Larson — he's this really cute boy in my grade. His sister is a cheerleader and is so awesome. . . . Anyway,

Brandon said you scored a touchdown. That's kind of cool." She went out through the lobby. "But you're still a dork!" she shouted back.

The parking lot in front of the school was deserted except for a few teachers' cars. A bunch of people were hanging out in the student parking lot around the side. I could hear their stereos and some of their loud voices. They were always there for a while after the game.

The school door opened behind me, and Isma came out. "Hey, I've been looking for you everywhere. You scored! Your first game and you scored a touchdown!" She squeezed my arm, showing more excitement about my big play than anyone else outside the team. "That's really cool, right?"

"I guess so," I said.

"You guess so?" She laughed. "You know so. So, Mr. Sports, will you walk me home?"

"Sure," I said. At the beginning of the last school year, her family had moved into one of the cool new houses in the west-side development. I'd never been to her house, but that neighborhood was sort of on the way to where I lived.

I pulled Scrappy out of the rack and walked it along as we started up the Lincoln Street hill. For a long time the only sound was the embarrassing clanking and rattling of my bicycle. This was our very first time hanging out together outside of school.

"We're still on for tomorrow, right?" she said.

"Yeah," I said. "And before you ask, yes, I will have the report written by then. It might actually not be so terrible either."

"I never thought it would be bad. You're a good writer. A smart guy. You don't give yourself enough credit."

What could I say to that? "What are you going to do tonight while I'm slaving away on this paper?"

"Oh, not much. I have some new comics to read."

"Wait. What? You read comics?"

She stopped. "What's wrong with that?"

"Like what kind of comics?"

"Spider-Man. Iron Man. Lots of Captain America."

I hadn't expected this at all. I used to read a lot of comics, mostly stuff I'd found in one of Dad's old trunks, but lately I'd turned my attention toward more serious books. "Wow," I said.

"What's so 'wow' about it? Just comics."

"I know, but not a lot of girls read about superheroes."

She hurried ahead of me. "I take back what I said about you being smart."

I jogged to catch up with her. "No, no. I think it's cool. I just didn't know that about you."

She stopped, looking right at me with her depths-of-space eyes. "There's a lot you don't know about me."

We stood very close to each other, and neither of us moved. Her smile made her nose crinkle, and I wondered what she was thinking.

Then a car rounded the corner and its headlights fell on us. The car's brights came on as it got closer, and in the glare I couldn't tell who it was.

The car stopped. "Woo, Wilson and Ass-ma!" Rhodes yelled out the window. The guys riding with him called out a bunch of crude jokes and other stupid crap. Rhodes pointed at me. "You got lucky tonight, scoring that touchdown that should have been mine. I'll see you in practice, loser!"

I took two steps toward the car to see if Rhodes felt like fighting about it. Isma grabbed my arm and held me back. "Not worth it," she said.

I bit my lip and let the car drive off. Isma was probably right.

"I hate those guys," I said.

"I know what you mean."

A short while later we were on her street. The houses here traded off the honor of winning Riverside's "Lawn of the Month" award in the *Riverside Reporter*. They were large, clean, newer homes, all with similar neutral shades of aluminum siding and brick fronts.

Isma stopped where a maple tree cast a shadow from the street-light. She pointed to the largest house at the end of the street, a big place with a two-car garage, a huge window in front, and a chimney for the fireplace. "That's where I live. Thanks for walking me home."

"Well, we're not really there yet," I said.

She laughed a little, but kept sneaking glances at her house. "Yeah, I know, but if you walked me up to the door, my . . . um . . . my little brother might see you, and then he'd make kissy noises and make a big deal out of it." She looked up at me. "Um . . . making a big deal out of you walking with me, not of us kissing." Then her eyes went wide, as if she'd just realized what she'd said. "Oh. Unh, not that we'd be kissing."

Why had she said that? Was she thinking this was like a date? "Yeah."

"Not that I wouldn't want to —"

"What?"

She wiped her forehead. "No, it's . . . You're fine. I don't know why I . . ." She punched me in the arm. "We're just walking. No big deal. Good luck on that paper, okay? I'll see you tomorrow." She ran off toward her house, stopping on her doorstep long enough to offer a little wave before she slipped inside.

"What just happened?" I whispered.

SEVEN

Back at home that night, even though it was late, I couldn't have slept if I tried. The dull ache in my sore muscles kept pulling me back to the memory of the smell of sweat and grass, the glare from the lights overhead, and the crowd cheering after I ran the ball into the end zone. From there my thoughts drifted to what had happened with Isma, the way she looked at me with her deep, dark eyes, the small electric space between us. I'd never had a night like this before.

In his second letter, Dad had talked about how he'd worked up the nerve to ask that girl, Hillary, to dance. How he'd almost missed out with her because he kept chickening out. Isma had talked about kissing. Did she want to kiss me? Had I botched it with Isma the way Ethan had thrown away his chance to go out with Raelyn last year? Did I even want a chance with Isma? Had I failed my second mission?

I shook my head. Isma and I only worked together on school projects. She was just a friend. Just a really pretty friend. Who probably never thought of me as anything more than a school partner.

Which reminded me of homework. I could always make more sense of books than about anything else. A ring of light kept the attic shadows at bay as I worked at my desk. The Civil War report almost wrote itself. When I finished, I thought about going to bed, but the warmth of my desk light shining on my books held me there, reading *Hamlet* for English.

After I finished the first act, I switched off the light and lay down on my bed to relax, with thoughts of tonight's game, and Isma, and my father spinning through my head.

I woke on Saturday morning about nine. Derek had agreed to stop by at ten to work on the roof, so I went downstairs to the kitchen. From the fridge, I downed the dregs of a two-liter bottle of Coke (hopelessly flat), hoping it would help wake me up.

"Morning, Mikey." Mom yawned as she came into the kitchen in her bathrobe. She ran her fingers back through her still-wet hair.

"What are you doing here?" I asked.

She slumped into a chair at the table. "I live here," she said.

"No, I mean, aren't you supposed to be at work?" If she were still here when Derek arrived to help with the roof, she'd worry about the leak. If she stayed long enough to discover I'd invited Isma over without permission . . . Well, Mom did not approve of guests.

"I told you. Stupid cutbacks at the home. They won't let me cover Saturday mornings anymore. Just a few hours in the afternoon."

At least she'd miss Isma. Maybe Derek could help me smooth things over with Mom about the roof. They knew each other from high school a long time ago.

"Cool." I started to leave the kitchen. "I'll be up in my room."

"Hang on a minute," Mom said. She motioned me toward a chair that she pushed back from the table with her foot. "We've hardly talked since school started. How did the first week go? How's work?"

I joined her at the table. "School's fine, Mom. Work's the same."

She leaned over and reached out to squeeze my hand. "It's your birthday in a few weeks," she said. "Is there something special you'd like?"

"Hunh. You mean besides a car?" I joked.

"Yes, besides the Ferrari I already have parked in the garage with a bow on the hood." She pushed my hand away and laughed. "Seriously, though."

"I seriously don't need anything," I said. I would have liked some books, and I could have used new clothes, but I'd get by. "Anyway, there are more important things to spend the money on besides me." The leaky roof came to mind.

"We'll see about that. There just might be a little surprise for you, mister."

I made some toast and had breakfast. After a few minutes I heard a vehicle pulling up out front. Of course Derek just had to show up early. I headed outside, leaving Mom to her cereal.

"Hey," I said as I jogged over to the Falcon. "Sorry for bothering you with this hassle."

"Oh, no problem. Heard you did real good in the game last night."

I checked over my shoulder to make sure Mom hadn't heard. "It was just one touchdown. We got killed."

"Still, good job." He stepped out of the truck but leaned over the seat to get something. When he turned back around, he held a paper sack in one arm, some sweet corn poking out the top. "Um, is your mom home?"

I frowned. "She's inside."

"Oh. Hmm." Derek looked back to the truck, then at the house, as if he couldn't decide what to do with his food. "It's just, I had all these extra vegetables. From my garden," he added suddenly. "And I can't eat all this. So I thought if your mom . . . I just . . . This was all ripe, and I didn't want it to go to waste."

"Michael?" Mom's voice came from behind me. I spun around to see her coming out on the porch.

"Mom." Great. I couldn't hide any of this now.

"Hi, Derek." She looked tired. "How are you?"

"Hey, Allison." He walked up the path to her. "These vegetables needed to be picked in the garden today. Some sweet corn. Cucumbers and stuff. I thought you might like them."

Mom took the sack. "Thanks so much." She smiled like she hadn't in a while. "It's good to see you again."

"Yeah! You too." They both looked down at the ground. Finally, I had to fake a cough to break the quiet. Derek looked at me. "Well, we're just going to take a look at the roof real quick. Maybe touch it up in the corner."

"Why?" Mom's whole body sagged as if the food had suddenly become much heavier. "Is there a problem? I don't have the money for new shingles."

"Mom, it's fine," I said. "There's just a spot where I noticed a shingle was missing. I wanted to get it patched so that it doesn't leak. It'll take . . ." I looked to Derek.

"About ten minutes, tops."

"Well, that's good." She gave the bag a shake. "Thanks for this, Derek. And for your help."

"Anytime," he said. Mom started toward the front door. "Oh, hey, Allison? I just . . . What are you up to tonight?"

Mom closed her eyes. "Mmm. I get a couple hours at the home this afternoon, but I have the worst headache. When I'm done there, I think I'll see if I can get some rest. Get to bed early."

"Yeah, you should do that." Derek wiped his forehead on his

sleeve. "There's a band down at the VFW. They play a bunch of old eighties and nineties songs. I was thinking about going to see 'em."

Wait a minute! I looked from Derek, who I swore was starting to sweat, to my mother, who actually took a step back. Was Derek asking my mom out? Like, on a date? Mom hadn't been on a date in my whole life. She was . . . she was, well, Mom.

She swallowed and nodded. "That sounds fun. You should really do that. I wish I could get out to see a band sometime." I looked back and forth between them again as the silence set in. "Well," Mom finally said, "thanks again for the food. Have fun tonight."

"Because I was thinking, maybe you could come with me," Derek burst out. "I mean, if you'd like to. 'Cause . . . Would you like to go? With me, to see this band? They're supposed to be good."

I didn't fit in so well at school, and so I had almost more embarrassing memories than our library had books. But I'd never been stuck in a situation quite as awkward as this one.

"I don't . . ." Mom's cheeks flared red.

Did I want Mom and Derek to go out? Well, why not? He was a cool guy, and it would be good for Mom to go do something. "You should go," I said.

"What?" Mom suddenly focused on me as if I'd just popped out of thin air.

"You have the night off anyway," I said. "I'll watch Mary . . . I guess."

Derek shrugged. "What do you say?"

She smiled. "I'll go."

"Really?" he said.

Mom nodded. "I'll go. Why not? It sounds fun."

"Great!" Derek laughed a little. "So I'll swing by at nine to pick you up?"

"Sounds good." Mom shifted the bag to her other hip. "See you then." She went back inside the house.

"What was that all about?" I asked Derek.

He stared at the front door for a moment. "Huh?"

"You just totally asked my mother out," I said.

"What?" he said. "No, it's just hanging out, like old times. Going to see a band. So it's . . . Let's go fix this."

Derek brought his extension ladder around to the corner of the house while I carried his bucket of tools. He climbed up to check out what was wrong. When he came back down, he frowned. "It doesn't look good, Michael. Every shingle up there is old and falling apart. I found a spot where one had fallen away and the tar paper underneath was torn. That's got to be your leak right there."

I pressed the heels of my hands to my eyes, dreading hearing about the thousands of dollars it would take to fix the roof.

"You can patch it, no problem, but it'll be a temporary fix. It's only a matter of time before more leaks spring up. Eventually, you'll have to face the fact that the house needs more serious, more permanent repairs."

I dropped my hands to my sides. "We don't have the money," I said quietly.

"I know." He patted me on the arm. "Let's not worry about that right now."

He handed me a tool belt with a hammer and nails. Then he gave me some shingles and explained how to patch the hole. I climbed the ladder, found the spot he'd mentioned, and lifted the bottoms of a couple shingles to slide the new ones underneath. Then I hammered in nails to lock it all in place. The color wasn't an exact match, but it was close enough, and a mismatched spot on the roof was the least of the troubles for this old house.

Back on the ground, I smiled as I handed Derek his hammer and tool belt. I felt good — tough. Sure, Derek told me how to patch the leak, but then he just held the ladder and I took care of the problem. Dad would have been proud.

I put Derek's tools in the cab as he put his ladder away and climbed in behind the wheel. "I got some stuff to do. Keep an eye on things next time it rains. Let me know if there's any more trouble."

I watched as he drove away. Derek made most other adults seem pretty lame by comparison, and I trusted him more than a lot of people. If Mom had to date someone, he'd be the best choice.

Now that I'd dealt with the roof, the time had come to move on to another project: getting ready for Isma to come over. Mom left for work, and then I had to get rid of Mary. I found her, as I often did, in the living room, slumped with one leg up over the arm of the faded recliner, flipping through the stations on TV.

"If you're not watching anything in particular, do you mind if we watch football?" I asked. "It's the Hawkeyes' first game of the season."

"Why can't we get better cable?" she asked, as if she hadn't heard me. "We don't get any good channels."

"It's kind of expensive to get the better package."

She stopped on some cartoon show and dropped the remote in her lap. Her head flopped back against the recliner as she sighed. "We have to do something about the cable. I'm so bored."

"I'll ask Mom about it. Now will you find the game coverage? I really want to watch the Hawks," I said. She made no effort to change the channel. Boredom had taken over. This was good. "Why don't you go out with your friends? Doesn't Crystal Rhodes go shopping about every weekend?"

"You're such an idiot. Yeah, it would be so fun to go to Iowa City and watch Crystal try on every cool outfit at the mall while I have no money and have to wear dork clothes."

"I just got paid at the farm. I might have a little extra if you want. You could get a shirt or . . . earrings or something."

She flashed me an excited look. "Really?" I shrugged. Then she narrowed her eyes. "Wait a sec. Why do you want to get rid of me so bad? What's going on?"

"No. Nothing. Just, you looked so bored and —"

"I'm always bored around here," Mary said. "You usually tell me to go read a stupid book."

I dropped down on the couch, and a little cloud of dust puffed out. Mary waved her hand in front of her face. "Ugh. Idiot. Anyway, Crystal isn't even going shopping this weekend. She has to visit her grandma in Illinois or something."

What was I supposed to do now? She'd be suspicious of anything I recommended that would get her out of the house. "Fine."

"What's going on?"

I might as well tell her. She would find out in a few hours anyway. "I have this group project on the Civil War for history. My partner, Isma, is coming over later so we can work on it."

Mary flashed her *gotcha* smile. "Isma Rafee? That weirdo Iraqi girl? You like Isma Rafee?"

"No!" I stood up. "I just told you, moron! We're working on a history project. And she's not Iraqi *or* weird."

"You sure are getting mad over someone who is just your school partner."

"I'm getting mad because you're a moron." I went to the arch between the living room and dining room. "So stay out of my way today because I want to clean this place up before she comes over."

"Yeah, yeah." Mary went back to flipping channels. "You want to impress your girlfriend. I know."

She didn't know how much I couldn't stand her sometimes.

EIGHT

I worked for hours to get the house ready, taking periodic breaks to make Mary turn the channel so I could at least check the score of the game. Our dusty little yard didn't have much grass, but after fighting to get our aged mower started, I cut the long weeds. I washed, dried, and put away the dishes. I scrubbed the toilet, sink, mirror, and shower. I vacuumed our rugs, mopped the scuffed wood floors, and dusted everything that needed dusting, which was everything. Mary wouldn't accept a bribe to run to ThriftyTown for Coke and pretzels, so I finally had to make an emergency run on Scrappy.

All of this made me pretty sweaty, so I cleaned myself up and changed clothes. At first I wondered if I shouldn't try to find a kind of dress-up shirt, but I only had a white, long-sleeve, button-down shirt with an irritating collar. A newer Roughriders T-shirt would have to do. Then I sat on the couch in the clean living room and waited. It was only three thirty, but I kept going to the window to peek up and down the street in case Isma came early.

"Mike. Sit down," Mary said. "I don't know how it is with two people as dorky as you and Isma, but a normal girl would be totally creeped out by the way you're acting."

I suppose she picked up her know-it-all attitude from hanging out with Rhodes's sister all the time. "I'm not acting any different," I said. "This is no big deal. Just a history assignment."

"Whatever." Mary went back to watching her show, where a couple was having an awkward conversation over a candlelit dinner.

I sat back down and tried to calm myself. She had a point. Why did I feel so nervous? I couldn't relax or get rid of that hollow feeling in my stomach. Was it because of Dad's second challenge that I was making a bigger deal out of this than it really was?

I heard Isma's footsteps on the porch before I saw her out the window. I waited to give her enough time to press the button so I could fake like the doorbell worked. Then I answered the door.

"Hi," I said. Isma looked great in dark jeans and a light blue T-shirt.

Mary stepped up behind me and to my right, pinching my arm. "Isma! Come in! Oh my gosh, that shirt looks *so* good on you. Where did you get it? I totally want a shirt like that." She pulled me back into the dining room.

Isma came in. "You must be Mary. It's nice to meet you. And the shirt? I can't remember. Somewhere at the mall, I guess." Her school bag was slung over her right shoulder and she held a big bowl covered in plastic wrap. "I brought a snack. We might get hungry."

"Oh, something from your country?" Mary asked.

Isma kept her grin, but I could tell the question annoyed her. "Um, it's caramel corn."

I chuckled.

Mary's cheeks flared red. "Oh. Yeah. Love that stuff. I'll shut the TV off and let you two have the living —"

Isma stepped back. "I don't want to be a bother if —"

"We'll just work on the project in my room," I said. "It's no problem."

I led her up the stairs and around the corner in the hallway, where I held aside the curtain over the doorway to the attic steps. "Right up here." I followed her up the steep stairs, keeping my eyes down so I wouldn't be staring at her backside.

When I came up out of the stairwell, Isma slowly spun around, taking in my rough, unfinished attic. When her turn brought her around to face me, she smiled and pushed back a strand of her black hair. "Is this really your room?"

"Yeah," I said. "Sorry. It's a small house. Only two real bedrooms. My mom and sister use those. I'm stuck up here."

"Yeah, but I love it." She put her book bag down on my bed. "It's like your own space, you know? You have your own floor of the house all to yourself. I have a bedroom with thin walls next to my little brother's room. I hear his stupid video games all the time." She ran her fingers along the spines of some books in my bookcase. "Are these all yours?"

"Some of them," I said. "A lot of them — the spy-thriller paperbacks, the Stephen Kings, and the Patrick O'Brians — belonged to my father. He . . . sort of gave them to me."

"Have you read them all?"

"Most of them."

"I'd want to read all the time too if I had a quiet, hidden-away place like this."

"Yeah, well . . ." I couldn't believe she saw my attic as something besides a dark, run-down slum-dump, that she understood what I liked about this place. "It's pretty quiet up here. Unless it rains. Then the drops sort of pound the roof."

"That sounds kind of nice," Isma said.

I watched her. "It can be," I said quietly. She looked away, and I went to flip on the light and switch on my desk lamp.

"What's on the other side of the curtain?" she asked.

"Oh, not much," I said. "Some storage space and . . . my gym."

"I thought you must have been working out. You have muscles. Can I see this gym?"

In the history of my whole life, no girl had ever noticed that I had muscles before. "I'll show you." I led her to the other side of the

94

curtain and pointed to the cement weights I had made. "They're not exactly Olympic quality, but between lifting here and the work I do on the farm . . . Well, they work okay, I guess."

"You must really love Hawkeye football." She motioned toward my posters hanging on the stacks of boxes.

"I never miss a game. Well, almost never."

She smiled. "Did you make these weights? That's so cool."

I didn't want to act super cocky. I shrugged. "It took forever to figure out how much concrete to pour for the different weights. So instead of the normal ten-, twenty-five-, thirty-five-, and forty-five-pounders, mine are like thirteen-and-a-half pounds." I lightly kicked a different weight. "That one is something like twenty-seven or twenty-eight. Best I could do, I guess."

She rested her warm hand on my bicep. A tingle went up my spine from her touch. "I wouldn't have expected a lot of this."

"I did a lot of curls. Bench press."

She dropped her hand from my arm. "No, I meant the books, the desk — that I can understand. But all the Hawkeye posters, the weights, your going out for *football* — that just seems to clash with the image I have of you."

I shrugged. "For a long time I convinced myself that all I needed were my books. But I've always liked football. It's a fun game. The posters? They help motivate me when I'm lifting, and they're a reminder of my future, hopefully at the University of Iowa."

"To play football?"

"No." I laughed. "I'm not close to that good. But they have a good English program, and one of the best writing programs in the country."

"Too bad those things don't get the kind of attention that sports do."

I pulled the curtain wall aside and led her to the other part of the attic. "That would be nice. It's just that the writing and everything is not as dramatic in the short term as football."

"Your gym took a lot of smarts and a lot of work. I'm impressed." She took another look around the attic. "Wow. That is a huge stereo." She crouched down in front of Dad's old CD-and-cassette player. It was one of those all-in-one units with a three-disc carousel on top and a double tape deck in front. Plus, for some reason, it had tons of blue, green, and red flashing lights. I joined her by the stereo and tapped the POWER button to bring it to life. The whirl of color started on its front panel and in its buttons.

Isma clapped her hands together. "What's it doing?"

I laughed. "It just does all that when it turns on. I guess in the nineties, this was supposed to look futuristic."

She looked at the shelves stacked high with CDs in their cases. "Are these all yours?"

"I guess so. I mean . . . they were my father's."

"He gave them to you? He's really generous."

I rubbed my hand across the back of my neck. "My dad died in the war in Afghanistan."

She stood up straight and put her hand over her mouth. "I'm so sorry."

"It's okay. It was a long time ago."

"I didn't know. I just thought your parents were divorced. It must be . . ." She reached out and brushed her hand down my arm. "I'm sorry. You must miss him very much."

It was very quiet for a moment. I hardly ever talked to people about Dad. It felt strangely good to tell Isma about him. I wanted to tell her more, but I didn't know what to say.

Finally Isma took a deep breath and smiled. "Play us something?"

I hit the button to start the last disc I had in. In a moment, Pink Floyd's "Wish You Were Here" filled the room.

I'd never shown anyone my attic or my gym. Nobody had ever listened to music up here with me. For a moment, I thought of the dance Dad had written about and the mission he'd set for me. Should I ask Isma to dance with me? I had zero experience with girls, and I'd never actually slow danced before. It looked easy enough, but even if Isma didn't think my request was weird and she said yes, I would probably mess it all up.

"Are you okay?" Isma asked. "You suddenly went all quiet."

"You said I must miss my dad very much." I pulled the two letters out from under *Hamlet* on my desk. "That's the thing. I do miss him, but now I've gotten these letters from him." The expression on her face told me she thought that sounded crazy. "Before he died, my dad wrote a bunch of letters for me to have before I turned sixteen. Someone is mailing them to me. I've received two so far."

"Wow," Isma said. "That must be so intense. Who's sending them?"

"I have no idea. Dad had planned to have one of his war buddies deliver them, but I found out that guy didn't make it home either. I think of the sender as the Mystery Mailer. There's no return address or note explaining anything."

Isma looked at the papers in my hands. "Did your dad leave you any clues?" Without thinking, I held the letters out to her. She took a step back. "No. No, I can't. Those words are between you and your father."

"No, it's cool," I said. "I want you to read them. I mean, if you want."

She slowly reached out and took the papers from me. "I'm . . . honored."

I didn't want to sit here watching her read. I remembered the soda downstairs. "Want a Coke?"

"Um, sure." She started reading, and I went downstairs to the kitchen.

Had I really just done that? Handed over my dad's letters? What if she thought I was weird for letting her read them? What if she didn't really want to read them, but didn't want to hurt my feelings about a serious subject like my father?

I went to the fridge and reached down to get two bottles. For some reason Riverside's grocery store, ThriftyTown, sold actual glass bottles of Coke. Soda tasted way better from a glass bottle, and suddenly I was very thirsty.

"How's your date?" Mary said from behind me.

I stood up. "It's not a date! We're working on a school project." I put the bottles on the counter and took the opener from a drawer.

"Whatever. She's cute. You should totally date her."

"I don't need relationship advice from my little sister." I pried the cap off one bottle. "Anyway, it's not like that. We're just —"

"You're so clueless. She totally likes you, Mike."

"Would you just leave me alone!" I felt the heat in my cheeks, and I took a deep breath to calm down. "She does not."

"Yeah, right." Mary made a big show of tossing back her hair and blinking her eyes really fast. "Oh, hi, Mikey," she said in a high-pitched voice as she leaned back against the counter like a model. "I brought you some caramel corn. Don't you think I'm — Oops! I mean, don't you think the caramel corn's — soooooo sssweet?"

"What happened to you?" Not long ago Mary had played with Barbies, and now she thought she knew enough to offer expert advice in romance. "You're only in seventh grade." I popped the top off the other bottle.

Mary stood up straight. "Yeah, and I'm the only one in this family who is living in modern times."

"You're not nearly as sophisticated as you —"

"Have you ever had a girlfriend? Or even held hands with a girl? *Kissed* a girl?"

I grabbed the Coke bottles and the bag of pretzels and headed out of the kitchen. "None of your business."

"Yeah, that's what I thought!" Mary called after me. "Don't ruin your one chance!"

"Is everything okay?" Isma asked when I returned to the attic. She had sat down on my bed. "I heard shouting."

"You heard my idiot sister." I placed the Cokes on the corner of my desk near Isma and sat down on my chair with the pretzel bag open in my lap. I tilted my head to the side and said in my best ditzy-girl voice, "I've learned that it's best to just, like, totally ignore her or whatever."

Isma laughed and handed Dad's letters back to me. "These are amazing, Mike. What a gift." She leaned closer. "Thanks for sharing them with me. It sounds like your father was a really great man. Did these letters convince you to play football?"

"They helped. It's just frustrating not knowing how many more letters might be coming or when they'll arrive."

"Have you thought about asking this Ed Hughes that your dad mentions?"

"I doubt he's sending them. Who would give letters like this to their boss?"

Isma shrugged. "It seems like the best lead you have so far. If you write down all the people your father lists in his letters, I'll help you research them at school."

"Sure," I said. "I don't think he mentions a lot of names, but it would be a start."

Neither of us said anything for a moment. The pretzel I ate seemed to crunch into the silence loud enough to shake the house. "So, about that report." She handed me the bowl of caramel corn. "Here," she said, holding out her hand for the papers I had next to me. "Trade you."

I gave her the report and dug into the caramel corn and pretzels while I watched her read. She'd come over, and we'd talked about everything, and she was sitting on my bed. She didn't really *need* to bring caramel corn for a school project. Could Mary be right? Could Isma like me? I took a drink. The soda tasted cold and sweet, burning the way Coke does.

Finally, she put my report down and had some soda. Light from the window sparkled on the glass and her lips shined a little.

"What did you think?"

"It's good. You're a good writer." She flipped through some papers in her binder. "I think a lot of the ideas in the report would make good points for our speech. We could have a PowerPoint slide for almost every one of your paragraphs." She pulled her laptop out of her bag, opened it, and booted it up.

"I hate doing slides," I said. "Last year I had three PowerPoint presentations and had to ride to school really early in the mornings to get on a computer. But at least I got there before Nick Rhodes or Matt Karn showed up in their cars, making fun of my bike."

"You shouldn't pay attention to those guys," she said.

"They're kind of hard to ignore sometimes."

Isma pressed her lips together. "They're such jerks." Our eyes met. Had she heard what Rhodes said about her in the library the other day? "It's crap what they do. Teachers think they can fix it by making us watch stupid videos about bullying."

"Or when they make us read stories about some kid getting beat up and then ask us, 'How would *you* feel if someone punched *you* to the ground and forced *you* to eat dog poop?'"

Isma laughed, stood up straight like a soldier, and saluted. " 'Gee, teacher, I was going to tape some little kids upside down to a flagpole, pour honey on them, and then dump fire ants all over them, but since I read this sad story, I will study instead. You've really turned me around on this one.'"

I laughed. "I think some of the guys who used to beat me up actually got their ideas for new bullying techniques directly from anti-bullying education."

"Used to beat you up?" Isma asked.

"All though elementary Clint and Adam were sometimes jerks, but in junior high I kind of drifted apart from my friends, and then things with those two got really bad. One day in eighth grade, they had me cornered by the bike rack, and nobody was around to help."

"Tell a trusted adult, right?" Isma said.

I chuckled. "Exactly. So I ran. Lots of times I could outrun them. They'd give up after they chased me and called me names for a while. This time they followed me all the way to the woods north of the school. I tripped on a rock or something and they caught up to me and started shoving me around. Escape was impossible, and I was tired of being beat up. So when Clint shoved me in the chest, I just lost it, decked him, then I kept going. I punched Adam in the nose and he backed up, then Clint came after me again and I slammed my fist into his stomach. Finally, they ran away." I paused, figuring I wouldn't tell her how I had been trembling and all full of adrenaline after they left. "And those guys haven't tried anything like that since that day."

"You're tougher than those guys. You scored a touchdown when none of them could. Anyway," she said, "let's get this speech written and this presentation ready!"

We went to work figuring out what each of us would talk about in our speech. While I wrote a lot of what we'd say, she put together the slides, until we'd finished what already seemed like the biggest, most complicated project of the year. We each had to practice our parts, but we could do that on our own, and we had over a week to get ready.

Only one thing remained, and it would be tricky to get Isma to go for it. "I still need to type my report," I said.

"You want to borrow my computer?"

I could have sworn she'd read my mind. "Wow," I answered. "If you're sure it's okay. It would really help me a lot."

"I trust you," she said. "Just make sure to get it back to me on Monday. If my dad starts to wonder where it is, I could be in trouble."

"Thanks," I said. "This is going to be cool. I'm glad we did this today."

Isma started putting papers back into her binder. "Me too!"

A loud, low car rumble came from outside. Mom's ancient Ford Escort with the worthless muffler! What time was it? Working and joking with Isma, I'd lost track of everything and totally forgotten about Mary and Mom.

"We should be all set," I said, standing up.

Isma stood too, and stretched her arms above her head. "Maybe we could meet sometime to practice our presentation."

Mom would park the car in the garage. No opener, so it would take her a moment to open and close the door. The back door to the house wouldn't latch, so we locked it to keep it from blowing open in the wind. Mom would have to walk around the house to go in the front door. It bought some time, but not a lot. "Sure. Here." I put my hand against Isma's back. "Let me walk you out." I had to hurry without letting Isma know I was hurrying, and I didn't even want her to go.

Down in the dining room, Mary put on a big, fake grin and looked at me with wide eyes. She didn't want Mom to catch us either. "Cool talking to you, Isma."

Isma stopped. I wanted to push her out the door, but then she'd be onto me. "Good to talk to you too," she said.

We were just paces from the front door when it opened. "I'm home, kids," Mom said in a tired voice. Mary groaned quietly behind us. "I'm actually going out tonight, but what do you say we call for a pizza and . . ."

She trailed off when she stepped inside and saw Isma. The silence lasted forever. Isma kept a brave, cheerful face, but even that started to fade in front of Mom's openmouthed surprise. Great. Mom would flip out, and Isma would think my whole family was completely screwed up.

The best I could do was try to act normal. "Mom, this is Isma Rafee. We were working on a project for school."

"Hello, Isma," Mom said. She stepped away from the door but didn't say anything more. Her look of surprise had faded to a sort of blank stare.

"It's nice to meet you, Mrs. Wilson," Isma said. Mom stood still and silent as a statue. Isma shot me a questioning glance. Maybe I should have prepared her in case this happened, but I didn't want to ruin the afternoon by trying to explain my mother.

"Well, I was just leaving," said Isma. "Good-bye, Mike. Have a good night."

She left before I could say anything.

"Bye, Isma!" Mary called. Mom closed the door behind her. "Well, that was messed up," Mary said to us. "Now someone else thinks we're really weird."

"Mary." Mom didn't even look at my sister. "Go to your room. I want to talk to your brother."

"Mom, you gotta relax," Mary said. "They weren't doing anything. He's, like, a total dork, and so is Isma . . . kind of . . . although she actually seems to know about fashion and —"

"Now!" Mom stomped her foot. The sound echoed through the room.

Mary rolled her eyes and marched up the stairs, stomping her feet on each step the whole way.

"You know I don't like you having people over," Mom said to me after the door to Mary's room slammed. "I especially don't like you having people over without permission. Sneaking around? Lying?"

"We weren't sneaking. I never —"

"I come home and find my son has some *girl* over, and who is this person in my house? I don't know. Could be anybody."

"Mom, Isma's all right."

"How do I know that?" She unslung her purse from her shoulder and dropped it on the dining room table. "I don't know anything about this girl because nobody *asks* me if she can come over, nobody *tells* me anything about this strange person. This is why you wanted me to go out tonight, isn't it? So you and her could —"

"It's no big deal, Mom. We were just working on —"

Mom glared at me and pointed toward the door through which Isma had just left. "She's one of *them*, Michael!"

I hoped maybe I was misunderstanding her. "One of who?"

"Those . . . people." She nearly spat when she said "people." "They killed your father and then . . ."

It was as if Nick Rhodes or Hailey Green or one of the other idiots at school had just possessed my mother's mind. How could she be saying what I thought she was saying? How could she even think that? "Isma is not —"

"The arguing! The disrespect!"

"Do you even know how Dad died?" I shouted. "Nobody will tell me. I wish —"

"He was killed in the war, Michael."

"Yeah, I get it. He died for no reason in a useless, endless war."

Mom stomped her foot. "Don't you *dare* say anything like that ever again! Your father died fighting for freedom."

"What does that mean? What actually happened to him?"

Her face screwed up like she was in pain. "What? I don't know. Why would I want to know every little detail —"

"Well, I can tell you this. He did not die fighting an American girl like Isma!" I didn't wait around to hear any more, but ran toward my attic.

"I forbid you from talking to or seeing that girl again!" Mom yelled after me.

I stopped for a moment in the hallway upstairs. I heard Mom call Derek, saying she couldn't go out that night. She claimed to be too tired.

I climbed the steps to my attic, tired of my mother.

NINE

Up in my attic, I put on one of Dad's old metal CDs. Then I cut loose on my punching bag, throwing the right side of my whole upper body forward to slam my fist into the fabric, then following it with a bunch of low jabs, right and left and right and left. I twisted my lower body around, turning my upper torso the opposite way for balance as I swept my right leg up in a kick. "Almost sixteen . . ." Another kick. "Can't have a simple homework meeting with a girl." I threw a fast series of punches, right-left, as fast as I could. "Can't date . . ." *Right-left, right-left.* "Hardly any friends." *Punch-punch.* A kick with the knee. "Got to sneak around to play football like a normal guy." *Punch-punch-punch-punch-punch.* "Never do *anything*!"

I pressed my fists to the side of my head so hard that my arms shook. A bead of sweat ran down my cheek.

"Mike?" Mary said quietly from the other side of the sheet.

I was not in the mood to listen to my snotty little sister's I-told-you-sos. "Go away!" The music stopped. "I said get out of here!"

"Trust me," she said, "the last thing I want to do is hang out in your weirdo attic. The mail came while you and Isma were . . . doing whatever you two were doing up here."

"We were just working on a project for —" Why explain myself to her? "Just leave!"

"You got another letter. Doesn't say from who."

I whisked the curtain aside and snatched the envelope from her fingers.

"Who keeps sending —"

"None of your business," I said. She always hated hearing about Dad, so why should she be in on his letters now?

"Whatever." She rolled her eyes. "In a normal family, people would just text or email."

"This isn't a normal family."

"I know." Mary stopped halfway down the stairs. "About Isma . . . What Mom said about her is way messed up."

She left me staring after her. Something was rotten in the state of Iowa when my sister and I actually agreed on something.

I looked at the new envelope in my hands. This one was thicker than the others, but it had been addressed with the same sloppy handwriting, the same Iowa City postmark, and no return address. Trying to calm myself, I sat down at my desk and opened the envelope. Again, no note had come from whoever had mailed this letter. I remembered Isma's suggestion about contacting Ed Hughes. Maybe that would lead to some answers.

For now, I took out the message that my father had written years ago. He had said that part of the point of these letters was to give me advice. I hoped he had some answers to all the questions I had about how I was supposed to handle life. About how I was supposed to deal with Mom.

Sunday, July 4, 2004 (329 Days Left)

Dear Michael,

Happy 4th of July! And greetings from my new home in the city of Farah. These have been a few of the craziest weeks of my life. If the rest of my time here goes like this, I will have many stories to tell when I get home. I only pray that I'll be able to tell you all of them in person.

Of course, if you're reading this . . .

We spent about three weeks in the city of Herat in northwest Afghanistan, where I last wrote to you. I miss that place already. The base there was a nice place with a great chow hall in the basement, rooms with air-conditioning, and showers available whenever we wanted them. Hot water, even. The city is pretty advanced as far as Afghanistan goes. A lot of the streets are paved, and we could even go to the little shops a few times.

That didn't last, since orders came down for us to pack up and prepare to move to Farah. So we drove south through the blazing-hot Afghan desert. If you've seen photographs of the surface of Mars, that was what it looked like out there.

Little Mikey, the seven-year-old version of you, who's at home right now as I write this, thinks I'm super brave. He thinks I'm fearless because I've gone to this war. Of course, that's how I acted when I left, so that I wouldn't scare you all. But now that you're old enough for the truth, I need you to know that I was terrified on the mission south to Farah. That was the first time when we were all really out in the open on our own. If the Taliban would have ambushed us along the road when all we had was one combat squad with some cooks and medics, and all of us in weak little civilian Toyota trucks, we'd have all been killed. The convoy made it safely, though.

The city of Farah is a crazy place. It's not as large as Herat, but it's a lot bigger than any of the villages we drove through on the way. It has two streets that have recently been paved, the bazaar road and one cross street. The rest are bumpy and made of dirt and rock. Almost all the buildings are one-story mud brick, all hidden away behind mud-brick walls.

I can't believe this is where I'll be living and working for the next year. Our base here isn't even finished yet. We have no air conditioners and it gets up to about 120 degrees some days. We have no refrigeration, so we're stuck with field rations for every meal. Our well isn't deep enough yet, so it often goes dry. Because of this, we get a shower once every three days, and then for a maximum of three minutes of water use. If the well goes dry on your scheduled shower day? Go pound sand. See you in three days.

I was down at the bazaar here in Farah yesterday and these two young Afghan men came up to me. You know how you can just tell when someone wants to fight? I knew they were mad about something. Now, I had my M16, and neither man seemed to have any weapons, but I couldn't be sure that they were unarmed, and I didn't know how many of their buddies were around. So I smiled, said "Hello, friend" in their language, and reached out to shake their hands. They wouldn't shake, but still acted mad. I kept smiling, kept calling them friends, and insisted they shake my hand. In the end, we were able to buy our stuff and leave without fighting and without having to be all arrogant while bossing people around.

Fighting is horrible, Michael. Never start a fight or be one of those guys who enjoys fighting. Still, at the same time, those people who say violence never solves anything are full of crap. When a fight is unavoidable, when you're being attacked, or when there's absolutely no way out of a situation without being totally dishonored, then make sure you WIN the fight. Fight one on one, never with a group. And unless you're wrestling around with a guy on the ground, never punch or kick a man who's down. Let a guy get up first. Tear into him hard and beat him until he gives up. Then stop immediately.

Of course, never, ever hit a woman. Not even if you think she deserves it. Actually, don't even think that, or joke about it *or allow others around you to joke about it. Even if a woman is attacking you, and you risk taking on some injuries to yourself, even then, never hit a woman.*

Our base is so far out west, so far away from our main base at Bagram, that it is hard to arrange support flights. That means all our food is shipped in by slow trucks, and the chaplain for our Iowa task force will only be visiting once or twice through the whole deployment. We had our first church service sitting in the blazing-hot ammo bunker that we've built. There we were, sitting on cans of 5.56 rounds or on crates of Claymore antipersonnel mines, saying the Lord's Prayer. It is a humble church, but I think every one of us meant those prayers more than at any other time in our lives.

Michael, I want you to go to church. Learn about Jesus. Read the Bible, so that you have your own understanding of the Lord and of right and wrong, not just what someone tells you to think. These things are important. I tell you, son, if I didn't have faith, I don't know how I'd make it through this. I've talked to your mother about making sure she gets you to church and Sunday school while I'm gone.

I remembered that! We used to go to the Methodist church all the time when I was a little kid. I think we only went once or twice after Dad died, though. Now that I'd grown up, maybe I could see about attending services again.

Speaking . . . or writing . . . of your mother. I know I've already asked you to help her and your sister out, but I can't stress that enough. I know that when you're a teenager, it can be a real challenge to get along with your mother.

I looked up from the page. Years ago, Dad had meant for me to be reading his advice about God somewhere close to this day. Was it God's will that I read what Dad had to say about Mom on the night she went crazy on me? Providence or coincidence, I welcomed his thoughts.

Your mother will annoy you. That's what mothers do. Remember the Bible says you should honor your father and mother. If you're reading this letter now, I've made it a lot easier to put up with me. But I'm telling you to respect your mom and be kind to her. Help her out, okay? ~~This deployment is rough on her.~~ *She* ~~hasn't been~~ *didn't handle this deployment so well.*

Your mom's had it rough all her life. Her father abandoned his family, and her mother wasn't so great to her. But your mom worked through all that. She's one of the hardest-working people I know. Maybe she's remarried by the time you get this. That would offer her a little help, but even then . . . Trust me, it's hard work raising two kids. If she's brought you up on her own, then she's working all day only to come home and work taking care of you, Mary, and the house. The next time you're mad at her, try to think of all she's done for you, of all she's sacrificed.

Likewise, go easy on your sister. She's younger than you, so don't expect her to be so mature. When your mom decides she's old enough to date, make sure her boyfriends are afraid of you.

That's your mission this time. Do something nice for your mom or sister or both. It should be something extra. So if you're already taking out the trash or washing the dishes on a

regular basis, find something more, maybe something unex-
pected that will really make their day. I'm sure you'll think of
something, but if you need help, remember you can always ask
Ortiz. He's a good guy. You can trust him.

Ortiz again. That part of Dad's plan hadn't worked out. Why was the
Mystery Mailer staying so quiet through all of this? Why wouldn't he
contact me?

Some nights Ortiz and me and some of the guys get together
to smoke cheap cigars and talk about life, politics, women,
the war, and everything. We call this group the Gentlemen's
Smoking Club. The GSC were talking on our first night in
Farah, and we were all feeling kind of down. There we were,
on this base that wasn't even close to finished. We don't have
many guys, we have few weapons, and we don't even have tac-
tical vehicles yet.

So I said to the guys, "Look. We're the Army National
Guard. Some of our equipment, like our radios and rifles, may
not be the newest and best, but we still get the job done. Out here
in the middle of nowhere, we've had to figure out how to han-
dle things on our own, like cowboys out on the range. We might
not always be completely sure how to solve a problem or carry
out the mission, but we do it anyway. It's the Cowboy Way."

Cookmaster (our cook — just about everybody out here
has a nickname. One poor kid in Bravo team is stuck being
called Weebly.) raised his paper coffee cup in the air and made
a toast. "Here's to the Cowboy Way."

Saddle up, Michael. Don't shy away from doing good
things because you're afraid or because you're not sure how, or
you're not sure if it will work out or not. Follow your heart.

Have the courage to do what you know to be right in life and in love. If you don't feel the courage, then just act like you do. Nobody will know the difference. I didn't make it, so it's up to you to live the Cowboy Way.

Love,

Dad

Do something nice for Mom or Mary? Right now, I was too angry to even begin to imagine how to complete this mission. I guess I'd have to figure it out. It was what Dad called the Cowboy Way.

TEN

"How was the Iowa game?" I asked Ethan as he sat down at the lunch table on Monday.

He smiled. "It was good. A win's a win. How was your weekend?"

I shrugged. "It started out okay," I said. I told him about Mom ruining the end of Isma's visit.

He ate a bite of beef and noodles and frowned. "Sorry about how it ended up, but dude, what's going on with you and Isma?"

"Not you too."

"Hanging out in your bedroom —"

"Working on a history project!" I said. "Hey, I talked to Raelyn on Friday before the game."

He waved a forkful of beef and noodles around. "And?"

"And you are going to be in the musical," I said.

Ethan dropped his fork. "I am not."

"She said Ms. Burke is desperate to get someone for these two little parts in the first and second acts. You're available, and being in this show will mean you'll get to hang out with Raelyn every night. As soon as her breakup with Moore is official, you can ask her to the dance. Who knows? You might even get to dance with her *in* the show."

"That's not the same thing."

"I thought you liked her."

Ethan leaned forward. "Dude, I think I love her."

"Then the quest's the quest." I smiled. "Take the part. Make it happen."

He closed his eyes. "I'm going to kill you."

"You're going to thank me."

Gabe and Monty joined us. "Rhodes was talking in bio this morning. He has seriously got it in for you, dude," Gabe said to me.

"What did I do?" I asked.

"I know, right?" said Monty. "He's mad because you scored a touchdown? How does that make sense?" He took a bite of the beef and noodles. "Mmm, this stuff's actually good. You gonna eat yours, Mike?" I pushed my tray toward him, and he snatched it up. "Thanks, man."

"Well, maybe if the guy didn't flip out and get us unsportsmanlike-conduct penalties, he wouldn't have to worry about it," Ethan said.

"You had some good tackles," Gabe said to Ethan. "And some good action on kickoff return."

Ethan grinned and showed off his bruises. "Yeah, but the thing is, kickoff return would be a lot better if we hadn't had to return so often. It's the only thing I do on the team where I wish I got less playing time."

The guys laughed. We told jokes and kept talking about the game for the rest of lunch.

When I went back to fifth-hour study hall, I read in my corner in the library. I was still deep into *Hamlet* when I looked up to see Isma standing over me. "Hey," I said, handing back her laptop. "Listen, about my mom. You have to understand that —"

"No, I get it. Parents are weird." She grabbed a chair and sat down.

"Well, I'm sorry. She shouldn't have been so —"

"Do you have the list we talked about? The people your dad mentioned in his letters?" Isma said quietly. I pulled it out of my backpack, and she took the paper from my hand to read over the names. "Taylor Ramsey, Todd Nelson, and Ed Hughes."

"These are the only people he's mentioned by first and last name. Except for Marcelo Ortiz, none of them are guys he served with, but I know Ortiz isn't who we're looking for."

"You think the Mystery Mailer is a soldier?"

"Or he was. It makes sense, doesn't it, that if Ortiz didn't survive to deliver the letters, they would be passed to someone else who was with my dad in Afghanistan?"

"I guess so," said Isma. "But they might have been sent to someone here in Riverside just as easily."

"Well, Hughes lives right in town. His phone number's listed."

"Have you called him?"

"Well, um . . . not yet." I rubbed the back of my neck. "I just . . . I mean, I will."

Isma looked up from the list. "It must be tough. The idea of calling these strangers to see if one of them is sending the letters. All of this, really." She leaned closer to me. "Maybe it's enough that you have the letters in the first place. Don't take this the wrong way, Mike, because I can't imagine how terrible it must be to lose a parent like you have, but in a way, you're really lucky. It's been a long war, and a lot of kids have lost parents. How many of them get letters from them? Maybe you should just read the letters as they come and be grateful for what you have."

I swallowed. "It's hard to explain," I whispered. "Before these letters, all I knew about my dad was that he'd been this brave guy who died in a war. I thought I knew him. I remembered some things about him from before he left, and he called a couple times while he was over there. But all I really remember was how he acted around his two little kids. Mary always says I didn't know him as well as I thought. The last couple of years I've wondered if maybe she was right. It may sound dumb, but it bugs me that I didn't even know how he died."

"It doesn't sound dumb at all," Isma said. "Your father was taken out of your life. You deserve to know how and maybe why."

I nodded. "These letters have shown me things about my father that I never knew before, things I'd never guess. I've got to find out who's sending them."

"Well then." Isma smiled and turned back to her computer, pulling up an online phone book. "Let's get started." She spoke with enthusiasm, but as we ran the names through several different people-finder websites, our chances of finding the right guys seemed to diminish. The sites turned up a bunch of guys named Taylor Ramsey, but none in the state of Iowa. A zillion people named Todd Nelson lived both in Iowa and around the country. The only guy we knew about for sure was Ed Hughes.

"What am I supposed to do, call or write letters to each one of these people?" I said. "Ask total strangers if they just happen to be mailing me letters from my dead dad?"

"We could try some of them, at least some of the Todd Nelsons in Iowa," Isma said. "It's a place to start." I must not have looked very hopeful, because she went on, "Don't give up. The Mystery Mailer might send you a note of his own. And I'll check in at the post office to ask if there's any way to find out more about the sender. I don't know, maybe there's some kind of code in all those wavy lines on a postmark."

She was reaching, and we both knew it. Still, nobody else would have cared enough to try. Having a partner in this made the difficult task of finding the truth much more enjoyable.

That night at football practice, Coach Carter had us all on one knee where we faced what the guys called the Volcano's Revenge. Coach paced back and forth in front of us, shouting every sentence like always. "The Big Three. Hard Work! You did not give me four quarters of your best work! Integrity! You did not do what was right at the game! We had sloppy plays and penalties! Team! You began yelling at each other! No unit cohesion!

"You men weren't tackling hard enough Friday night. That is my fault. I accept the responsibility. I have failed to properly train you. I have failed to properly motivate you. I will remedy this situation today. Today, we will not run drills at half speed. We will not go full contact. Today is double contact! All day. You will learn to take the fight to our opponent, and come this Friday night, when we head over to Kalona, we're going to show the Pioneers what hitting's all about!"

A brutal and endless series of sprints and tackling drills followed. Then I had extra running to do after practice. After my day wrapped up with a rough night on the farm, I was hungry, tired, bruised, and filthy.

My spirits picked up as soon as I walked in the door at home. Mary was standing in the dining room, waving an envelope in front of her. "Okay, this is getting weird. Who is writing to you all the time?"

"Isma," I said, snatching the envelope from her fingers.

Mary laughed. "Yeah, right. That address is so not a girl's handwriting, and it's from Iowa City."

I walked right past her and went up to my attic to read the letter.

Dear Michael,

I'm not supposed to be writing this right now because I'm on guard duty, roasting in the blazing heat in a cement room at the top of a two-story tower. My job is to stare at the empty, dead desert to make sure that it stays empty and dead. To do that we have to keep our eyes open and staring out the window. So writing letters is against the rules.

Reading books on guard duty is also against the rules. We must be staring at nothing at all times. It kind of drives me nuts. Anyway, that brings me to the first thing I guess I want to tell you. Always have a book going. Always take it with you. That way, if you get stuck someplace, like the dentist's waiting room, you'll have something to read besides those terrible magazines.

I smiled after I read that part, amazed at how often Dad would tell me to do something that I already did all the time. Working hard in school? Reading? No problem. I was my father's son.

In all this heat, we sweat constantly. When we come back from missions in forty pounds of body armor, our uniforms are soaked so much that they look like we wore them swimming. That and the low rations have actually made me lose quite a bit of weight. If you are like I was in high school, you work out pretty hard. You're in good shape. You're also constantly hungry, and it's hard for you to gain weight. That will change at about age twenty. It will be like someone flipped a switch, and suddenly, it will be a challenge to keep off the fat. Be ready. Watch what you eat. Keep working out.

You should find someone to work out with. That way you'll always have a spotter and someone to make you go to the gym on the days you'd rather take it easy. For me that guy was Todd Nelson. I mentioned him in an earlier letter. It's kind of cool how we met. Near the start of my sophomore year, Nelson, this big senior, steps up to where I was sitting in the cafeteria. He tells me I'm in his way and I need to move, but there was plenty of room for him to go around. When I told him this, he said he'd have to make me move.

Remember how I told you about not fighting unless you were attacked or unless your honor was absolutely on the line? Well, I figured this was one of those times. I shot up out of my chair and faced him. "Fine." I shoved him hard in the chest, knocking him back a couple steps. "See if you can make me." I thought for sure he was going to punch me, and then I'd have to hit him back.

Instead, he laughed a little and slapped me on the shoulder. He said, "You got guts, kid."

I tell you all this because friendship can be a tricky thing. Nelson turned out to be one of my best friends that year. He really helped change things for me for the better back then. I was sad and angry about the death of my parents and pretty much everything else. Somehow during all that time I spent hanging out with him, I started to see the good in life too. I hope you have lots of friends and that you're making many more.

Just . . . be careful who you trust. Don't share all your deepest secrets with just anyone. I think lots of times in high school, because it's the first time you have the chance to be independent with people who like you and seem to understand you, you feel like you can tell those people anything. When your mother and I started going out, I told a couple guys some things about our relationship that I thought they would keep quiet. After your mother found out what I'd said to them, she was so angry, I thought I'd lose her. Sometimes people seem more trustworthy than they really are.

Still, once you are absolutely sure that you've found a real, trustworthy, loyal friend, do all you can for him. You'll never make friends like the ones you make in high school. Later in life, like when you start a new job or go off to college, you can reinvent yourself, decide who you want to be and then BE that person. But your high school friends do a lot of growing up with you. In your case, they'll know you basically since you were in diapers. You can't fake the funk with those guys.

I miss you all. This is easily the longest I've ever been away from home. In fact, apart from basic training, I haven't been away from your mother for about fifteen years. That may seem like a long time, but it feels like it's just flown by.

It was actually Todd Nelson who introduced us. We'd just won a great game, and I got invited to the victory party out at Nature Spot for the first time. Your mom was the only freshman on the cheerleading squad, and when I saw her sitting across the fire from me, I couldn't keep my eyes off her, she was so beautiful. But I didn't have the guts to go talk to her. Nelson was fearless, though, and physically dragged me over to sit on the log with her, making the introductions.

Allison and I talked for a long time. Then, as the party was winding down, I walked her home. We held hands for the very first time that night, and we've been together ever since. She's an amazing woman. So beautiful, hardworking, with the ability to cope with a lot of pain in her life.

I met your mother and had some of the best times of my life with my friends at parties. Your mission, then, is to go to a *party, or to throw one if you have to. Be safe, be smart, but have fun. The thought of you doing all of that as a young man helps keep me going through this tough time.*

. . . And now I hear the sound of someone climbing up the metal steps of the guard tower. I have to stop writing before I'm caught.

Love,
Dad

I went to our old phone in the dining room. With Mary in the living room watching TV, I was grateful for the long cord on the receiver so I could call from the kitchen in relative privacy. I dialed Ed Hughes's number, then held my finger over the button to hang up. There was still time to get out of this right while it was ringing.

Someone picked up. "This is Ed," came the voice. "Hello?"

I quickly put the receiver to my face. "Um, hello, Mr. Hughes. This is Michael Wilson."

"Mark's boy?"

"Yes. I'm sorry to bother you, but I —"

"No bother at all. Wow, I was wondering if you'd ever call. How the heck are you? What can I do for you?" He sounded upbeat, excited maybe. My heart beat faster. Could this be it? Was he hoping I'd figure out that he'd been mailing the letters?

My damp hands slipped a little on the plastic phone. "I'm, um, I'm fine, actually. This is going to sound crazy, but I'd like to find out if you know —"

"About your old man? You bet I do. You know, your dad died a hero, fighting for our freedom."

My spirits sank upon hearing the same old lines. "Did he ever leave you letters to send to me?" I said.

"Well, no," Hughes went on. "He never left me anything. If he had, I would have given it to you or your mother years ago. But he was a terrific worker."

We talked for a little while longer. Ed told me more about what a great employee Dad had been, how he'd sometimes sing old classic rock songs on the job. It wasn't the information I'd been hoping for, but I loved knowing more about my father.

After my conversation with Ed, I started calling Todd Nelsons. Several of them lived in Iowa City, where all the letters had been postmarked, so I figured I'd start there. I found the right guy on my second try.

"Little Mikey Wilson?" said Todd. "How can you possibly be old enough to even use a telephone? You know your numbers and everything?"

I laughed politely. "Do you have a few moments to talk?" I asked. "I could call back later if —"

"No, no, this is fine. Wow. So the time has finally come."

That could mean anything, and I forced myself not to get my hopes up. "I know you're busy, so I'll get right to the point," I said. "I want to know if my dad gave you letters years ago for you to mail to me this year."

"You're getting letters from your dad?"

Was he playing dumb to throw me off the trail? But why would anyone do that? "Yes, I am. Do you know who is sending them?"

"Wow, kid, I wish I did. Sorry. Me and your dad were great friends. He tell you 'bout the time we was four-wheeling in my parents' pasture, and I crashed the thing and broke my leg?"

"No, he didn't," I said.

Todd laughed. "It was a bad break, bone sticking out through the skin and blood everywhere. No cell phones in them days, you see.

Couldn't call for help. Your old man bandaged me up with his own shirt, and then carried me over a mile all the way back to my folks' house. I almost passed out from the pain while your dad ran the whole way with me on his back. If I'd have been alone, I probably would have bled out and died. Great man, your father.

"I wish I would have done a better job staying in touch after I graduated high school. I kept telling myself, 'I'll call him tomorrow. Next week. I'll go visit him next month.' That's how it goes, I guess. People drift apart, keep putting things off. Then one day it was too late." There was quiet on the line for a moment. "Still, we remember him for who he was and the good he did, right? He was a great friend to me. A hero, when you get right down to it."

It was a disappointment that Todd Nelson wasn't the Mystery Mailer, but it turned out that he was a pretty nice guy. He and I went on for a while longer, reminiscing about my father and the good times they'd had together. I was glad Dad had given me the opportunity to talk to him.

At football practice Tuesday night, Coach broke us up into groups. Offensive ends were with the receivers and quarterbacks. The drill was that the receiver or end would run a pass route, Karn or Gabe would throw him the pass, then the receiver had to run upfield, and a guy from a different line had to tackle him. After you did the tackle, you were up to catch.

It was a brutal drill. Coach kept yelling at each guy to hit harder. I waited in line. Someone stepped right up behind me so that his face mask hit the back of my helmet. "You're dead, Wilson," Rhodes said. "I'm going to knock the snot out of you."

I took a deep breath and rubbed my sweaty palms on my pants over my thigh pads. Coach blew the whistle and Karn dropped back to pass as Clint Stewart ran out from the line of scrimmage. He caught a quick pass and I launched forward. Clint tried a pathetic attempt at a juke step to fake me out, but all it did was slow him down. I hit him low and ran forward, dumping him on his back hard and then running for the loose ball. I dropped down to wrap my body around it.

"Good work, Wilson! That's what I want to see! Let's go! Your turn." Coach slapped his clipboard against his thigh.

I went to stand next to the quarterback. Karn shot me a nasty grin. Coach blew the whistle and I ran out, but Karn threw a high, wobbly pass that took forever in the air. I caught it and tried to move upfield, but Rhodes had started his approach earlier than he was supposed to. I had just enough time to grab the ball and drop my shoulders a little bit before he crushed into my gut and put me down.

Rhodes got up in my face, glaring at me through our face masks. "Dead, Wilson. You should quit the team."

I pushed him off me. He'd knocked the wind from me and it hurt when I got up. I wanted another turn. "Coach!" I tried to yell. I waved at him, but he was checking something on his clipboard.

Rhodes took his position for the next pass. It was Monty's chance to tackle the receiver. Coach wasn't watching, so I pushed Monty aside. "I'll pay you back," I whispered to him. Monty grinned and let me have the shot.

Coach blew the whistle and Rhodes ran his route. Karn hit him square in the chest with a perfect short pass. I bolted for the guy. In the second before we collided, I could see Rhodes's glare. I knew he wasn't going to try to fake me out or sidestep me. He would try to come through me, and I would hurt him.

The crushing hit rattled us both, but I pumped my legs, wrapped my arms around his thighs, and kept driving. Rhodes fell right at the point of contact. It wasn't as good a tackle as I'd thrown on Clint, but

I'd taken Rhodes down. I stood up and jogged back toward the end of the line.

"Wilson!" Coach Carter shouted. "Did you just go twice?"

"Sorry, Coach," I said. "I messed up."

"Yeah, you messed up! Looks like you messed up Rhodes here! Get up, Rhodes!"

Nick stood up and walked out of the way so the next two could go. I couldn't help but grin when I saw him limping a little.

Through the rest of the week, it took everything I had to keep slogging through school, farmwork, and tough football practices. Thursday night's team supper was in Iowa City, and without a ride, I couldn't go.

I kept waiting for a new letter and rereading the ones Dad had already sent. I wondered how I would complete my missions to take a chance with a girl and to do something nice for Mom and Mary, while I struggled with my first mission of football.

Friday night in Kalona went much better than our first game. Two early touchdowns put us in the lead twelve to zero going into halftime. Both defenses held up well until near the end of the third quarter, when a Pioneer fullback broke through and scored on a forty-yard run. After that, the defensive battle continued until the game ended with the Roughriders winning twelve to seven. It was so close that Coach didn't rotate subs in. I only played on kickoff and kick return, so I had three kickoff plays and two return plays, making sure to drill at least one Pioneer per play. Derek had come out to watch me, but I had so few minutes on the field that I almost regretted him wasting his time driving the seven miles to see the game.

I made it home before Mom got off work and went to my attic to finish the study guide for the second act of *Hamlet*. After a while, a knock on wood sounded behind me. I jumped in my chair and spun around to see Mom's head and shoulders above floor level on the staircase. "Whatcha doing?"

"Geez, Mom, don't you knock?"

"I just did." She came in and sat on the end of my bed. I slid my chair back to keep my bruised arms out of sight. She looked around. "Why do you keep it so dark up here? Why not turn on the overhead light?"

"I like it like this."

"All gloomy and depressing?"

Actually, I liked the way the circle of light from my desk lamp focused me on my reading. "You want the light on?"

"No," she said. "You can leave it off. That's fine. It's a little weird to sit here, where it's mostly dark, but that's fine."

I rubbed my eyes. I hated it when she did the "that's fine" guilt-trip routine. "If that's fine, then I'll leave the light off."

Mom closed her eyes and took a deep breath. "The reason I came up here is that I've been thinking."

"Angels and ministers of grace defend us." I stole that line from *Hamlet.*

"You're a good boy, Mikey. I know that things have been kind of tense between us lately, and . . . I want you to know that no matter how old you are, you'll always be my boy. I'll always love you."

"I know, Mom, and —"

"Just — just hear me out on this, okay?" She held her hand up. "You're a good boy, and you help me so much. Sometimes I don't show enough appreciation, and I'm sorry about that. I got to thinking about how we argued about that Muslim girl. I was a little unreasonable, and I wanted to say I'm sorry."

A *little* unreasonable?

"It's not so much that she's a Muslim," Mom said, "but that you just sneaked her over here without my permission. You know I don't like people coming over and seeing our run-down house."

"I'm sorry I didn't ask, Mom, but the house isn't that bad."

"It's embarrassing, Michael."

"Isma thought my attic was cool. What was embarrassing was how you acted when you met her."

"I know. I know. I'm sorry. But Mikey, soon you'll be reaching that age where you start thinking about girls more."

Soon? I'd start thinking about girls *soon*? How young did she think I was?

"Your body is changing and you might notice strange feelings when . . ."

I stood up, scraping my metal chair across the wood floor as loud as I could. There were plenty of times I wished I could have a real conversation with my mother, but no way did I want to listen to her talk about the birds and the bees. "Like I said, Mom, I'm really sorry. It won't happen again. But you know, I have a ton of reading for English class. I should get to it."

"All I'm saying is you don't have to rush to get a girlfriend and everything. Think about all the pretty girls you'll meet in college. Right now you need to focus on school."

How could she offer advice that was so completely the opposite of what Dad had said? He wanted me to enjoy my time in high school, while she didn't want me to have a life until college. Anyway, for the hundred millionth time, Isma and I were *not going out*. I struggled to keep my voice even. "We were only working on a school project." Even if Isma and I did start dating, did Mom think we'd get married immediately so that I'd never go out with any of those college girls? Maybe she did. After all, that's what happened with her and Dad.

"Just take your time. Don't be in such a rush to grow up." Mom stood up and hugged me. "You're such a good boy, Mikey. But if you're going to read, make sure you have more light. It's not good for your eyes, reading when it's so dark like this."

"I will, Mom." I forced a smile. "Thanks for coming up here and everything."

She gave a little finger wave and went downstairs. When she was gone, I sat down at my desk. Dad had asked me to be patient with her. I was trying.

ELEVEN

On Monday, Isma and I were picked first to deliver our talk on the Civil War, its causes, and its important battles. I thought I would be more nervous, but Isma's early preparation had, well . . . prepared us. Still, I didn't relax fully until Isma finally switched to the last slide.

"Although statistics are incomplete, most estimates suggest that over 620,000 men died in the Civil War," she said.

"An estimate of the total number of dead and wounded is about 1.1 million," I continued. "With Americans killing Americans, it was the deadliest war by far in American history."

"To put it into perspective, while the Civil War cost 620,000 lives," Isma said, "in our wars in both Iraq and Afghanistan, only about 6,280 have died. That's —"

"Because of people like you," Clint Stewart whispered.

Isma stared at Clint openmouthed, her hands tightly gripping her note cards. I waited for some outrage from Coach Carter, but he only glanced up from the notes he'd been writing, looking confused. He must have missed Clint's comment.

I spoke up quickly to keep us going. "That's only about one percent of the Civil War casualties. It's still too many losses, but it gives you an idea of the terrible carnage of the Civil War. Its cost in human life and in resources was really —"

"Really sick," Isma said. She glared at Clint.

★ ★ ★

I welcomed the silence in my library corner during fifth-hour study hall the next day. Monday's practice had been tough, and rereading Dad's letters had kept me up late after that. Somehow when I read Dad's letters, I could almost remember the deep sound of his voice, the way he walked, and his smile. Safe behind the wooden dividers on the table, I sat back in my seat and closed my eyes.

"Sleeping?"

I opened my eyes and sat up straight. Isma dragged a chair behind the study barrier, flopped down, and folded her arms. It was the first time I'd seen her since history the day before.

"You're still mad," I said.

"About what?"

"About Clint and —"

"Clint's an idiot." She scowled like she'd just tasted something awful.

"I know. I can't believe he said that."

Isma leaned closer. "I can't believe Mr. Carter would let him get away with it."

I slid my chair back a little. "I don't think Coach let him get away with it. He just didn't hear it."

"Are you kidding? Of course he heard it. He's a jerk."

"He's not so bad. Anyway, there's no way he heard Clint."

"Oh no." Isma sighed. "I knew it."

"What?"

"You're becoming one of them."

"One of who?"

"You're becoming a sports person. A disciple in the temple of sports worship."

"Because I'm on the football team?"

"Because you're on the football team, screaming with guys like Clint and his crowd, defending the coach, even though he barely teaches us anything and he's super strict with everyone but his football players."

"Whoa," I said. "First, don't lump me in with those guys." I held my arms out. "I got bruises all over from going up against idiots like that. And I'm just playing for fun. That's all it is. Not sports worship. Just fun."

"To you, maybe, but not to the rest of this school or town. These books?" She motioned at the shelves behind us. "Next year Mrs. Potter won't be able to buy as many because her purchasing budget is being cut."

"How do you know —"

"School board meeting report," Isma said. "It was in the paper last week. But despite library cuts, they did manage to find enough money for some big new machine for the weight room." I almost said something, but she didn't slow down. "Do you know that a starting teacher in this school makes about twenty-six thousand dollars a year? The football coach makes twelve thousand extra just for coaching a nine-game season, a little under half of a first-year teacher's full salary for working way less than a quarter of the year. When I factor in what they pay the other coaches, plus all the money for equipment and facilities, it really makes me wonder why the school claims it can't afford a full-time art teacher."

"That's because not as many kids take art class," I said.

"Not as many kids *can* take art. There are only three art classes offered. I like art. I'm good at it. Zillions of people make their careers in the visual arts or graphic design. This school offers basically nothing for them."

Even though she was angry and pointing at me, her dark eyes still held a certain kindness. Her long dark hair fell about her shoulders. I couldn't stop looking at her. Forget Hailey Green or the Dinsler cousins on the cheerleading squad, with all their makeup and their fake tans. Isma looked great without even trying. Why had it taken me so long to realize that?

"In the next ten years, nobody from this school will go on to play professional sports. Not even major college sports. Yet the school offers everything, spends every stupid penny it has, just so kids can play dumb games."

"Miss Rafee." Mrs. Potter appeared around the corner of the table's privacy wall. "While I sympathize with your outrage, you will remember that this is a library, and as such, you will keep your voice down."

"Sorry, Mrs. Potter," Isma whispered.

Mrs. Potter nodded, looked at us both for a moment, and walked away with a smile.

"Whoops," Isma said. "Mom's always telling me that I argue too much. She's always like, 'Don't be so opinionated all the time.' Daddy's different. Some nights we'll sit in his study for hours debating issues. I guess my argumentative side comes from him. He keeps telling me I should be a lawyer or run for Congress someday." She shook her head. "Yeah, right, as if anyone would vote for me."

"I'd vote for you."

"Really?"

"Yeah, you're smart, you actually research your opinions, and . . ." I trailed off when I noticed her watching me with her deep brown eyes.

She tilted her chin down a little. "And what?"

I could feel my heart beating heavier in my chest. "And . . . you're really . . . cool."

"Thanks," she said without taking her eyes off me. "You're sweet."

I didn't know what would happen between Isma and me, but more and more, I had the feeling that this good thing we had would take its course.

The bell rang, startling me from my thoughts. It just wouldn't take its course right now.

When Friday morning rolled around, I felt pretty good, dressed in my Roughriders jersey for our home football game against the Lone Tree Lumberjacks. (Yeah, that was their real mascot.) I had the plays figured out and hoped to get more playing time than last week.

"A monk wears robes. Sports worshippers wear football jerseys." Isma elbowed me in the hall on the way to sixth-hour English.

I laughed. "You coming to the game tonight?"

She slowed down. "We've been over this. I'm forced to go to the home games because of band, remember? The band must play music to praise the sports gods that the school worships."

"Okay, okay." I held my hands up to surrender. "I don't want to argue."

"That's smart of you." Then her joking mood became serious. "Plus, you know, after the last home game" — she twirled a strand of hair around her finger — "it was kind of nice having someone to walk home with. I was thinking, since it's on your way and all, maybe we could walk together again tonight?"

"Sure. Meet you at the same place after the game?"

For something so simple, Isma sure looked happy. "Great, see you then." She went into the classroom.

Clint cut between us, blocking my way to the door. " 'Great, see you then,' " he said in a high-pitched mocking voice. "Getting desperate, huh, Wilson?"

I wanted to punch him, but I remembered Dad's advice about trying to avoid fights, and Ms. Burke came out in the hall just then. "Gentlemen, let's hurry up. We have a lot to cover today."

I followed Clint into the room, wishing he could be on the opposing team tonight. The guy deserved some wicked hard hits.

TWELVE

The Lumberjacks scored only a few plays after they received the kickoff. Coach Carter called the offense into a quick huddle on the field while the officials set up the Lone Tree kickoff. Rhodes threw his helmet down and stepped away, kicking the ground. Coach grabbed his arm and pulled him back, shouting in his face so loud I could hear him from where I stood on the sidelines, even if I couldn't make out the words.

"Nick's got to calm down," Laura said to Kelsey behind me.

"When he gets like this, he starts messing up," Kelsey agreed.

We had a decent kick return, bringing the ball up to our thirty-five. But when Karn dropped back to pass on our first down, he threw a ten-yarder right to Rhodes, who dropped it. On the next play, Sullivan swept right and the play looked good, but Rhodes didn't hold his block and the linebacker knocked Tony back almost to the line of scrimmage.

As the guys ran back to the huddle after the play, Rhodes straight-armed a Lone Tree player in the shoulder and shouted something at him. The ref threw the flag and sent us back to our own twenty-yard line.

"Wilson!" Coach Carter yelled. "Get in there for Rhodes!"

I sprinted for the huddle. "Rhodes! Rhodes!" I called.

"What?" Nick shouted.

"What do you mean, 'What?'" Sullivan said. "He's subbing in for you. Get off the field!"

Rhodes swore as he jogged off toward the sidelines. The play was called in and we were about to break the huddle.

"Whoa, wait a sec, guys." Sullivan held his hands out in front of him, and we all leaned in to focus. "We're off to a rocky start, but they're only up by six and we got a whole game. Throwing a fit won't help us. Throwing a hard hit will. This is the best football team Riverside's had in years, because you guys are the best players we've had in years. Don't get mad. Just do what you know how to do."

Dozer punched the side of his own helmet. "Yeah! It's go time!"

McKay shouted, "Let's do it!"

We broke the huddle and set up quickly to avoid a delay-of-game penalty. Sullivan would be running right between Dozer and me, with the defensive end lined up right over me. I didn't know whether to block him to the inside or try to push him out.

Dozer slapped my elbow to get my attention. He jerked his head toward the D-end. "This guy's mine."

Wait. The defense wasn't lined up the way they were in the playbook I'd studied. Should I go for the linebacker way inside or shoot out to the cornerback? How was I supposed to know who to block?

Karn called out the cadence and McKay snapped the ball. I rushed forward with Dozer and we crushed the end from both sides. He groaned as he fell. The cornerback came down fast, so I ran to collide with him, risking a look toward the middle to see Tony on his way upfield. I cut back fast and launched myself at a safety. "Go! Go! Go!" I yelled at Sullivan.

The safety sloughed me off quick enough, but not before Sullivan whizzed by him. He passed midfield to the Lone Tree forty-five before the other safety tripped him up and brought him down.

Back in our huddle, the intensity had returned. Dozer head-butted me, screaming something I couldn't understand. Sullivan brought his fists crashing down on top of my shoulder pads. "That's how we do it, Roughriders! Nice blocks, Wilson!"

I barely had time to process what had just happened before we set up another play. This one called for a pass, only I couldn't remember exactly what route I was supposed to run, and I had no time to ask. At the snap, I ran out ten yards and then cut inside for a cross pattern, hoping I had it right.

I didn't. The left-side wide receiver, Chris Moore, ran straight toward me. I'd entered his sector, doubling up the coverage on us. I kicked back outside as fast as I could, trying to get open.

A defensive lineman cut through our line on our left side. Karn fled to his right and launched the ball straight toward me. I caught it and took a few steps upfield before two Lumberjacks collided with me on either side and dropped me on the spot. Dull pain seared through my arms and chest, but I forgot about it when the ref whistled the play dead and moved the chains for another first down.

On the next play, Drew Hamilton had a gain of seven on a quick run up the middle.

"Yeeee-ah, boys! Inside the twenty now!" Karn shouted in the huddle. He called out a pass play. "*Now* you run the cross pattern, Wilson."

"Got it," I said.

Dozer slapped me on the helmet.

"Let's punch it in," said Cody.

After the snap, I ran my route but the back was all over me. Karn threw the ball to Clint, who caught it and went down on the Lone Tree eight-yard line. On the next play, Sullivan swept out to the left and put the ball into the end zone in the left corner. Our point-after-touchdown kick made the score seven to six.

Coach put Rhodes in when the defense took over, so I found myself on the sidelines again.

"Water, Mike?"

I turned around and accepted a water bottle from Laura. It was the first time I'd really seen the crowd that had come out to watch us. A sea of people flooded the stands, with more high school, junior high, and elementary groups sitting or standing in clusters on the hill. The only high school people in the bleachers were in the band, with Isma sitting near the front, holding her clarinet. I watched her for a while, hoping she'd see me or even wave. But that was stupid, and I needed to focus on the game.

Just as I turned to face the field again, I did see someone else I knew. About a dozen feet over from the band, halfway up in the stands, Derek Harris waved in my direction and clapped. One second later, everyone in the stands rushed to their feet, shouting and applauding. Lone Tree had fumbled, and we'd recovered the ball on their forty.

"Wilson! Stop screwing around!" Coach Carter shouted, and motioned me out onto the field. I'd thought Rhodes would go back in, but I ran to join my celebrating teammates.

"Let's go. Let's go." Karn clapped his hands in the huddle. "Two minutes in the quarter. See if we can score."

He called out the play and we went to the line. This time I had to run a corner pattern. I'd never run a route this deep in a game. I let out a breath.

McKay snapped the ball. I burst ahead as fast as I could and then angled out. When I checked to see if Karn would be passing to me, the ball was already coming, and the cornerback and safety were closing in on me. I kept running, snagged the ball, then slowed a few steps and spun outside the cornerback.

I ran as fast as I could, willing my legs to speed up. But the safety would have me in a moment. If he didn't, the other safety was angling to take me down before the end zone.

Then, just like in my first game, Sullivan came out of nowhere from behind me. "Keep running!" he shouted. He threw out an arm to knock away the first safety and then stayed with me. "All the way, Wilson! I got ya! I got this guy up here. Just go!"

Sullivan bumped the last defender off course, and I ran into the end zone. The whistle blew and the ref threw his hands straight up in the touchdown sign. The crowd in the stands went crazy, stomping the bleachers and screaming. The band struck up the school fight song.

"Touchdown, Roughriders!" the announcer said over the loudspeaker. "Number forty-two, Mike Wilson, with a forty-yard touchdown completion."

Sullivan ran up and clamped me in a bear hug. "Yeah, buddy! Touchdown, kid! That's how we do it!"

"Thanks for the block," I said.

"Don't thank me yet! We're just getting started!"

Sullivan spoke the truth. The momentum had changed. We went for the two-point conversion, making the score fifteen to six. We didn't look back. Hamilton picked up on a long run. Sullivan scored a touchdown after the team fought for a series of short gains. By halftime we were up thirty to six.

We jogged toward the locker room as a group, passing the marching band on its way to the field. I caught Isma's eye, and she smiled at me. I wanted to jump up in the air and scream like Dozer or Cody.

Then Rhodes shoved me into the doorframe as he pushed by to enter the locker room. I rushed ahead to hit him back, but Ethan grabbed my arm. "Not now. Not here. You know why he's mad," he said. "Let's focus on winning this game. Let him make himself look like an idiot if he wants."

What he said made a lot of sense, but my whole body coursed with anger as I entered the locker room. We all drank water and Coach went over some defensive adjustments. "We have a strong lead," he said, "but that doesn't mean this game is over. That doesn't mean we can relax."

Rhodes raised his hand. "Coach?"

Carter ignored him. "Wilson, you're in at tight end until I tell you otherwise. Keep up the good work out there." Rhodes glared at me. I tried to hold back my grin. Coach looked around at all of us. "Now let's get out there and give those Lumberjacks another heavy-hitting half of hard-core football!"

On the way to the field, Rhodes elbowed me in the ribs, but didn't get a very good shot. I took Ethan's advice and let it go.

Dozer didn't. "Knock it off, Rhodes, or I'll do the same to you!"

Sullivan jogged out beside me. "You having fun out there?"

"Yeah. A couple times I didn't know who I was supposed to block or which route to run, though."

"That don't matter as long as you just hit somebody hard." McKay slapped his big beefy arm on my back.

Seniors had never talked to me like this before. Now they were . . . Well, they seemed to actually want me on the team.

"Wipe that stupid grin off your face already," Sullivan said. "We got a game to finish." He slammed his fist down on my shoulder pad and ran on ahead.

The second half went a lot like the first. Lone Tree stopped our offensive drive at the top of the half and scored after a series of short drives. We scored twice more, making the final count forty-four to fourteen.

The celebration in the locker room after the game surpassed the one at Kalona. Coach gave us a quick talk, then we cranked up the music as the guys whooped and shouted and recounted the best parts of the game.

Cody Arnath sat in front of his locker in just his jeans, with an ice pack on his shoulder. He elbowed Dozer. "You know that guy who kept trying to cut block me? When he came in low like that, I finally just grabbed him by the back of the helmet and yanked him forward to the ground." He laughed. "You should have seen the big clump of mud and grass that came up in his face mask."

"I saw you put that guy down," said Hamilton. "Took him out good. That was my touchdown run."

I knew Isma was probably waiting for me out front, so I showered and dressed quickly, groaning against the pain in my ribs and arms as I squeezed into my T-shirt and jacket. I wanted to celebrate too, but no matter how well I'd played tonight, I still didn't know these people well enough to feel comfortable joining in.

"Hey, Wilson." Karn stopped me before I left the locker room. He still wore his football pants and his disgusting lucky game shirt. He leaned forward, and with his smell, I wished he hadn't. "Good game, man. Couple of real good catches there."

"You made it easy," I said. "You threw it right to me. So, thanks." Karn nodded and went back to the others. I went out of the stifling locker room into the cool gym, unable to hold back my smile.

THIRTEEN

Isma met me outside the school. She was shivering a little, with her arms wrapped around herself against the autumn chill, but she smiled when she saw me. Suddenly I didn't want to see anyone else even half as much as I wanted to see her right then.

"I actually watched the whole game this time," she said. "I guess if you absolutely must play frivolous games, it's at least good that you were great."

"I wouldn't say I was great," I said. I wouldn't say it, maybe, but inside I felt it.

We started walking. "Some of the guys in band actually understand what's going on out there, and they told me you did a touchdown and caught some passes."

"Yeah, I did, but that's just playing the game."

"It's okay to admit you did a good job, you know."

Before I could answer, a car pulled up beside us in the parking lot. The window went down and McKay called out, "Hey, Wilson. We're heading out to Nature Spot for a little celebration. A couple of guys plus most of the cheerleaders are out there already. There's drinks and burgers and hot dogs and stuff."

Dozer leaned forward in the passenger seat. "Yeah, man. Get in. It's gonna be a blast."

All freshman year I'd told myself that I didn't want to go out partying. When I saw high school people having fun driving around in their cars, or when on Monday mornings I heard whispers about weekend adventures, I had always reminded myself that I'd never get out of this town, never go to college, unless I studied a lot.

But that night, I wanted to discover firsthand what Dad had been talking about when he mentioned Nature Spot in his letters. More than anything, I wanted to complete the mission from his most recent letter: to go to a party.

Isma shifted her weight next to me. More than *almost* anything, I wanted to. I couldn't promise to walk Isma home and then just ditch her. Unless maybe . . . "Can Isma come too?"

McKay looked confused. "Um, I guess. Sure. Whatever. Just get in. We gotta get out there before everything's gone."

Isma took a step toward me. "I can't go. Mom and Dad are expecting me."

I sighed, but then remembered my own mother. "Yeah, I'll have to pass," I said, trying to conceal my disappointment. "Thanks, though, man."

"You're missing out!" McKay said. They sped off out of the parking lot.

I grabbed Scrappy from the rack and Isma and I started for her house. Neither of us said anything for the first two blocks. The silence made the walk uncomfortable, especially when Isma usually had so much to say.

"Um, was band fun tonight?" I finally said.

"I guess."

I risked a look at her but she stared straight ahead.

"You have big plans for the weekend?"

"Nope."

Our last walk had gone much better than this one. "Are you —"

"Mike." She spoke clearly and calmly, as if giving a speech for a class. "If you want to go party with those guys, don't let me stop you."

"What are you talking —"

"Oh, please. You almost scrambled to jump in the stupid car with Dozer and McKay, even if it meant you had to drag along your weirdo girl —" She stopped herself, and I looked at her with wide eyes. Had she been about to say what I think she'd almost said? She went on, "Your weirdo friend."

This was unfair. "You're not weird. And I asked if you could come. What's so bad about that? They said it was cool if you came too."

"Come on! You heard the way he said it." She made air quotes with her fingers and spoke in a deep, dumb-sounding voice. " 'I guess she can come. Whatever.' "

"I don't get it," I said. "You want to go to the party? I thought you said —"

"No!" She stopped and faced me. "I don't want to be with those guys as they act like a bunch of idiots. I don't care to watch the cheerleaders and other female sports worshippers hang on them while they recount their glories in a stupid game. I don't want to listen to girls like the Dinsler cousins and Hailey Green faking like they're nice, saying crap like, 'Oh, Isma, that's such a pretty shirt. Did you get that at such and such store in the mall?' They're such jerks to people like us all the time, and I don't understand why you want to impress them so much!"

We'd stopped by the side of the road, where we were mostly shaded from the nearby streetlight under a big oak tree. I dropped Scrappy to the pavement. "Whoa," I said. "Isma, don't worry about it. I can't go to the party anyway. My mom will be freaking out that I'm home so late as it is." I disagreed with her us-versus-them mentality, but I couldn't say so right now.

"I just . . . you know . . ." Isma wiped at a tear on her cheek. "We were going to walk home together and I'm . . . tired of being second best, you know? Tired of being a consolation prize, someone to hang out with when there's nothing else to do."

I brushed a stray strand of dark hair back from her face and worried for a moment that she'd step back or push my hand away. She only watched me. A breeze blew, rattling the changing leaves in the branches above us, making the light from the streetlamp dance with the shadows.

"I'm tired of being so alone," she whispered, stepping a little closer to me.

Somehow my hands slid around her back. She looked up at me and I leaned toward her. Our lips pressed together, warm and electric. We parted a little, but our foreheads still touched, and I could breathe her breath. Then we kissed again and our mouths opened and I could taste and feel her everywhere.

For years my companions had always been books. I'd read how Romeo kissed Juliet, how Katniss kissed Peeta in *The Hunger Games*, and how Gatsby kissed Daisy in *The Great Gatsby*. I'd read hundreds of storybook kisses. None of them were as perfect as this kiss with Isma.

When we somehow finally stopped, we still stood close, and I let out a slow breath as I stared into her dark eyes. "You're not alone, Isma," I whispered. And I realized that for the first time in a long time, neither was I.

She shivered. "I've never kissed a boy before."

It had been a first for me too. I smiled, slipped my jacket off, and put it over her shoulders.

She made a small effort to squirm away. "I'm not some helpless girl who can't remember her own jacket and —"

"I know you're not." Pulling the coat tighter around her, I leaned in to kiss her again, and this time I felt her warm fingers press my cheek.

I picked up Scrappy and gripped the handlebars with one hand so that I could take Isma's soft hand in my other. My arm grew tired from the constant adjustments I had to make guiding the bike that way, but it was worth it to hold on to her. She rubbed her thumb against mine as we walked, and each movement warmed my whole body.

When we reached her block, she squeezed my hand. "I've got to go."

"I wish you didn't have to."

"I know. But we better say good-bye here. If my parents see us together . . ." She let the thought trail off, but I understood her completely. My mother would be even worse. "Thanks for walking me home," she said.

I wanted to thank her for the kiss. For holding my hand. For everything. I wanted to tell her how I felt, but I didn't know what to say. "I . . . uh . . ."

She smiled in that cute way she had that wrinkled her nose. Then she quickly kissed me on the cheek and backed away toward her house. "Good night," she whispered with a little wave before running home.

"Good night, Isma," I said quietly, pressing my fingers to my cheek where her lips had been.

FOURTEEN

The next morning, I woke in the light from a single sunbeam shining in through my tiny attic window. The muscles in my arms and chest ached when I stretched, but the warmth in my chest spread through me, reducing the pain to a mere reminder of the wonder of last night. Dad's second mission had been to take a risk and make a move with a girl. I smiled and whispered, "Mission accomplished."

I threw the old quilt off me, quickly rolled out of bed, and ran so fast toward the stereo that I slid to a stop in my socks on the wood floor. My finger traced down the line of Dad's CD collection until I found a disc I hadn't listened to in a long time. It had this cheesy old song that fit today perfectly.

When the first notes hit and the deep voice started, I closed my eyes and I imagined Isma there with me. Why couldn't she really be here right now? She'd actually liked my attic. We'd been alone up here for hours and all we'd done is studied. We could have been dancing. I found myself swaying along to the music, slowly spinning in a circle as I sang along.

My darlin', I can't get enough of your love, babe
Girl, I don't know, I don't know why
Can't get enough of your love, babe

"Oh. My. Gosh," came the sound of Mary's voice.
I jumped and slammed my hand down on the OPEN button

on the CD carousel. The disc inside spun out of control, probably scratching.

"You've *got* to knock! I told you that! You can't keep sneaking up here!" I shouted.

Mary laughed. "You're such a dork. Is this what you do all the time, dance around to *terrible* music and make out with invisible girls?"

"Shut up. Just get out."

"It makes sense, though, since that's the only kind you could ever get."

"Well, you weren't there last night when —"

"You bet I wasn't there last night." Mary put her finger in her mouth like she was gagging herself. Then she stopped and stared at me seriously. "Wait. What are you smiling about?"

My cheeks flared hot and I knew I had to be bright red. "Nothing. I wasn't smiling."

"What happened?" She climbed the rest of the steps out of the stairwell into my attic. "What did you do?"

"Nothing."

Mary pressed a finger to her lips. "Hmm." She held the finger up. "Fact. My dorky, never-been-kissed brother had Isma Rafee up in his bedroom to" — she coughed — "study . . . or . . . whatever."

"We didn't do —"

"Fact." Mary held a second finger up. "My dorky, never-been-kissed brother has been spotted walking alone with Isma Rafee after football games."

"Wait. How did you —"

"I have my sources. Fact. My dorky, never-been-kissed brother is caught dancing around to the stupidest old music in the world the day after he has a great football game and is seen walking alone with Isma Rafee." She clapped her hands to her cheeks and looked at me with wide eyes. "Could it be?"

"Will you just leave?"

"Is it possible?"

"Get out of here!"

"I think Michael M. Wilson might have actually found a girl willing to" — she grabbed her stomach, bent over, and heaved like she was about to vomit — "willing to kiss him." Then she stood up straight and stared at me.

"Yeah." What was I supposed to say to that? "You're an idiot. Get out of here."

"You did kiss her! Wow. What was it like?"

"I'm not talking about this with my sister," I said.

"Well, you were dancing around, so it must have been pretty good."

I pressed the heels of my hands to my eyes. "What did you even come up here for?"

"Oh. Yeah. Mom's taking off for work, but she said we're supposed to rake and bag the leaves."

I rolled my eyes and pointed at the stairs. "I'll be down in a minute."

"Except that I'm going shopping with Tara and Crystal. So . . . it looks like you're going to have to do the raking yourself."

"Yeah, right," I said. "For once you're going to have to get off your spoiled butt and help out around —"

"And you're going to give me twenty bucks."

"You're dreaming."

Mary started dancing around the room, making kissy faces. "You're right, Mikey. I guess that instead of taking your twenty bucks shopping, I'll just stay home and tell Mom all about football and your hot make-out session with Isma." She made a big, long, sucking kissing sound and smacked her lips. Then she put her fist under her chin and looked up like she was in deep thought.

"She might be so mad that she won't allow you to get your license next week."

I sighed. I hated my sister. Just once I wanted to see her not get something she wanted. But she had me cornered. I pulled a twenty-dollar bill from my wallet, crumpled it, and threw the paper ball at her. Somehow I didn't think that a blackmailed payout to my sister was what Dad had in mind when he told me to do something nice for her.

She picked up the bill and smoothed it out. "Thank you, Isma. I like her, Mike. I really do." She slipped the bill in her pocket. "Here. Trade you." She pulled out an envelope. "Another letter came for you yesterday afternoon." She left it on my floor as she went downstairs.

Yes! I snatched the letter up and hurried to my desk. For once the Mystery Mailer had perfect timing.

Tuesday, August 31, 2004 (271 Days Left)

Dear Michael,

It's been over a month since I last wrote to you. We've been busy. Second squad drove armored Humvees out from Kandahar, so we now have tactical vehicles. My squad has named our Humvee "Rawhide" after this old Western TV show. We sing the theme song as we launch every mission. More importantly, we have more guys who can help us cover guard duty, so we can get a little more sleep.

Our base is getting closer to done. Construction on the barracks will be finished soon and then we will all move into three-man rooms, or two-man rooms for us team leaders. The barracks are supposed to have a big latrine with actual real, working showers that should have hot water and everything.

One big thing happened. One night we were all just hanging around talking after chow. There's not a lot else to do. Suddenly, we heard this far-off explosion. This sounds like a big deal, but it's really not. Explosions and gunshots go off all the time here in Afghanistan. Who knows why. Anyway, we all paused for a second, but it was far away and nothing else happened, so we went back to talking. About ten minutes later, there was a white flash and a much bigger boom. It was still far away. We weren't under direct attack or anything, but a minute or two after that, the lieutenant came running out of the ~~TOC~~ Tactical Operations Center, telling us to get our armor and helmets on. He'd got a call from the local hajji governor's office saying the UN compound in Farah had been bombed once, and then when Afghans went to help the victims, a second explosion had gone off.

Every spare man went to the walls to guard our base in case of attack, but my squad was assigned to protect our medics and a physician's assistant — a female captain attached to us from an active-duty unit — while we went into town to see if we could help.

All of the usual joking that we did when we rolled out on a mission was replaced by nerves and a cold quiet. A crowd of Afghans had gathered around the blast site, but many of them scattered when they saw us pull up. This was unusual. Most of the time, a crowd would gather wherever we went. If they were running, did they know something we didn't? Were they expecting another Taliban attack?

The captain and the three medics did a great job. They ran right up to the blast site to help. Let me tell you, it wasn't pretty. Bits of shrapnel had shredded through a couple nearby cars, and even a poor donkey that called out in agony until an Afghan put it down. There was . . . stuff . . . body parts everywhere. I told my guys not to look at it, and I made sure they kept a sharp eye out as they stood in a security perimeter around the area. In the darkening evening, there were too many shadows for the Taliban to hide in. Our medical people helped patch up a couple Afghans, and then it was time to head back to base.

I forced myself to stay sharp and focused on our mission the whole time, but back at our base, I thanked God that we all made it back to base safe. I kept thinking that if we'd been there a few minutes earlier or if there had been a third bomb, it could have been my parts thrown all around the area. I thanked God, as I do every day here, for the gift of being able to live one more day.

Outside of that bombing, life has been pretty routine. Yes, I know that sounds crazy, but that's how things go here, I guess. Ortiz has even been complaining about being bored.

I get letters sometimes that thank me for my service and call me a hero. I appreciate it, but I wish they wouldn't say those things. I'm no hero. I'm a scared guy just doing my job in a war. That's it. I didn't enlist to defend freedom or protect my country, though those things mean a lot to me now. I signed up for the Guard the first time because I was flat broke, and they were offering a $10,000 sign-on bonus, plus G.I. Bill money for college that I or someone in my family could use. The ten grand helped me and your mom buy the house. A fixer-upper, true, but a place of our own.

I reenlisted in the Guard about six months after you were born because we were short on cash, and we needed the $15,000 reenlistment bonus. Your mom had been talking about college, maybe to be a nurse or something, so I figured she could use my G.I. Bill. That was nine months before the 9/11 attacks, so there were no wars or anything at that time, but your mom was furious that I re-upped. If you're reading *this, I guess she was right. I should have listened to her and got out of the Guard. Then maybe I could tell you all this in person. Still, I want you to know that I don't regret anything I've done for you, Mary, or your mother. I'm proud of our family.*

This war has taught me that it is a big world with more places to go and more kinds of jobs and lives than your high school guidance counselor ever tells you about. If you're willing to travel and take risks, Mike, you'll find endless opportunities, and I hope you get to grab all of those. Don't rush to be burdened by a house payment. Don't hurry to take out a loan to buy a car. The more stuff you buy — especially the more stuff you borrow money to buy — the harder it is for you to take advantage of certain opportunities.

Use high school as a time to explore a lot of your interests. Find that one great future that you want in life and then work as hard as you can to achieve it. Even if you think your goal is just a silly dream, never be one of those people who gave up on what they wanted. ALWAYS HOLD ON TO YOUR DREAM!

To that end, I want you to do really great in school, and so your mission with this letter is to ace a school assignment. Do your best. Earn that A. Then keep on going. It will make all the difference in the long run.

I wish I could be there with you now. I'd love to hear about all the fun you're having.

Love,
Dad

Again, I couldn't hold back my grin at the thought of how in sync I was with so much of what Dad wanted for me. I always did my best in school. If my mission was to earn an A on an assignment, I probably only had to wait for Coach Carter's grade to come back for the

Civil War presentation. Or else I'd study to ace the next English quiz on *Hamlet*. This mission shouldn't be too much of a problem.

What troubled me was the idea that Mom had been mad at Dad for reenlisting. I'd never known that. I'd thought that, except for not having a lot of money, my family had always been happy, sort of ideal. At least that was what I remembered from when Dad was alive. That's how it had felt on the trip to the Mark Twain Cave, and when Mom and Dad smiled at Mary and me on the kiddie rides at the county fair in Iowa City. I'd never considered that Mom might not have wanted him to be in the Guard.

Dad said he wasn't a hero, yet he'd gone to a Taliban bomb site with his unit as if it were no big deal. Is that what everyone meant when they said he'd been a hero — that it hardly fazed him to do a whole bunch of scary things? The superheroes in Dad's old comics that I used to read acted like that, casually fighting powerful villains on a regular schedule, but in Spider-Man and the New Warriors, the heroes always fought with a clear purpose, to save the day. What had my dad been fighting for? He said himself that he wasn't there to defend freedom, so apart from improving a base in Afghanistan and responding to this bombing, what was he supposed to be doing? What was it all for?

After a few hours of raking leaves, I headed out to Derek's farm on Scrappy. Annie rushed out of the ditch and ran along beside me as I rode. She barked and opened her mouth in a doggie smile, as though she knew about Isma and the football victory.

"Hey! There he is! Touchdown Wilson!" Derek rolled out from under the Falcon when I came into the shop.

"I swear all you ever do is mess around with this old truck," I said as I got off my bike.

"Whoa!" Derek stood up and patted the Falcon's fender. "Don't listen to him. With all the work I've put in on this truck, it's hardly old anymore. New shocks. Engine work. Some reinforcing in the body. Replaced the windshield. New stereo and rewired speakers. Completely new transmission. Muffler. Well, the whole exhaust system. The brakes are fixed up. I even have tires on order. The Falcon is back, baby!" He slapped the fender again. "Good as new! Better. They don't make 'em like this anymore."

I had to laugh. That truck was over thirty years old. "I'll believe all that 'good as new' stuff when I see it in action."

"You got your permit, right?"

"Sure, but I haven't had the chance to drive much since —"

The keys came flying at me, and I caught them. Derek climbed into the truck on the passenger side. I slid in behind the wheel. "Are you sure about this?" I said.

"Yeah." Derek pointed out the door of the shop. "It needs a test drive."

I put the key in, turned it, and gave it some gas. The engine fired up and the rumble shook through me. The Falcon sounded good. It sounded hungry.

"Let's go!" Derek rolled down his window.

I shifted into drive and rolled out of the shop, stopping before the highway at the end of the gravel driveway. "Which way?"

"Let's head to town."

I hit the gas and the tires spun out in the gravel before we shot ahead.

Derek laughed. "Easy, there. The Falcon's got a lot of juice under the hood. It doesn't take much to get it going." He smiled as he watched me drive. "What do you think?"

"It's pretty awesome," I said.

He tapped a button to turn on the radio. *"Three forty. Twenty minutes until four o'clock. It's sunshine and sixty-eight degrees here*

*in downtown Riverside. I want to give a shout-out to the mighty
Riverside Roughriders football team for bringing home a big win
last night against Lone Tree. Great work, guys. Keep it here on the
one to count on for today's news and the best of yesterday's music.
K Double R P, 102.3 FM."*

"I love this station," Derek said.

"I know. You listen to it all the time."

"He was right, though. It was a great win. I saw you play. Wow!
You were really looking tough out there. You laid on some hard hits!"

"Thanks for coming to the game."

"Oh, come on. Don't be so modest."

"What do you want me to say?"

"Tell me about it! Was it fun? It looked fun. You gotta be having
fun out there."

It was nice to get some congratulations from a grown-up. "Yeah,"
I said. "I'm pretty sore this morning, but the game was great."

"Your dad would be proud."

I rolled down the window and let the breeze blow through my
hair. "I know he would."

Nobody spoke for a while. KRRP was playing an old song by the
Doors. As we crossed the English River, Derek sat up. "Watching
that game last night sure brought back a lot of memories."

I hooked a left to bring us onto the highway that led into town.
"You played?"

"Not as well as you, but yeah. I remember me and some of the
guys drove over to Lone Tree once at like two in the morning the night
before we played them. They got that big Lumberjack statue out in
front of the school, and we spray-painted the whole thing bright red."
He frowned. "Course I think we ended up losing that night in overtime, but it was still all sorts of fun. I heard it took them forever to get
the paint off the statue, and even then, for years there was still the

faintest trace of red." Derek grinned. "Keep that kind of between the two of us, okay? They never did find out who did that."

"Sounds pretty crazy," I said.

"It was great. Hanging out with the guys. Parties at Nature Spot." I looked at him to see if he was serious. "Hey, eyes on the road, buddy." He pointed ahead. "Don't look so surprised. You think you kids are the first to find that place?"

Thanks to Dad's letters, I knew people my age hadn't found the place, but I didn't say anything.

"Officer Mitchell knows about every one of those parties, but he gets tired of the long walk down the railroad tracks to bust them." He laughed and patted the armrest on his door. "But he busted one of our parties once. I got away just in time. Found your mother on her way out there and got her back to town without getting caught."

Dad had told me that Mom used to go to parties, but I never imagined she'd almost been busted at one. Derek must have seen my look of surprise.

"Your mom is cooler than you think," he said. "You should see if she'd come to one of your games. I bet she'd like that."

"No way!" I turned right onto Weigand Street to head up toward the square. "The second she found out I'd gone behind her back to play football, she'd pull me off the team and prevent me from getting my license."

"It's your call, buddy. It just doesn't seem right, keeping her in the dark like that. Maybe if she saw you were playing and everything was fine, she wouldn't be so worried about it."

I'd heard enough of this. "Do you like my mom or something?"

"I told you, we've been friends for —"

"That's not what I mean and you know it. You two almost went out the other night. Plus you're always taking her side. Do you want to date her or something?"

He ran his hand back through his hair. "I just want to help her get out and enjoy life a little, you know?"

Thinking of Mom dating again was really weird, but there had to be a lot of guys who would be worse for her than Derek. "I think you two should go out. . . . I mean, if you both want to. I don't have a problem with it or anything. But I can't risk telling her about football. She's" — how could I explain this? — "out of touch with reality."

"Or she's had a little too much reality," he said quietly. There was a short silence. "We better head back to the farm. We have some bales to stack." He hesitated a moment. "Just don't be too hard on her, okay?"

I gripped the steering wheel tight as I turned the Falcon back toward the highway. "Don't be too hard on your mother." Everybody kept telling me that. Maybe someone should tell my mom not to be too hard on *me* for a change.

FIFTEEN

On Monday, I wondered how things would be between Isma and me. Would we act differently around each other now that we had kissed? Would we sit together at lunch? It turned out I needn't have worried. She preferred to eat with her friends from the band, and apart from a few shared, knowing smiles, our relationship was mostly the same, only better now that we'd made it romantic.

At practice that night, Coach started the team on our regular warm-up run. "Wilson!" he shouted. "No more extra running! You're caught up!" A few of the guys actually clapped. Some of them slapped me on the back or on the helmet as they ran past me, saying, "Good work, man," or "Keep it up."

Nick Rhodes hadn't clapped. Our battles at practice continued, only he came at me even more, and I hit him back twice as hard. Sometimes he'd win, tackling me or keeping me covered as I ran a pass route. Other times I got the upper hand. I loved throwing a block hard enough to knock him down.

Ethan found me in the lunch line on Wednesday. "Things still cool with you and Isma?"

"Yep," I said. "Nothing's changed in the last two days." On Monday, I'd told him about Isma and me kissing. He'd been more than appropriately impressed.

The line shuffled ahead, and Ethan and I grabbed our trays.

"Man, you're like a total genius with women," he said.

"No, I'm not."

"But you were right, dude. Thanks for making me join the musical."

"Fun?" I asked. We picked up milk and silverware.

"It is, actually." He smiled. "But more than that, Raelyn is finally starting to believe that Chris cheated on her. She was almost crying about it when I walked her home last night." He sounded giddy.

"That's . . . good to hear, I guess."

"I think she's going to break up with him! It's really happening."

"I'm happy for you, buddy." I slapped him on the arm before the lunch ladies dumped chicken patties and green beans on our trays.

During study hall on Thursday, I signed out to the library and went back to my corner.

"Hi," Isma said, already sitting back there when I rounded the dividers. "Mind if I join you in your secret spot?"

"It's not my spot. It's everybody's library." I pulled a chair around and sat down close to her. Every time I'd seen her since Friday night, there had been more warmth in her smile, a knowing look that said we had something special between us. I hoped she felt the same connection when she looked at me.

"Yeah, right," said Isma. "Nobody else ever sits back here."

I took her hands in mine. "Okay, then it can be *our* spot."

"That sounds so dorky," she said, but she didn't pull away.

Isma had a point. This resembled a scene from one of those horrible romantic comedies that Mary liked to watch, but I didn't care. She squeezed my hands and I squeezed hers back. I wanted to kiss her again. Isma, football, and Dad's letters were about all I had thought of all week.

Only, thinking of the letters made me start to worry. If the Mystery Mailer knew about Dad's plan to make sure I got all his letters before my sixteenth birthday, and if no more came before Saturday, that meant I probably already had all the letters from my father that I'd ever get. And I still had so many questions.

"You okay?" Isma asked.

I smiled at her. "I'm great," I said.

"Ready for the game tomorrow?"

"Yeah. Away game at Traer."

She rubbed her thumbs on my hands. "Are they good?"

"Yeah, they're a tough team." She looked away from me. She had something on her mind. "Why are you asking?"

"Well, there's this pep bus that goes to the away games," she said. "More sports worship. But it only costs two bucks, and I thought I might go."

"Since when do you care about the game?"

She pulled her hands away. "If you don't want me to go, just say —"

I put my hand on her knee. "No, no! I want you to go. I'm just surprised." Then I added, before she might misunderstand me, "Happily surprised!"

She rolled her eyes. "Well, for some reason these games are important to you, and I don't feel like spending another Friday night putting up with my annoying brother."

"Better than Mary, I promise you. This morning she —"

She placed one finger to my lips to quiet me, but I kissed it instead. She giggled. "I was thinking, if you weren't busy Saturday night, you could, you know, come over to my house." She shrugged. "We could hang out. Or my brother has a million video games. Or whatever."

The thought of that "whatever" made my heart beat heavier.

"Unless you don't want to," she said.

I snapped out of fantasyland and back to the library. "What?"

"If you don't want to come over —"

"I'd love to —"

"— I totally get it."

"— come over."

"It might be a little weird, since you've never —"

"No, not weird at all —"

"— even been to my house and —"

I placed my finger to her lips. She kissed it and laughed. "Isma," I said, "I'd love to come over. Saturday night sounds perfect."

"Oh, that sounds so perfect." Rhodes spoke in a stupid high-pitched voice. He leaned on the wooden study partitions. "You could put on one of those blue body-tent things and Mikey here could crawl up inside. You two could talk about jihad or suck on each other's fingers or whatever you freaks do."

I stood up so fast my chair fell back. "Get out of here."

"I just came back here to look at some of these lame poems and lookie what I found." He ran his fingers along the books. "Dorks in love."

Rhodes had finally crossed the honor line Dad had written about. I took a step toward him.

"Michael, don't. It's not worth it," Isma said.

Rhodes got up off the divider and moved close enough that I could crack him one right there. My legs felt rubbery and my fists were tight. I wanted to knock him out so bad my shoulder twitched.

"Yeah, Mikey, there's no need to stop being a lady." He grinned. "Or maybe you're going to let your little raghead girlfriend fight your battles for you." He put his hand to his chin and squinted his eyes like he was thinking real hard. "But they never stand up and fight, do they? They stick with the roadside bombs and suicide attacks."

"Come on, Mike. Let's go." Isma put her hand on my shoulder, but I jerked away.

"You go," I said. "I got to take care of something."

Rhodes glared at me. "We have a problem. You're in my tight end spot."

"Only problem is you can't keep yourself under control on the field."

"Gentlemen!" Mrs. Potter had come out of nowhere and stood watching us with her hands on her hips. "I suggest you *both* get yourselves under control right now," she said in her no-nonsense librarian power voice. "Mr. Rhodes, are you looking for a particular book back here?"

"Naw." He didn't take his eyes off me. "Just looking around when I found these two —"

"Then you will move along right now."

"Sure," he said. "See you around, Mikey." He walked off.

I turned back to Isma, but she had vanished. I only saw a flash of her hair as she slipped out through the library doors.

"Michael," said Mrs. Potter.

Here it came. Mrs. Potter was usually the kindest, most helpful person in the school. She was *really* nice, not fake nice like the school secretary, who never stopped giggling. But when Mrs. Potter was mad, everybody knew it, and she could bring anyone in the school nearly to tears. I folded my arms across my chest and waited for the onslaught.

"Take a deep breath, Mike."

I managed to look at her. She seemed relaxed.

"I didn't do anything," I said.

She waved her hand dismissively. "The problem was what you were about to do."

"Sorry," I said.

"Think about all you have to lose by getting into a fight. First, you'd be disturbing my library, which is the *worst* thing you could possibly do. But if you got in a fight, you'd probably also be suspended, and then you wouldn't be able to play football. Can you think of anyone who'd be happy about that?"

"He was the one who started —"

"Whoa! I'm not talking about any specific person," she said. "I was asking a question."

I doubted that very much, but I didn't want to push my luck with her.

"You think about that, and think about how Isma would have felt to see you two fighting it out. She didn't look very happy."

Why was Isma mad at me? Rhodes had started all this. "This wasn't my —"

She held up a hand. "Just think about it." She lowered her hand very slowly. "Calm down. And think about it."

I did think about it all the way down the hallway after the bell rang, searching the crowd for Isma. I was still thinking about it when Rhodes shoulder-checked me right into Laura Tammerin. I crashed into her chest, knocking her books out of her hands.

"Hey!" Laura said. "Watch where you're going!"

Rhodes elbowed Clint, pointed at me, and laughed as the two of them headed down the hall. For a second I almost ran after him, but Laura was crouching down to pick up her books, and I figured I should help her.

She must have seen Nick laughing, because when I handed her binder and algebra book to her, she rolled her eyes. "Forget about that guy. He's an idiot, and he's just jealous that you've been getting so much playing time."

"Sorry about that," I said as we stood up together.

"I'm a big girl. I can handle it." She tossed her hair back over her shoulder. "Are you going to the team supper tonight?"

"I don't have a ride."

"It's at Piggly's."

"Oh." I never found out the location until Thursday-night practice. "Then I can probably go."

"And don't worry about the next time it's in Iowa City and you need a ride." She brushed against me as she walked past. "I got you covered."

The crowd in the hallway was starting to thin out. I'd missed my chance to try to smooth things over with Isma. I rushed to class, sliding into my desk just as the bell rang.

English usually held my attention even more than my other classes, but that day my thoughts kept drifting to the memory of that idiot Rhodes. We read the second half of act four of *Hamlet*, where Hamlet had this big awesome speech. I felt like standing up on my desk and shouting the last lines at Rhodes: "O, from this time forth, my thoughts be bloody, or be nothing worth!"

And then in the next scene Hamlet's girlfriend, Ophelia, went totally crazy. Isma surely wasn't going to put on a huge dress and drown in a stream, but her anger made about as much sense to me as the weird, insane songs Ophelia sang.

Isma ignored me through history, and after class, I hurried to catch up with her. "Can we talk for a second?" I asked, gently grabbing her elbow.

She pulled her arm away from me. "I don't want to talk right now, okay?" She picked up her pace and faded into the crowd.

"Uh-oh, Mikey's got twouble wit his wittle girlfwiend." Clint wiped pretend tears from his cheeks. I took a deep breath and walked in the other direction, wishing that tonight were a contact practice.

The practice breezed by light and quick, though, and afterward, I cleaned up, dressed, and headed to the bike rack to get Scrappy. I stopped two steps outside the front doors of the school. Isma sat on the bike rack, reading something in her binder.

"Hey, I'm really sorry for whatever I did," I said as I approached.

She snapped her binder shut. "That's really not much of an apology." I opened my mouth to speak, but she continued, "I don't need you or anyone else fighting for me."

"Hey, Rhodes is the guy who —"

"He's a moron. Not worth fighting over the stupid things he says."

I bit my lip. Her attitude was getting on my nerves. "I'm not just going to sit back and do nothing while he calls you a terrorist."

"Shouldn't that be my decision?" she said. "He says all Muslims are violent, dangerous people. Maybe he believes it. I don't know. But if I get in a fight with him, or if you fight him on my behalf, even if you win, I'll still lose because it'll be confirming everything he said about Muslim violence. So no fights, okay?"

"I'm sorry," I said.

She reached over and squeezed my hand. "No need to apologize. I'm not mad. I wasn't mad all afternoon. I just needed a private place and time to explain all this." She stood up. "You've got that sports-supper-cult thing tonight, so I'll leave you alone." She kissed me on the cheek and headed off toward home. I watched her walk away for a while before I pulled Scrappy out of the rack.

"Hey there, Mike Wilson!" Mr. Pineeda greeted me as I came in through the oinking door wearing my Roughriders jersey. "I've been hearing some great things about you Saturday mornings at Piggly's Old Timers' Coffee Club. They say the mighty Roughriders have a new tight end. They say he's quick and tough." He slapped me on the back and pointed toward the team room with his other hand. "Your teammates are in there. Keep it up, young man!"

When I entered the room, Sullivan looked up at me from where he sat in a sea of red jerseys at a table with Dozer, McKay, Cody, Hamilton, and Rhodes. He nodded, and I nodded back.

I went to the empty seat next to Ethan. He put a red plastic cup down in front of me and poured some Mountain Dew from the pitcher on the table. "You ready for tomorrow night?"

"Think so."

"Dude, you better *know* so. Traer's going to be tough."

I felt a hand slide across my upper back as Laura sat down in the chair next to me and motioned across the room. Kendra stood there with her arms folded over her chest and her head cocked to the side, trying to look like she absolutely didn't care about all the guys making pig snorts and squeals at her. Laura said, "What has to be tough is being Kendra Hanson in that stupid rubber pig snout. I don't know why she keeps working here. Nothing is worth that kind of humiliation."

Kendra and I barely knew each other. She was a freshman and we didn't have any classes together. But her father worked as the night janitor at the elementary school, and her family lived in a trailer that made my house look like a castle. I knew why she worked here.

"Mike," Laura whispered, "if we win tomorrow night, you have to come out to Nature Spot. Me and Kelsey were just out there getting the fire pit ready. It's going to be awesome."

"I'll do my best," I said, though I had no idea how I would get out there without getting in trouble with Mom. Then I noticed Ethan pretending to be focused on some of the plaques on the wall, as if he wasn't listening. "Ethan and I might stop by."

"Oh," she said, sounding surprised. "Yeah, totally bring Ethan. It's going to be a blast. You'll see."

Monty joined our table, and later Kelsey Hughes sat down too. I had a great night eating, talking, laughing, and being a part of the team.

SIXTEEN

What I learned that Friday night at the game was that sometimes Coach Carter called it exactly right. The Traer Tigers were almost as good as Dysart. Their defense moved cat-quick in the secondary and they had a big, powerful line. We nearly went into the locker room at halftime without scoring, but managed a touchdown and extra point late in the second quarter to tie the game at seven.

The second half went even worse. Traer received and scored early. After that, the Tiger defense had us pinned down. We couldn't get much of anything going offensively. They sacked Matt Karn several times.

Finally, with less than a minute left in the game, Sullivan broke loose with a forty-yard run. They took him down on the five. On second down, Coach called in a pass play, and Karn did a great job dodging the defensive back who broke through our line. Just after the game clock expired, he connected with Chris Moore for a touchdown, making the score thirteen to fourteen.

We waited for the next play in the huddle. When Ethan came running onto the field, we knew Coach wanted us to kick the extra point, tie the game, and try to win it in overtime.

Karn kicked at the ground. "Oh, come on. We can do this. Let's go for two and win the game."

"No way," said Cody. "We do what Coach says. We'll get them in overtime."

"You have to do what he says," said Hamilton. "If you try for the conversion, he'll run us to death next week for ignoring his plan."

"Come on, guys!" Dozer shouted. "Man up! Let's go for it!"

"We can't!" Cody said.

I couldn't believe they were arguing about this right now. We needed to hurry to avoid a delay-of-game penalty.

"I'm the center. The choice is mine," McKay said. He locked eyes with Karn. "High snap on one. That's what you're getting. Be ready."

"No way, man. It won't —" Cody started.

"No time for this," Sullivan said. "Receivers, get open in the end zone. Everybody else" — he slapped Karn on the shoulder — "let's give the man time."

Everyone on my team had lost their minds. We were going for a last-second unorganized pass play against the toughest defense we'd seen yet. If we scored, we won the game. If we didn't, we would lose, and Coach would kill us for not going for the tie.

Karn called out the cadence and McKay snapped the ball. I exploded forward, juke-stepping around one defender and rolling out to get open. One of the backs followed me deeper into the end zone while another moved up on me. I sped up to pass the second defender on my right, then cut to the left at the last second. It worked. I'd scraped off my trail defender for the seconds I needed to cut back inside.

Behind our line, Sullivan checked one rushing defensive lineman. Ethan moved up to block another. Karn launched the pass in my direction, but a little high. I ran up a few steps and jumped to grab the ball out of the air.

Someone slammed into me from behind, putting me on the ground, but I had the ball. I was in. The ref on the sidelines put both hands up in the air. We'd just won the game fifteen to fourteen.

"My thoughts be bloody, or be nothing worth!" I screamed as I stood up and tossed the ball to the referee. Sullivan found me first, gripping me in a bear hug and swinging me around. Ethan punched me in the side of the helmet. More and more screaming Roughriders joined in. Even Karn grabbed me by my face mask and pulled me forward until my helmet hit his. "You are awesome!" he shouted.

"Dude, it was your pass!" I said.

Coach eventually got us to calm down and get through the line, slapping fives and saying "Good game" to each guy on the other team.

"I got one question before we clean up and get out of here," Coach said back in the locker room. "And think carefully about how you answer me. What happened on that last point-after play?"

"Sorry, Coach," said McKay. "My hand slipped on the ball. I sent back a bad snap. I'm just glad it worked out."

Coach narrowed his eyes and didn't say anything. "At practice this week . . ." He rubbed his chin. I don't think anyone in that locker room moved. A painful-looking smile cracked across his face. "I want you to do some extra snaps, McKay."

I wasn't the only one who let out the breath he'd been holding.

"Sure thing, Coach," said McKay. "Won't happen again."

"Good win, men. Let's get cleaned up and head home!"

We erupted into our usual celebration.

After we got off the bus back at school and stowed our gear away in the locker room, Dozer put his arm around my shoulder. "You're coming out tonight." It was not a question, and his tone did not invite disagreement.

"I'll do my best," I said.

He poked me in the chest. "You better." Then he smiled. "Oh, and nice catch."

For the first time in years, people really wanted me around. I couldn't hold back my grin as I looked at all these guys who used to be big dangerous juniors and seniors to me, guys I had always secretly feared. Now they seemed like people, maybe almost like friends. My teammates had given me the best early birthday present I could have hoped for.

After both of the last two games I had avoided the crowd in the senior parking lot by going through the school and out the front door, but after tonight's game, I had to admit, I wanted to be noticed. I went out the side door.

The lot was mostly empty, but there were still three cars and a couple pickups. Some rough metal played from someone's car stereo. People were gathered around talking and laughing. A big cooler full of ice and Gatorade sat on the sidewalk. Hopefully Gatorade or soda was all they had in there. Surely the guys wouldn't be stupid enough to bring anything they weren't supposed to have to the school parking lot.

Nicky Dinsler sat on the hood of Eddie Bracken's car with her feet on the bumper. Bracken stepped between her knees and whispered something in her ear.

Gabe sat next to Maria Vasquez on the big metal toolbox behind the cab in the bed of his pickup. She tried to tickle his side, but he picked her up with one arm under her knees and the other under her shoulders. "Oooh," she squealed and laughed. "Gabe, put me down!"

Gabe jiggled her like he was about to drop her down to the pavement. "You want down?"

She screamed and kicked her legs. "Put me down on the truck!"

He swung her back to the bed of the truck and stood her back up again. Then he put his arms around her and leaned in to kiss her.

Cody sat in his pickup with the door open and his legs hanging down. "Hey, Wilson, good job!" he shouted to me.

"Yeah, way to go, stud!" Erica Larson called to me from where she sat on the trunk of Hamilton's Dodge Stratus.

"Nice catch, Wilson!" Hamilton said.

I didn't want to act like I'd come out there to show off, so I just waved and kept walking toward the front of the school, where I found Isma waiting by the bike rack again.

"Hey! You were great!" She threw her arms around me. I squeezed her back. "I saw your catch!"

"It was crazy," I said. "We didn't even really have a play. At the last second, the guys decided to go for two."

"Go for two?"

"They decided to pass into the end zone for two points instead of kicking for one point. One point would have only tied it up. We needed two."

She looked so beautiful when she grinned like that and her nose wrinkled. "So you won the game!"

"Whoa! Sullivan had some good runs. Chris Moore scored the last touchdown." I pulled Scrappy out of the rack and noticed at once that someone had flattened both tires. "Great," I said, looking down at the rubber bulging on the bottom of the rims. I leaned it against the rack and bent down to make sure the tires hadn't been slashed.

"They both went flat on the same day?" Isma said.

"Someone let the air out of them," I said. It had to be Rhodes.

"Why would —"

"It doesn't matter. I can pump them up again. It's just kind of a pain." Any other time, I would have been really mad about this, but tonight, I couldn't be angry for long. To make sure the rims didn't tear up the empty tires, I carried Scrappy as we walked.

"Are you still coming over tomorrow?" Isma asked.

"Wouldn't miss it," I said. I would sneak out after Mom went to work, or I would say that I had to work longer on the farm. Either way, I wouldn't let Isma down.

The talk came fun and easy, the way it always did with Isma. The warm fullness in my chest spread out through my body in electric tingles when we stopped and stood close together under the big maple on the corner of her block. I don't know if she leaned forward to kiss me or if I pulled her to me and kissed her, but when our lips touched, I didn't want the moment to end.

When she gently stepped away from me a few minutes later, I tried to hold on to her with my hands at her waist, my fingers hooking under her belt. She took my hands in hers and kissed them. "Good night," she whispered, and I watched as she ran away from our tree to her front door, stopping again to wave before she vanished inside.

At home, after I put my bike in the shed, I went around to the front door. As soon as I entered the dining room, though, I knew that all the wonder of the night was about to be taken away.

Mom gasped and hung the phone up on the wall. "Do you know that I was just about to call the police? Where have you been?"

"Mom, calm down. I was just —"

"It's almost eleven! I've been out of my mind with worry. Where were you?"

"Working! I was at the farm."

"I *called* the farm! Nobody answered, so I was left to wait and pace around the house, imagining you hit by a semi or chewed up in a combine or —"

"Mom!" I shouted. "I'm fine! I said I was working." I felt a little bad lying, but I had to get her calmed down. We wouldn't have this problem if she would just relax and let me do things. "We were out in the field, not sitting by the phone!"

"Until ten forty-five? And you didn't even call?"

"It's harvest time, Mom. There's a lot to do out there."

Mary came halfway down the stairs, but stayed out of Mom's sight. She pointed at her wrist as though she had a watch and then shot me a look like, *What were you thinking being out so late?* I glared at her.

"I don't know if it's so good for you to keep working out there." Mom started pacing the room.

"Mom, it's okay. I'm fine. We need the money."

"I expect you to call if you're going to be out that late again."

I pressed my hands to my face. "Yeah. Fine. I'll call. Sorry you were so worried."

She pushed aside some laundry on the cluttered dining room table and sat down, resting her head in her hands. "Michael, you're sixteen tomorrow. I know I promised I would take you to get your license, but after tonight, I'm really not so sure. I'm worried that you're going through one of these rebellious-teenager stages."

Oh no. I couldn't handle this. The law said I was old enough for a license. How could she just decide by herself that I couldn't get it?

"I'm really sorry, Mom. I have to go to work tomorrow after we get my license. I promise I'll talk to Derek about cutting back my hours some so I'm not out so late." I'd resorted to another lie, but I could think of no other way to save this situation. "I'm really sorry."

"Okay, Michael," she said. "We'll get you your license tomorrow, but then we're going to have a serious talk about your responsibilities and my expectations."

She sounded like she'd granted me some amazing favor. It made me sick, but I knew what she really wanted to hear.

"Wow. Thanks, Mom," I said. I took it one step further by going to her side to hug her. "Good night."

I went upstairs, taking care to make plenty of noise on every step so Mom would know I went all the way to my attic. I nearly punched the wall when I got there, but stopped myself so Mom wouldn't hear me throwing a fit. I wasn't a rebellious teenager. I only wanted to be a normal one. In about an hour, I would be sixteen, and she still treated me like I was Mary's age. All I wanted was my license and the chance to have some friends, maybe a girlfriend, like everyone else. Like what Dad said he wanted for me.

I took a seat at my desk, waiting for a while to make sure Mom had time to settle in. I looked over my books. How many Friday nights had I spent up here alone, trying to convince myself that they were all I needed? I'd read some good poems and great novels. But a lot of what Dad had said about the fun of high school had begun to make sense to me, and I wanted to get out to experience it.

I stretched my neck and sore arms, closed my eyes, and took a deep breath to try to relax. I would make something happen tonight. Mom had no idea how much of a rebellious teenager I could be.

Mom often watched TV in the living room after she finished work, and she always had the volume up way too loud. I could just barely hear it all the way up here. She was watching something or she'd fallen asleep watching something. Either way, if I went down the squeaky stairs and out the front door, I'd probably be caught. I wished I lived in one of those houses in the movies where a handy tree branch came right up to my bedroom window, but I didn't have a normal bedroom, and the tiny windows in the attic didn't open.

But the window in the upstairs hallway did. I carried my shoes down the steps from my attic to the upper level. Then I slid the old-fashioned window up just a crack to see if it would make any noise. It wobbled a bit in the frame, so I had to push it up slowly and keep it steady. Then I popped out the screen, carefully lowering it to the roof of the back room below. I slipped one leg out and placed my foot on the roof.

"Where do you think you're going?" Mary said in a loud whisper. She stood outside her bedroom door with her hands on her hips.

"Shhh! Be quiet," I whispered.

She came closer to the window. "Mom will kill you! Or she'll throw a fit and I'll be the one stuck here dealing with it."

"She'll never know."

"She will!" Mary whispered. "Because I'm telling her."

She went toward the stairs but I grabbed her by the wrist and pulled her back to me. "No you won't!" I hissed. "And I won't pay you any money or do anything to buy your silence. You're going to stay out of my business, go back to your room, and forget that you ever saw this." Mary's eyes were wide. She flinched and looked at her wrist until I relaxed my grip a little. "Not one word, got it?"

She nodded and I let her go. "You always try to tell me what Dad would have thought we should or shouldn't do," she said, rubbing her wrist. "I wonder what he would say about you sneaking out." She didn't wait for me to answer, but went back to her room.

I stepped down onto the roof of the back room, closed the window, put the screen back in, and then put my shoes on. The roof was almost flat, and after I lowered myself onto my stomach with my legs dangling over the edge, I slid down a little before I dropped to the backyard. Since we lived on a dead end right next to the fields, the walk to the old railroad tracks was easy. With my arms up to shield my face from the sharp, dry leaves of the cornstalks, I cut across the rows, climbed over a barbed-wire fence, and then went up the slope to the tracks.

Mary could talk all she wanted about Dad, but I knew better than anyone what he thought I should do. He'd told me to honor my mother, to take care of my mother and sister. Well, I did. I'd calmed Mom down tonight. I worked hard and paid for a lot of stuff around the house. Show me another kid in my grade who did that. I helped my sister more than any other brother ever had to. And what did I get? Constant reprimands from my mother and even from Mary. When would the time come for me to do something for me?

Tonight. When I completed the fourth mission Dad had given me. I took off down the tracks toward the party at Nature Spot.

SEVENTEEN

The stars shined bright in the dark sky overhead — the same stars my father had seen when he'd made his way down these same abandoned train tracks to Nature Spot years ago. When he was my age, he'd crossed this same big limestone bridge that spanned the English River. People called it the Runaway Bridge. I'd heard a bunch of different stories about why people called it that, but tonight, as I sneaked out of my house, the name made perfect sense.

Scrub brush and small trees lining each side of the tracks cast the railway bed in dark shadows. A tiny bit of light from the sliver of moon kept me from tripping on too many of the wooden railroad ties. I'd been walking forever. Everyone said Nature Spot could be found just off the railroad tracks a few miles south of town. It had to be coming up soon.

Finally, I thought I heard something, a whoop or a scream, maybe laughter. Soon the sound of music echoed toward me, getting louder as I approached. I stepped out onto a much smaller stone bridge.

This bridge crossed a little creek that ran through a clearing surrounded by tall oaks. In the middle of the clearing, people talked and drank as they sat on logs or wooden stumps around a fire pit. A new guy in my class named Hunter Thorson played guitar and watched the sparks rising from the fire up into the dark.

"Don't do it! You're too heavy. It won't hold you." Nicky Dinsler laughed from somewhere.

I followed the sound of her voice overhead to where she and Eddie Bracken stood in what was left of an old tree house. Long ago, someone had built a large platform about a dozen feet from the ground around a tree that had grown up in three tall trunks. One of the tree house's walls had fallen away and most of the roof had collapsed, but the remnants of a whole room were up there.

Eddie walked a few steps out onto the plank floor of a shaky old rope bridge. Then he ran across the fifteen feet of rattling bridge to a second, smaller platform in the branches of an oak.

Cody Arnath was in the trees too. He went from this second platform along a solid bridge to another decaying tree house in a third tree. He grabbed a rope that hung from one of the top branches. "Roughriderrrrrrs!" he shouted. Then he jumped, wrapped his legs around the rope, and swung out away from the platform. "Mount up!"

Chris Moore waded out into Wolf Creek with his jeans rolled up. "The water's way too cold."

Erica Larson, still wearing her cheerleading uniform, stopped midstream, the water just above her knees. She drank from a can for a moment, then wiped her mouth. "Would you toughen up? Just give yourself a chance to get used to it."

Sarah Carnahan finished rolling up her jeans on the bank and then stepped out into the creek. "It's freezing!" she screamed. She laughed and joined Chris, gently rubbing his back when he put his arm around her. Chris and Sarah seemed pretty happy together. "Erica," Sarah said, "if Coach finds out you wore that uniform out here, she'll kill you."

"She won't find out. Anyway, we got to wear these more. Be proud! Cheer it out, girl!" Erica pounded the rest of her drink and dropped the can in the water, waving as it floated downstream.

Nature Spot. I'd heard so much about it, but now that I'd arrived, what should I do? What did people do at parties? Just talk and drink?

I felt completely out of place. Nobody seemed to have seen me yet, and for a moment I thought about turning around and going back home. But I had a mission to complete for Dad. He and his fellow soldiers didn't always know what they were doing in Afghanistan, but they never turned around and went home. It wasn't the Cowboy Way.

Careful not to slip on the loose gravel, I slowly shuffled down the slope from the tracks. Chris nodded to me from the water. "Mike! You made it. Cool."

"That was a great catch there, near the end," I said. "You saved us."

Chris laughed. "Yeah, same to you!"

Cody's swing wound down and he skidded to a stop on the ground. "Wilson!" He reached out his fist and I bumped it. He pointed to a crowd of people gathered around a wooden plank suspended over two fifty-gallon barrels. "Drinks over there. Get 'em while they're cold, dude." He slapped me on the back and ran toward the tree houses with the rope in hand.

I tried to walk casually, like I knew where to go and what to do. A bunch of these people weren't on the football team, and though I'd seen them around school and knew most of their names, I didn't really know them as people. By the time I reached the edge of the group by the drinks, I had begun to wish I'd never come. I'd gone through all this trouble to get out here, and for what? To stand around like a helpless, unwanted idiot.

"Hey, Mike, good to see you." Raelyn and Ethan stepped up beside me. I fought to hold back my laugh, both because I was so relieved to have someone to talk to, and because of the ridiculously happy look on Ethan's face.

"Thanks," I said. "This place is great. But I'm kind of surprised to see you here."

"Why?" she asked a little sharply. Ethan fired a death stare at me.

"Um . . . no reason." How could I mention the Chris Moore thing delicately? I was stupid for starting to bring it up. On the other hand, maybe I could take the fall to help Ethan. "Just . . . so I guess you and Chris —"

"I swear, if one more person mentions that tonight, I will explode," Raelyn said. "Yeah, I used to come out here because me and him were going out, but I'm not going to stop just because we broke up." Ethan sneaked a thumbs-up at me from behind her, but snapped his hand down when she turned to him. "Come on, Ethan." She led him away.

"Mike!" Laura pushed through the crowd, almost dropping the bottle of whatever cherry-red stuff she'd been drinking. She threw her arms around my neck and squeezed me. "I'm so happy you could come!"

I patted her on the back. "Hey, Laura."

She backed away from me a little but kept her hands on my shoulders. "Seriously" — she shook her head as she said the word — "it's awesome you're here. You were *totally*" — she wobbled a little — "awesome tonight."

Laura pulled me close to her side, kind of hanging on my shoulders with her arm draped around me as she walked us around Nature Spot. "Isn't this place great?" She pointed with her bottle to show it off. "Just hanging out, celebrating the win, and having some drinks with friends."

Cody whooped as he swung from the rope again.

"And swinging from ropes out of the tree houses," I said. "Who built them, anyway?"

Laura laughed. "Nobody knows. They've been here forever. Come on, let's get you a drink!" She dropped her arm from my shoulder and led me through the crowd. All sorts of different bottles occupied the wood plank. I also spotted the cooler that had been outside the school.

"Just a Gatorade would be great. I'm kind of dehydrated after the game," I said, hoping I didn't sound completely lame.

"What?" Laura frowned. "You sure?"

"Yeah."

She shrugged and handed me a red Gatorade. Over by the fire, people clapped as Hunter finished a song. A few people asked him to play another one. He chugged the rest of his drink before crushing the can and tossing it in the fire. Then he went back to strumming his guitar, launching into the introduction to Pink Floyd's "Wish You Were Here."

"I can't believe it," I whispered to Laura. "I know this song."

"Yeah, I think Hunter's really talented."

He let the introduction roll off his guitar for a moment before he started singing. After a couple lines, Dozer came back from the trees to stand next to Hunter and McKay. He held up his drink and joined in.

This was awesome. I joined the guys, who were swaying back and forth as they sang, and I added my voice to the mix. Dozer put his arms over each of our shoulders. Laura followed and slid into the huddle, and then a few others, including quiet Sullivan, completed our swaying, singing circle.

As I belted out the lines, someone's fingers rubbed the back of my neck. For one second I looked at Dozer, but when he swayed away, he nearly fell down, so I knew it wasn't him. I turned to Laura, who grinned at me with her eyes half closed.

When the song ended and the group broke up, I took a seat on a log with Laura, Dozer, McKay, and Sullivan. Hunter pointed his guitar toward me. "You really knew the song, man."

"My dad left me a bunch of CDs," I said.

"You're still listening to CDs?" Rhodes said as he came into the circle and sat on a rock across the fire from me.

"Yeah," I said.

"Stone Age," said Rhodes.

"I got a bunch of CDs in my car," said Sullivan. "Anyway, who cares about that? What I want to know is did anyone see that explosive hit Moore put on number seventeen in the third quarter?"

"Dude, that was awesome," said Hamilton. He held up a finger in a *wait a second* gesture, burped, took a long drink, and then continued. "I'll admit that I messed up and missed my tackle right there. I was mad about that, but then *boom!* Moore comes flying in so fast, I didn't even know who hit the Traer guy at first. That guy just said 'uuuh.'" Hamilton laughed. "Just like that, like, 'uuuh,' and then he went down."

We all laughed. Everything that Dad had said about having fun with great high school friends made perfect sense now. I had something in common with people. I only wished Isma could be here with me.

Laura pulled on my arm until I stood up and followed her. She led me away from the fire and whispered, "Let's get you something better than that Gatorade."

"I'm good, seriously. I just —"

She tripped and nearly fell, but I caught her just in time. She had one hand on each of my shoulders and pulled herself up until her face was close to mine. I could smell her drink on her breath. Her eyes were half closed again as she smiled. "You're really cute."

No girl had ever told me that in my whole life, especially not a pretty and popular older girl like Laura Tammerin. Of course, no girl had hung on me quite this way either. She leaned toward me and closed her eyes.

My mouth fell open in surprise. She wanted to kiss me? Dad had warned me about having more girls than I could handle. Why hadn't he told me what to do about it? And what about Isma? I ducked my head to the side to dodge her kiss.

"Oops." Laura grinned at me with her eyes nearly closed. "I missed."

I helped her back to the log bench and sat her down before she could try again.

Hailey Green had joined the circle by now. She looked completely gorgeous, wearing brown boots, jeans, and one of those sweaters that hung down off the shoulder with a tank top underneath, like she had arrived for a fashion shoot and not a party. She smiled. "That was a great catch tonight." Was she talking to me? "Hello?" She laughed. "You okay, Mike?"

I'd assumed she was talking to Moore. She'd barely said three sentences to me since junior high. "Sorry," I said. "Um, thanks. I got lucky. Plus, there were a lot of plays to go around. The whole team did great."

"That's 'cause we got a team of studs," Hailey said. "So, Mike, are you, like, *dating* that Isma girl? Going to the homecoming dance with her or something?"

Where did this come from? "What?"

"I heard she's *way* into you," said Hailey.

I didn't want to talk about Isma and me. "I don't know how much she likes me. And we're not really dating. Just friends."

"She's, like, weird." Hailey tipped back her bottle of passion-berry punch and took a long drink.

Eddie came to the circle, holding hands with Nicky, whose hair was a little messed up. "Are you talking about that Muslim girl?" Nicky said. "She's in my study hall, always drawing pictures. Trying to be all arty or whatever."

I bit my lip. They had a problem with art? Why did they have to make fun of her about it? Guys could get to know each other while playing football and figure out how to get along. It seemed different with girls. Queens like Hailey Green and Nicky Dinsler seemed to have a list of rules long enough to stretch all the way back to town.

Eddie nodded. "Her little brother is in my brother's class. My bro says that kid is the weirdest in the fifth grade."

"Must run in the family," said Dozer. He must have noticed the expression on my face. "Sorry, dude, but she is a little . . ." He waved his hand in a little circle. "She ain't bad-looking, though."

"Gross!" someone shouted.

"She's not that bad," I said quietly. I knew that even if I tried to explain what made Isma great, they'd never change their minds. So why should I make a scene and mess up this good time?

"Do you guys realize that we only really need to win two more games to make the playoffs in our district?" Sullivan sat on the ground, leaning back against a log, watching sparks fly up out of the fire until they winked out in the night. "I got another letter this afternoon from the University of Dubuque."

"Another for your collection? How many does that make now?" said Hamilton.

"It doesn't matter," said Sullivan. "None of the letters matter unless we make the playoffs and do really well. My family doesn't have the money to pay for my college, so it's either I pull off this football-scholarship thing or go into a pile of debt."

Karn tossed his empty can into the glowing embers of the fire. "Don't worry about it. We've got this."

"The kid could have dropped the ball tonight." Sullivan nodded at me. "You could have been sacked, Matt. That game was way too close."

"Yeah, but it worked out," said Dozer. "This is important to us too, man. You got to trust us."

"I am trusting you guys," said Sullivan. "I'm trusting you with my whole future."

A cold drink splashed on my head and I jumped to my feet. The freezing liquid ran down my face and onto my shirt. I wiped my eyes, tasting whatever strong stuff had been mixed with the cherry Kool-Aid that would now stain one of my best T-shirts and my only jacket.

"Whoa," Dozer said. "Not cool, dude."

Was he talking to me? Of course it wasn't cool.

"What? It was an accident. I tripped," someone said behind me.

Nick Rhodes. I spun around to see him holding an empty red plastic cup. I scrambled to his side of the log. "What is your problem?"

"I think you know." Rhodes gave me a little shove in the chest.

My heart pounded so heavy, I could feel it in my ears. Dad would tell me to throttle this guy, and he'd get no argument from me. I clenched my fists. This time I'd punch him, knock him out, break his jaw. I'd throw him to the dirt like tossing a bale on the farm.

But Isma and Mrs. Potter had both told me not to fight. And Nick had a lot of friends in this group. He'd been hanging out with these people for years, and I'd only come onto the scene a few weeks ago. If I beat up their buddy, this could be the last time anyone invited me anywhere.

Rhodes pushed me again and I stepped back.

"Dude, chill. Leave him alone," said Eddie. "Can't we just have fun?"

"I want to know how this freak even got here." Rhodes pushed me a third time. I shoved him back. He cocked his fist, but Sullivan rushed him and grabbed his arm.

Dozer had stood up too and held his other arm. "Calm down, man. What's your problem?"

"You guys letting this loser out here is my problem!"

Dozer twisted Rhodes's arm behind his back until he gasped at the pain. Then Dozer swung him around and flung him to the ground. He pulled him up by the front of his T-shirt until their faces were inches apart. A little vein throbbed on the side of Dozer's head. "Knock it off or get out of here! This is supposed to be a party." His bulging biceps twitched. "Next time you want to fight someone out here, you fight me! Got it?" Dozer pushed him back to the ground.

Nobody moved or said anything. A log popped on the fire. Wolf Creek gurgled as it churned through rocks by the little bridge. Rhodes rose to his feet. He glared at me, then glanced at Dozer before heading off into the shadows, up the slope to the tracks. "This isn't over, Wilson!" he yelled back.

A bunch of snappy, tough-sounding replies echoed through my head. *It's over when I say it's over!* Or *I'll be ready!* Or *Bring it on!* I didn't say any of them. Instead, I sat down on the log and tried to act casual, even though I was soaked by Nick's drink.

Hunter Thorson strummed his guitar. "That's too bad. I was hoping for a fight." He laughed. "I love a good fight." He launched into a song, which seemed to be a signal for people to go for drinks and relax. Dozer grabbed two more drinks and sat back down while Sullivan poked the fire with a stick.

"Hey, man," I said quietly to Dozer. "Thanks."

He looked at me for a moment, then chugged like a madman before throwing the empty can into the fire. He put his hand to his stomach, wrinkled his nose, and belched long and deep before blowing it at McKay. McKay laughed and punched him in the shoulder, but Dozer only cracked open another and chugged again.

I wanted to go home and get out of my wet clothes, but nothing would have pleased Rhodes more than knowing I'd left early, so I just stayed close to the fire to get dry. The party rolled on. After a while,

I got another Gatorade and sat down on the end of a log next to Ethan. "Rhodes is an idiot, man," he said. Then he leaned toward me and whispered, "You could take him."

"Maybe someday," I said. "But who cares about that? How are things with the quest? Where is she, anyway?"

"Raelyn had to go home, but the quest is a success. I have a homecoming date," Ethan said. "I'm getting her back. I can hardly believe it."

I pushed his shoulder. "That's great, buddy. I knew you'd do it."

"You did not. You thought it was crazy to keep talking to her, waiting for her to come around."

"Well, I knew it would be good for you to be in the musical with her."

"You're right." Ethan raised a glass to me. "Hey, thanks for getting me invited to this. You're pretty cool, dude."

"What? It's mostly for football guys. I didn't do anything."

"You used your influence with Laura. I appreciate it. This is fun. I like this new you. I always knew that people would like you if you only made a little effort to let them get to know you."

I was about to answer when Laura crouched down in front of him. "I think you're in my seat, Jonesy."

Ethan raised an eyebrow at me and gave up his spot. Laura sat down. "You should have just knocked him out," she whispered.

"Who, Ethan? Naw, he's a good friend."

Laura laughed a little more than the joke deserved and leaned against me. "You're so funny! But you know who I mean. That was stupid what he did, and you should beat him up." She rested her head on my shoulder.

"Oh, you know. No big deal. Best to forget about it." I wouldn't forget it, but I wished everyone else would.

She rubbed her hand up and down my back. "But your shirt's all stained."

The back rub felt good, but it didn't feel right. I checked my watch. It was after two in the morning, September 22. I was sixteen years old.

"It's late," I whispered to Laura. "I have to go."

She pouted. "Oooh, are you sure?"

I stood up. "Thanks for a good time, everybody." I waved as I headed out. "See you later."

A small chorus of "good nights" followed me up the slope toward the tracks. I let out a little sigh of relief when Laura waved and stayed sitting. For a moment, I was worried she'd follow me.

Even though I was walking along flat railroad tracks, remembering the ups and downs of the night felt like a roller coaster. I stopped on the Runaway Bridge as a cool breeze blew through my hair. I smiled, looked at the stars, and whispered to myself, "Happy birthday."

EIGHTEEN

"Congratulations." Mom held up her glass of water in a toast. We were in the Brown Bottle restaurant in Iowa City. "How does it feel to be a driver?"

"Pretty good," I answered.

"Was the test hard? Were you nervous?"

"Not really. I mean, I guess I worried a little that they'd randomly pick me to go drive with the DOT lady."

Mom smiled. "Yeah, she didn't look very pleasant."

"I think that's a job requirement for working for the DOT. But the test was kind of easy. Stuff about road signs and right-of-way."

She pulled a small, wrapped box out of her purse and set it down in front of me. "Happy birthday," she said.

I held it up and smiled. "Okay if I open it?"

"Yeah, come on. Hurry up."

I ripped off the paper, popped open the little box, and pulled out a black leather wallet. "Hey, thanks, Mom." My family was never very big on presents, so this was pretty great.

"The guy at the store said this has a fifteen-year guarantee. It was kind of pricey, but that little canvas kiddie wallet you've had forever is falling apart, and I figured you needed something to put your new license in. Go on, try it out."

I slipped my new driver's license into a pocket with a little plastic window and showed it to Mom. She squeezed my hand. "Thanks. This is great," I said.

The waitress approached the table with our food. "Here you go, lunch-portion spaghetti." She put Mom's plate down. "And for you. Careful, that's real hot." She placed the small steak in front of me.

After she'd gone, Mom closed her eyes as she took a bite of a meatball. "Wow," she said. "That's really good. I haven't been here in a long time. The food's still great."

"And the waitresses don't wear plastic pig snouts."

Mom laughed. "That place is too much. But yes, it is nice to see normal waitresses."

"You've been here before?"

"Oh, yes. Your dad and me used to come here once or twice a year, at least back when we were first dating. We ate here the night he asked me to marry him. He had flowers delivered and put on the table." She smiled and little wrinkles creased the corners of her eyes. "One thing I loved about him. He was such a romantic."

Outside of D-Day, this was more than Mom ever talked about Dad. "Sounds like you two used to have a lot of fun together."

She held a bite of spaghetti twirled on her fork as she stared out the window. "We did. We really did. For a while."

I wanted to ask more about him, but I couldn't rush her. "All those nights at Nature Spot . . ."

Her attention snapped back to me. "What do you know about that?"

"Nothing, really," I started.

"Because if kids are still going to Nature Spot, I want you to stay away from there."

I twisted my napkin in my lap. "Mom, no . . . I mean, yeah. I've heard people talking about the place, but it's, like, exclusively for football guys. I'd never go there."

"Good."

We turned our attention to our lunches. I gnawed my steak. If I could help her recover her good mood, maybe she'd open up to talking. "So did Dad propose here in the restaurant?"

A faint smile returned to Mom's face. "No. We went for a walk down by the river. He said, 'I want to spend the rest of my life with you.' Then he went down on one knee, held out the ring, and asked me to marry him."

"Sounds cool, Mom." Now. She had a smile on her face. Now was my chance. "Did Dad ever send any letters? Like from the war?"

"Why would you —"

"I'm just curious."

"Well, he did in the beginning. But things started to . . . Anyway. That was a long time ago."

I couldn't quit now. "Did Dad have any good friends? I mean, before he shipped out to the war, were there guys he hung out with in town? Someone he trusted, maybe."

"What?" She shook her head. "I don't know. Not really. He worked a lot. Why are you asking me so much about your dad lately? We were having a nice lunch. Let's not spoil it, okay?"

She'd put the topic away. Again. We didn't talk about that, or much of anything else, for the rest of lunch.

With my brand-new license in my pocket, I should have been the one driving home. But Mom said it was best not to start driving in Iowa City traffic, so I sat in the passenger seat. I had a full stomach and nothing to do, so I blinked in the bright sunlight, trying to stay awake after my late night.

Mom squeezed my forearm, and I jerked my head up and opened my eyes wide. "Listen, Mikey, I want to say sorry about blowing up at you last night. I should have known you were just working. I know you won't leave me waiting up without calling again. You work so hard. You're such a good boy. I need to learn to trust you more."

A spring that had long ago popped through the worn upholstery poked me in the thigh as I slid down lower in my seat.

' "I can't believe you're already sixteen with a license," Mom said. "You're growing up so fast. It seems like just yesterday that you were a little boy, tottering around the house on wobbly little legs, carrying Binky Bear. Whatever happened to Binky Bear? Do you still have him? You two were so *cute* together. I'd come into you and Mary's room and hear you talking to him. 'Binky Bear,' you'd say . . ."

I sat up and looked out my window while she went on, stuck in the past as usual. My movement made the stupid spring poke into me harder.

". . . Did you hear me?"

"What? Sorry, I must have spaced out a little."

"I was trying to tell you that this is an intermediate license. You can have this license and drive unsupervised with certain limits, provided you have signed parental permission. I checked with the Department of Transportation. At any time, I can write a letter to them telling them I've changed my mind. Then your license is revoked."

I folded my arms over my chest. "Is this part of learning to trust me more?"

"Think of it as your chance to prove to me that I can trust you."

I reached forward and cranked the heater down a quarter turn.

"What are you doing?" Mom maxed out the heater again. "It's cold."

I wiped the dampness above my lip and felt the sweat under my arms. In a strange way, her overprotectiveness made me feel better about sneaking out last night.

* * *

In the early afternoon, I rode up the hill to the farm. Until I could afford a car, Scrappy remained my only ride. I lurched forward and nearly racked myself on my seat when all resistance in the pedals gave way. The bike had thrown its chain again.

I walked the rest of the way to the farm.

"Chain trouble?" Derek called to me from the front yard where he stood next to the open door of the Falcon. He wore nicer jeans, a pair of good Nikes, and a decent sweatshirt, not his work clothes.

I threw the bike down in the grass by the windmill. He had washed and waxed the Falcon until it shined in the sun. It looked amazing, almost like new.

Derek leaned into the cab and put a black-and-orange FOR SALE sign in the window. "What's up?"

"It's my birthday," I said. "Had lunch with Mom. Got my license."

"I thought your big day was coming up. Happy birthday!" He rubbed a rag on a spot on the Falcon's hood. "You get any presents today?"

I held up the wallet. "Something to keep my license in."

"Nice. A lot more grown-up." Derek gestured to the truck. "What do you think?"

"I can't believe you're selling the Falcon after all that work you put into it. Why?"

He patted the panel by the pickup's bed. "I had to fix it up or I'd never sell it."

"It looks great," I said. "Wish I had enough money saved up. I'd buy it." There was a little silence. "So, do you have work for me today?"

"What?" Derek looked surprised. "Oh. Yeah, I did have something I needed you to do. But something just came up. Sorry about that. I would have called you before you rode all the way out here, but you were already gone before I knew about this business."

"Oh," I said. That was weird. "Is everything okay?"

"Oh yeah!" He laughed. "Everything's fine, really. So, you say you'd be interested in buying the truck? I'd really like to get it off my hands. What will you give me for it?"

"Yeah, right," I said.

Derek walked around to the front of the truck, keeping his gaze locked on the vehicle. "Come on, how much?"

"I don't have enough," I said.

"How much you got?"

Why would he even bother asking me? This was stupid. "About five hundred fifty."

"I'll take eight hundred."

"There you go, then," I said. "I don't have enough."

"You give me five-fifty next time you come to work, I'll take twenty bucks a week from what you earn working here. You'll have her paid for in about a year or so."

I looked at the sky-blue Falcon shining in the sun, a pickup with the cool old-style Chevy body and big new tires. If I said yes, could I really be driving home in my own vehicle, not riding that bike like a little kid? But it wasn't right. "Just the improvements you've made to it in the last few months are worth more than eight hundred. I can't pay so little." I slowly let out a breath. "Sorry, I'm going to have to pass."

"It doesn't matter what work I've done on the truck. If you don't buy it, I won't get much more than eight hundred anyway."

"Yeah, but you'd get more."

"Eight hundred is fine with me, really. Or, if you're worried about paying it off, maybe I could go down to seven."

"Seven? No way. Derek, don't rip yourself off on this."

"Would you just buy the thing!" He slapped the hood. I'd heard Derek swear before when he hit his thumb with a hammer or something, but he'd never shouted at me like this. "I want to sell you a truck. Would you let me sell you a truck? It's a fair enough price, believe me. You're sixteen. You've worked hard to earn a vehicle of your own so you don't have to ride that bike. You're gonna have to start thinking of yourself for once, Mike."

I didn't move. I'm not sure I breathed. What could I do? Why was Derek so set on selling me the truck so cheap? Because he felt sorry for me?

He pointed to the garage on the house. "The truck I drive now is getting old. I'm going to make it my farm truck and buy a new one or maybe a car for driving around. So I have to get rid of the Falcon, and it will take me forever to sell it, probably to some guy who won't even take care of it. I'd rather you had it."

"Eight hundred?" I said. I could have my own vehicle.

"Eight hundred," Derek said. He held out his hand and we shook to seal the deal.

He said he trusted me to bring the money when I came to work Monday after football practice. Then he signed over the title deed and explained insurance, license plates, and registration. I'd have to figure something out for the insurance, but I'd make it work. I put Scrappy in the bed of the pickup and climbed up on the bench seat behind the wheel of my truck.

I strapped myself in and started the engine. The Falcon fired up, and I could feel the power of her engine vibrating through me. "Hey, thanks a lot," I called out the window to Derek. "I really appreciate this." I put the truck in gear and rolled out onto the road.

Hardly able to believe I was free to drive around on my own, I hooked a right up Weigand Street and headed for the square. On my second lap around the square, Ethan emerged from Williams

Hardware, carrying a small paper sack. I honked the horn and pulled into a diagonal parking spot in front of him.

"What's up?" Ethan said as he approached my window. "Where did you get this?"

"I just bought her from Derek Harris. Got a great deal. What are you doing?"

"Oh, man, my dad sent me to buy some more drywall screws. He's finally finishing the back bedroom in the basement. Don't know why he doesn't get them himself since he can drive and all."

"Want a ride?"

Ethan smiled and looked the truck over. "You sure it's safe?"

I laughed. "Shut up and get in before I change my mind."

He went around and climbed up in the passenger side. "Geez, this thing's an antique."

"Beats walking," I said, a little irritated.

"No . . . I mean, yeah. It's cool, though. We should take this baby out for a little bottle tag sometime."

I'd seen some of the guys playing bottle tag. They drove around with different teams in different cars, each trying to throw an empty soda bottle to hit the other group's car. Whichever car got hit was "it." "Yeah, that would be cool. Gabe has his license, right?"

"He does," said Ethan. He patted the seat. "Bench seat like this could be real handy for dates. You and Isma planning on taking advantage of this?"

"Yeah, you know, especially since I just bought this today, I've never actually walked up to her and asked if she'd like to mess around in my truck." I spoke in a jokey way, but the idea of parking with Isma had already occurred to me.

"Well, like I said last night, it's good that you've been cool lately, Mike," Ethan said as I turned the Falcon onto his street.

"Thanks, I think?"

"I mean it's good to see you getting out more, doing things, talking to people. For a while there you kind of vanished."

I knew exactly what he meant, and I smiled as I pulled over to drop him off. "Give me a call sometime. We'll play bottle tag or go up to Iowa City. Catch a movie or something."

"Yeah, man. Cool." Ethan shut the truck door and went up the path to his house.

With the window down, the cool air blew through my hair as I drove off. I was sixteen. I had a license and my own truck. Anything could happen. Anything at all.

NINETEEN

After driving around town for a while, I went home to clean up, check the mail (not yet delivered), and change clothes. Then I drove to Isma's house. It looked even nicer in the daylight, a newer brown house with a brick front and a chimney on the side. A big cement driveway led to a double-car garage. I pulled over and parked on the side of the road, accidentally bumping the curb a little with my tire.

I leaned forward and checked my hair in the mirror. I made sure nothing was stuck in my teeth and my breath wasn't nasty. I was wearing my jeans with no holes and I'd found a sweater in the back of my closet that I could still fit into if I kept pulling it down at the bottom. I didn't want her parents thinking I was a slob.

The path from the street to Isma's front door probably measured about twenty feet, but the walk seemed like twenty miles. My mouth felt dry, and I licked my lips while wiping my palms on my jeans.

"Relax," I whispered to myself as I pressed the doorbell button. "It's just Isma."

The door flew open at once and Isma came out on the little cement porch. This was definitely not *just* Isma. She wore dark jeans and a gray V-neck shirt with a white shirt underneath that fit kind of close and showed off her figure a little. She leaned against the door frame and grinned at me for a moment, then she flung herself forward and hugged me. "I'm so glad you're here," she said.

I looked past her through the open front door to see if her parents were watching. Nobody was there. Slipping my hands to her waist, I gently tried to push her back a little. "Um . . . Isma, maybe we shouldn't . . . you know, right here."

She sprang back and checked the street as if someone in the neighborhood might see us. "You're right."

"How do you like it?" I pointed to the Falcon.

"That's yours? You got a truck?"

"Yeah, I just sort of bought it from Derek Harris, the guy I work for."

"I love it. It's old and cool. You don't see that color much." Isma took my hand. "Come on." She pulled me into the house, throwing the door shut behind us. My back hit the door as Isma pounced, kissing me deep with her soft hands on my cheeks. She felt good, and I gave in for a moment, closing my eyes and sliding my hands to the small of her back. Then my brain reactivated and I knew I had to push her away again before her parents caught us like this.

Isma backed up first, but still leaned close. "Happy birthday."

The living room was empty, and I couldn't see anyone in the dining room through the archway. "What if your mom and dad see us?" I whispered.

She slipped her hands into her pockets and tilted her head in a sort of pout. "Nobody's here," she said.

"Huh?"

She laughed and took both my hands in hers. "Relax. My brother's birthday was Tuesday. Usually the most my parents will do is a small party at home or maybe something at Riverside Roller Rink, but for months he begged to take some of his friends to Laser Tag Pizza Funland in Iowa City. They gave in, I think just to shut him up."

Iowa City was about fifteen minutes north. Fifteen minutes there, the laser party, pizza, and fifteen minutes back meant maybe two hours. Two hours at Isma's house. Alone. With Isma.

"Cool," I said.

"So," said Isma, "this is my house." She motioned at the room we stood in. I took off my shoes and followed her. "The boring sitting room," she said. A fancy red rug with many-colored swirls and patterns like flowers decorated the center of a smooth, polished wood floor. The leather couch and recliner weren't faded and torn like our old, ratty furniture in the living room at home. A few large books rested on top of a coffee table in front of the couch.

"Where's the TV?" I asked.

"Not in here. That's why I call it the boring sitting room. Come on." She took my hand and led me through an arch.

Just past the dining room with its big shiny wooden table gleamed the richest kitchen I'd ever seen outside of TV. The polished rock countertops reflected the shine off the metal appliances. They even had a dishwasher and one of those cool refrigerators with a water-and-ice thing in the door. "This is a really nice place," I said.

Isma opened one of the refrigerator doors and reached inside. "You hungry?" She pulled out a frozen pizza.

"Always," I said.

She put the pizza on the counter and took two brown glass bottles from the fridge. "Root beer?"

I nodded, and she popped the tops on the bottles and handed me one. "Can I help with the pizza?" I asked.

Isma laughed. "While I appreciate your noble attempt to avoid sexism, I think unwrapping the pizza, slapping it on a pan, and tossing it in the oven is really a one-person job. Besides, you're my guest. Relax." She pressed some buttons on the oven. "This will take some time to heat up. I'll show you my room."

I followed her down the hall, looking at the framed family photos and a strange painting that looked like random splashes of color on a bright white background.

Isma's room resembled a museum. Paintings and photographs dominated almost all the available wall space. A few paintings were incredibly detailed, with colored swirls and lines like the rug in the sitting room, all neatly signed in the corner by Isma. One photo showed a white building that looked like a pyramid with a rectangular tower at the top. I stepped up to look at it more closely. An arched opening ran through the middle of the pyramid at the bottom, and a fountain sprayed columns of water in the air in front of the structure.

"The Azadi Tower in Tehran, Iran," Isma said. "Isn't it beautiful? I've only visited Iran once, when I was a little girl. I barely remember it. I keep this picture up as a reminder of what a great place Iran is, no matter how many drones our president sends to spy on it."

A closet took up one wall of the room. Another wall featured a little brown desk with her laptop, lamp, and a few comic books. I noticed that her light-switch plate was a pink sparkly unicorn, the switch right in the middle of its belly. She sat down on her bed in the corner.

"Cool room," I said. "Except . . . you know . . . nice unicorn."

"Oh my gosh." Isma put her face in her hands. "Oh my gosh. Don't look at that stupid thing. I'm so embarrassed." She peeked at me from behind her hands. "When I was really little, I had a thing for unicorns. They made me feel really magical or something. I had a unicorn lamp on my desk, unicorn toys, a unicorn stuffed animal, and yes, that switch-cover thing. Daddy somehow thought I still wanted it up when we moved here, even though I got rid of all that stuff. I've been meaning to take it down for a long time now. But I hardly notice it." She frowned at me. "Who notices switch-plate covers besides you? And it's not like anyone ever comes in here."

I held my hands up in surrender. "It's okay." I couldn't hold back my laugh. "No, it's cool. Really."

She stood up and put her hands on her hips. "Okay, if you're going to make fun of my unicorn-light thing, I am going to see if the oven is hot enough to put the pizza in."

She left me alone in her bedroom, so I looked around. Each rug painting must have taken about a hundred different colors, and the patterns repeated in the weaves of the rug, so she would have had to get each little flower, every swirl and splash of color, exactly right. I knew she loved art, but I didn't know she had this level of talent.

A big white paper on her desk caught my eye. Isma had made a pencil sketch of the two of us walking along the street, holding hands. It looked so much like us that I would have thought she'd traced it from a photograph if I didn't know better. Somehow she'd even drawn the lighting and shade right, with beams from the streetlight shining down through the leaves in the tree above.

"It's hot enough," Isma said.

I jumped and spun around. "Huh?"

"The oven was heated up, so I put the pizza in." She sat on her bed and patted the space next to her. From where I stood by her desk, I could see down her shirt if I looked. If I were that kind of guy. Which I wasn't, I reminded myself.

"Have a seat." She patted the bed again.

We'd kissed, but I had never made out with a girl, not on her bed and everything. I hadn't expected her to be this direct. "This is a pretty good plan you came up with."

"What do you mean?" She sat back with her hands on the bed a little behind her, shaking her head to toss her hair back.

I sat down next to her and leaned toward her. "To get me alone here like this."

"*What?*" She slid back until she hit the wall, and burst into laughter.

"What?" I sat up straight. "What's so funny?"

"You thought . . ." She put her hands to her face again for a moment, then slowly drew them down to look at me. "You thought this was . . . all . . ." She pointed back and forth from me to her. "You thought this was all to *seduce* you?"

My cheeks felt hot. I was such an idiot. "No, I didn't think . . . I mean . . ." I started to slide off the bed, but she grabbed my hand and pulled me back until we were sitting close. She kissed me on the cheek, and then our lips met. She smiled. "You're so cute." She placed her hand on my cheek. "But I just wanted to show you something."

She bent down and pulled a leather-covered album from under the bed, resting it on her lap and running her hand over it. "I've never shown this to anyone. Not my parents or my brother, definitely not anyone at school."

She opened the book. More of her art lit up the page, but instead of pictures of rugs, a woman with wings soared through the sky, with a city built on a floating island in the background behind her. She wore silver armor and carried a short shining sword in one hand and some futuristic gun in the other. "This is one of my original characters. I call her Ariana."

She flipped the page and showed me a picture of Iron Man in a desert village blasting away at some thugs with guns. "I loved in the first Iron Man movie how he goes and fights those Taliban guys. I wanted to see more of that, so I drew it."

On the facing page, Captain America ran up a hill. Vehicles exploded in the distance and bullets bounced off his red, white, and blue shield. I looked at the full-color drawings carefully. "These are great! They're just like the real thing. Unbelievable."

"Why? Can't girls like comics?"

"No," I said. "I mean, yes. They can like whatever they want. I meant, the pictures are unbelievably good. And a lot of girls just don't like comics . . . usually."

Isma turned back to the winged warrior woman. "That's because all the girls in the comic books have huge boobs and tiny waists. No real woman could ever look like that. Comic book girls make Barbie dolls look like scale models for medical school." She tapped Ariana's chest. "See, her armor is just a gently curved plate, not two ridiculous steel cones."

She showed me a new spread with two more pictures of Captain America, one showing him swinging from a rope over fire, the other with him standing in a city, lifting his shield to hold back an angry mob, while three darker-skinned kids huddled behind him.

"You really like Captain America?" I asked.

"Yeah, why not?"

"Nothing. I'm surprised, that's all. I just always thought —"

"What? Because my parents come from Iran? I was born *here*. Why can't I like Captain America? Why can't he be my hero too? Who decided —"

I put a finger to her lips. "I just always thought he was kind of boring. A guy running around with only a shield? Spider-Man and Superman were a lot more fun."

"Cn I twk nw?" she mumbled against my finger, and then kissed it. I took my finger from her lips. "Sorry," she said. "I don't mean to argue all the time."

She went to the back of the album and slipped a wrinkled Captain America comic book out of a pouch. The cover showed a giant Captain standing in the background with the ruins of the World Trade Center towers in New York City in front of him. He was looking down, pressing his hand to his eyes as if he was crying.

"This is why he's my favorite. I found this copy in a box of back issues at Wizards Comic Shop in Iowa City a few years ago." Isma turned the pages of the comic book, showing Captain America dressed in normal clothes, digging through the 9/11 wreckage for survivors. "Here." She tapped a page where a white guy attacked a darker-skinned man with a knife. "This guy who was born in New York, but whose father comes from Jordan, is about to get stabbed by this other man who just lost someone on 9/11." The next page showed Captain America blocking the knife with his shield. He stood there with light shining from behind him as the white guy collapsed to his knees, crying. "Captain America says that Americans should stick together no matter what country their parents came from." She didn't say anything for a moment. "Anyway, I always liked comics, but after I read this one, my favorite was Captain America, and I decided that what I want to do with my life is draw for Marvel or DC or some other comics company."

She showed me more of her art, a mix of characters from comics and TV, plus a lot of superheroes she made up. When we'd seen them all, she closed the book. "What do you think?" she whispered.

"They're all amazing," I said. "How do you make all those pictures so realistic and everything? When I try to draw people, I'm stuck with stick figures or blobs that sort of look like cows." She laughed. "You're really good, Isma. Incredible. My dad left me a bunch of his old comic books. Some Fantastic Four, Spider-Man, and this cool super team he really liked, the New Warriors, the heroes for the nineties. I even found a drawing that I guess he'd made of the New Warriors beating up the Fantastic Four. His picture was pretty realistic, but it wasn't half as good as yours."

"You still read your dad's old comics?"

"I've read most of them. Now I read from the college-bound section of the library so someday I can get into a good university."

Isma got up on her hands and knees, leaning close to me and smiling. "You're always so focused on the future. Don't forget to enjoy the here and now." She leaned forward, and we kissed. My hands slid around her lower back. She ran her fingers up the back of my neck and through my hair. The more we kissed, the more I wanted to kiss her. Our breathing came on heavy and we held each other closer.

"Isma," I whispered when we'd parted for a moment. We kissed again. "Isma." I gently eased her back.

"What?" She looked concerned. "Is something wrong?"

For the first time in a long time, everything seemed perfect, and I had no worries about my timing, no hesitation. "Will you go to the homecoming dance with me?"

She didn't answer right away. "Okay," she said, as if I'd just asked her the most casual question. Then she laughed. "I'd love to. It will be great."

I placed my fingers under her chin to kiss her. Once again, we lost ourselves with each other.

When the timer on the oven beeped, I wanted that oven and all the ovens in the world to die fiery deaths and go away. "Come on." She grinned so her nose wrinkled. "I'm hungry."

A few minutes later, we sat at the dining room table having pizza and soda, talking easily like we did at school, as if we hadn't been totally making out moments ago. I filled her in about Dad's most recent letter. We laughed about the way our science teacher, Mr. Dettmering, would get so far off the subject during his lectures. We complained about the school lunches. We hung out for a long time, a great time, made even better since we kept stealing kisses, and I could still feel where her fingers had been on my shoulders and neck.

"I'm so excited about the homecoming dance," Isma said. "I wasn't allowed to go last year, so I just sat around in my room."

"I went," I said. "Wish I hadn't. I had no date and felt like such a loser."

"Well, not this year," she said. "We'll have tons of fun. There's this dress I saw at the mall. If I could convince Mom that it's okay —"

Headlights flashed in the front window as a car pulled in the driveway. I heard the rumble of the garage door opening.

"They're early!" Isma jumped up from her chair. "Quick! You have to get out of here."

So her parents didn't know I was going to be here? There was no doubt I was in trouble. If I went running out the front door, they would only think worse of me. Plus, maybe if I stuck around, I could take some of the heat that would otherwise fall on Isma. "They've already seen my truck parked outside," I said. "They'll know someone is here. Anyway, better to talk to them than to just run away."

She grabbed my arm and pulled me out of the chair. "They'll think the truck belongs to the neighbors or something. And you don't know my parents."

"Isma?" A voice came from the living room as the front door opened.

"Oh no," Isma whispered, wide-eyed.

"Isma, how many times have I told you not to leave your shoes in the middle . . ." Isma's mom came into the living room and froze at the sight of me. She dropped the mail she'd been carrying, the envelopes fluttering to the floor.

A moment later a boy came running in from the door to the garage. "I want to go back already! I was the best shooter." He stopped when he saw me. "Who are you?"

A tall man with dark skin, a thick, round middle, and gray flecks in his short-cropped black hair followed the boy into the room. He looked at me, then Isma, then me again.

"Majid, go to your room, please," said Isma's mother.

"What did I do? I didn't do anything! I shouldn't have to —"

"Now!" the woman shouted.

Majid sighed and glared at me as he went down the hall. His door slammed a moment later.

The two adults in the living room stared at the two of us in the dining room. Nobody moved for a long time. I gripped the back of the chair so hard my fingers hurt. I'd invited Isma to my house without permission. Now she'd done the same thing. I watched Isma's dad watching me, considering the gap between him and my shoes by the door. Could I make it to them before he caught me? Forget the shoes. They were the cheapest brand possible, already falling apart. I could leave them and still escape with my life.

"Mom, Dad, this is Mike," Isma said.

Isma's mother motioned toward the hallway. "Isma, come with me, please."

Isma shifted her weight. "We were just having pizza."

Her father coughed. "Do as your mother says."

She shot me a look that said . . . what? *I'm so scared* or *I'm sorry about this* or *I can't believe this is happening*? I couldn't tell what she meant because I was trying to give *her* a look that said, *Don't you dare leave me here with your big, scary father.*

"*Now*, Isma," the woman said more forcefully.

Isma sighed and followed her mother.

"I cannot believe you have betrayed our trust like this." Her mother's voice echoed down the hallway before a door closed. Isma's muffled protests came next, followed by her mother, louder than she'd been since she got home: "Right now you will be quiet and listen to me!"

Isma's dad frowned in the direction of the argument. I felt like I should say something.

"I'm really sorry about all this, Mr. Rafee. We really were just having pizza. I didn't mean to cause so much trouble. I guess I should be going."

"You may call me Asad," he said. He probably wanted me to know his name before he killed me. "And your name is?"

"Huh?" I said. "Oh. Mike — Michael Wilson." Then I added, "Sir."

"When you call me 'sir,' I feel like I'm teaching in my classroom at the university. Please." He held his hand up. "Really. Call me Asad."

"Yes . . . Asad."

"You're not even listening to me!" Isma shouted from the other room.

"Follow me," said Isma's dad.

He led me down a different hallway and opened a door, motioning me inside and closing it after us. This seemed to be his study. A shiny wooden desk rested in the middle of the room. Three-foot-tall cupboards were attached to the bottom of the walls. Above them stood bookshelves packed with hundreds of books. I would have given just about anything for a library like this, and normally I would want to read all the book spines to make a quick inventory of the collection, but tonight I stood there, unable to move.

Isma's dad pointed to one of two short-backed leather chairs in front of his desk. "Please sit down."

I obeyed immediately. Mr. Rafee took a crystal bottle as big around as a basketball at the bottom from a ledge behind his desk. A golden-brown liquid filled half of the bottle. He picked up a short crystal glass from a tray, then he poured himself a drink, put the bottle back down on his desk, and sat down behind it.

"Mike. Are you and my daughter dating?" He closed his eyes and sniffed his drink as he swirled it around in his glass. "Are you . . . romantically involved, or whatever the kids call it today?"

The phrase "romantically involved" sounded like a psychological disorder or something. I swallowed and licked my lips. "I like her," I said quietly.

He took a sip and his face screwed up like the drink burned. It must have, because I could smell it from where I sat. He wiped his forehead on his sleeve, polished off the drink, and thumped the glass down on his desk. When he smiled, I actually thought I might live. "Isma has told me some good things about you. From what I hear, you are a hard worker. Smart. A good writer. Isma's mother would probably like her to go to school and come home, talking to no boys in between." He watched me as if waiting for me to say something. "That was . . . a bit of an exaggeration. A joke. But my wife is very reluctant to allow Isma to date, to go to the movies and do a lot of the things you young people do.

"Me?" He poured himself another drink and took a swallow. "As much as I wish she could stay a little girl forever, I know she is growing up. It's only natural that she's going to be interested in boys. So . . ." He held his glass up in front of him and looked at me. "It's good to see she's with a nice young man like you." His look turned serious. "But my wife and I must ask you please to not come over to our house ever again without our knowledge and permission."

I nodded. It sounded like a fair deal to me.

Several awkward minutes later, Isma and I were closely supervised back in the living room. "Um, good-bye," I said to Isma as I put on my shoes. I nodded to Asad and to Isma's mother. "It was . . . uh . . . nice meeting you."

"Likewise," said Asad. Isma's mom was silent.

I jogged out and climbed into the Falcon, strapping in, firing up the engine, and pulling the knob for the headlights. A light clicked on in one of the house windows and Isma came to the glass and waved. I waved back from my dark cab, but there was no way she could have seen me, so I flashed my headlights a few times before I drove away.

TWENTY

That night, after driving around in the Falcon thinking about Isma and life and the Falcon and Isma for a long time, I beat Mom home to find Mary in the living room with some reality show on TV. "Hey, Mary, slobbing around watching crap again?" I said.

"From now on I'm not going to answer people when they're being stupid."

I decided not to let my spoiled sister ruin the best birthday I'd had in years. "That's nice. Have fun being your bored and miserable little self."

"Whatever," Mary said. "Package came for you today. It's on your bed. Who keeps sending you stuff?"

I wish I knew.

I rushed upstairs to my attic and grabbed the package (a whole package!), a big plain cardboard box with no return address. I sat down on my weight bench and shifted the box in my hands. It weighed more than I had expected. Dad had said he wanted me to have all the letters by my sixteenth birthday. There had to be hundreds of letters packed in this box. I guess the Mystery Mailer liked waiting until the last minute.

I pulled off the tape and opened the box, but I did not find a huge stack of letters. Instead, I pulled out a rectangular plastic computer thing — the size of a toaster, but half as thick. It had power and USB cables coming out of it. A hard drive? A huge hard drive. It had to be three or four terabytes. I checked the sticker on the back. Two hundred fifty megabytes? I'd seen fifty-gigabyte thumb drives at the store with two hundred times the memory of this old thing. I might actually be able to fit two hundred of those thumb drives into the hard-drive case.

A faded tan canvas bag, like a small briefcase with a shoulder strap, lined the bottom of the box. Flipping it over, I ran my fingers along the sewn-on WILSON name ribbon. Two patches had been added on either side of the name tape, with red bull skulls on a black field that was rounded at the bottom and sort of squared off at the top. Inside the bag, I found another letter from Dad. Maybe his last letter.

Once again, I searched for a message from whoever kept mailing all of this stuff. Nothing.

Wednesday, September 22, 2004 (249 Days Left)
Dear Michael,

Happy birthday, little buddy. Today you are eight years old! Of course, if you're reading this, you're not so little anymore. You're sixteen and a sophomore in high school, and I hope you're having the best times of your life. Gosh, it's hard for me to wrap my mind around all that now.

I keep thinking of what you might get for your birthday. Maybe you got clothes or money for new clothes. That's good. It's important to look cool. But don't be the guy who pays money for an expensive T-shirt with the store's logo written across your chest. The store should pay YOU for that kind of advertising. Be the guy who is cool and confident enough to wear a shirt with no writing on it that you buy from the sale rack at the end of the season.

Oh, and learn how to tie a necktie. It's important.

Things for me and my guys have gotten a lot better here. First squad, fourth squad, and a mortar squad from our platoon have come out from Kandahar. Now we finally have enough guys to fill a decent duty rotation so that we can get some real sleep some nights. With the Humvees and the other squads here, we're settling into something like a routine. We're really getting the hang of this.

We are living in our barracks now with hot showers and flush toilets. We have a washer and dryer for our clothes, so we don't have to spend hours hand-washing our uniforms anymore. The chow hall is finished, so we have real food, or as real as the Army ever gives us. Field rations are only for long-range missions now. All of this is possible because the Afghan construction workers have finished work on our base.

That's another thing. We don't call the Afghans "hajjis" anymore. We were talking to our interpreter, Shiaraqa, and he told us that a hajji is a Muslim who has made a trip called the hajj all the way to Mecca, in Saudi Arabia. In places like Afghanistan, a hajji is a big deal. He's highly respected. Since our mission is to help these people, and since we're a lot safer if they're not mad at us, most of the guys have stopped calling them "hajji" and just say "Afghan" now.

To understand this war, you need to know that the Afghans are good people. They've helped us out, saved our lives, plenty of times. The Taliban are monsters. Brutal. Inhuman. But they are the tiniest fraction of the real Afghan population, like gangs or the Mafia in America. The Afghans are a great people. I've learned that Afghanistan used to be a pretty cool, peaceful place. Americans and Europeans used to vacation here. Their culture has been interrupted by wars that were not *the people's fault. We're trying to help them restore what they've lost.*

Have I told you about the guys I'm serving with? Maybe not. I'm with these guys so much that I guess I take it for granted that people at home know them too.

Our third squad leader is Staff Sergeant Joe Pratt. He's a good guy, a great leader. Cares about his soldiers. Like I wrote before, I'm the alpha team leader, with three guys in my team. One is Specialist Fredrickson, who likes to be called "Fast Freddy." Then I have this young kid, Private First Class Matthew Gardner, who's eighteen or nineteen and got called up for the war like a day or so after he got home from basic training. My other guy is Corporal Christopher Andrews, the only black guy in the company.

Bravo team is led by Sergeant Sweet. My friend Sergeant Ortiz is in his team along with a specialist and a PFC, but lately he's been upset because one of his guys had to go all the way back to the hospital at Bagram to have his appendix taken out and to deal with other weird medical problems. Meanwhile, he's stuck with MacDonald from the mortar squad, kind of an annoying guy. He's from Riverside, believe it or not, but a couple years younger than me. Anyway, those are my guys, my family over here.

Jackpot! MacDonald, a guy who at least used to live in Riverside. Almost a perfect clue. Though, still — "You gotta be kidding me, Dad," I whispered. He'd given first and last names for almost everybody in his team, but hardly mentioned the Bravo team guys.

That was okay. It would be easy to find MacDonald here in town. The name didn't sound too familiar, but I could find it in the phone book or run a search for it easy enough. If that failed, I'd look up the number for Dad's armory and start asking for the other guys he just mentioned.

Two hundred forty-nine days. I trick myself into thinking the time is winding down by saying things like, "We're in the lower half of the two hundreds now!" Drives my guys crazy, especially when they have to pull six-hour shifts for guard duty.

Wait a minute. Two hundred forty-nine days? I somehow hadn't thought about the day count and the date when I read the date on the first page. It bothered me now, though. I was supposed to get Dad's last letter by my sixteenth birthday. This couldn't be the last letter, could it? Was the Mystery Mailer slacking off? There had to be more letters to come.

And thinking about the day count . . . Dad had been killed August 28, 2005. If he only had two hundred forty-nine days in September of '04, he should have been home well before the day he died over there. Something wasn't adding up. Maybe the letter would offer more clues.

That's the thing about the Army. It forces time on us, gives us time to think with fewer distractions. Ed, my boss back home, has a cellular telephone and a pager. They go off all the time, even when he's out with friends. He has the radio on all day and likes to keep it loud enough to be heard over the noise of the hammers and saws. He says that when he gets home, he has to sit at his computer messing with his email for over an hour. It's like the guy is constantly connected to other people. That's no way to live.

The Army is different. Lots of times it strips life down to just me, my boys, and the world around us. Sometimes, when we're out in nature and it's all quiet, we notice the beauty that surrounds us. The other day there were actually some clouds for once, and the sun came up over the mountain, shining white beams of light down on the desert. It was beautiful and felt like God watching over us. But we see that view from behind walls topped with razor wire, and we remember we're a long way from home.

Sometimes we have to hurry to do some missions. Lots of times I'm scared, but sometimes life makes more sense with fewer things distracting me from thoughts about what really matters.

What matters is you, little buddy. Well, you, Mary, and your mom. That's the price of all this time. We always, always, always miss the ones we love.

What I'm trying to say with all of this is that I hope you'll take some quiet time to pray, to think about your life, where it's been, and where it's going. I hope, and I pray, that you're happy with your life. That you're taking steps to move it in the right direction.

Oh, and your mission for this letter? Easy. It's your birthday, and you're sixteen. Go get yourself a driver's license. Maybe someday you'll be able to get a car. Be safe, and have fun.

Happy birthday.

Love,

Dad

"I *am* having fun, Dad. Things are finally starting to work out," I whispered. I prayed, for the first time in a while, that somehow Dad might hear my words.

P.S. PFC Gardner came back from leave with this fancy new digital camera that doesn't even need film. It also shoots video. I'm going to try to make some video letters for you soon.

I picked up the big hard drive. Were these videos? Of what? My father? What would it be like to see him again, to hear his voice and see him talking to me? If I hadn't been in so much trouble when I left Isma's house, I might have been able to call her and ask to borrow her computer so I could watch the videos. Now I'd have to lug this thing to school and use one of the computers in the library. That meant I'd have to wait until Monday.

The letter had raised more questions than it answered. Dad's day count was all messed up, and I had no idea if he had any more messages for me. But he'd given me names of people I could try to contact who might be able to tell me what I needed to know about him. Best of all, if the hard drive contained what I thought it did, my dad had sent me videos. I would get another chance for my father to talk to me directly. I could never have imagined a better birthday present.

"Mary and I are going shopping for groceries and some things," Mom said late Sunday morning.

I looked up from the phone book, which had been no help at all. "Hey, do you know anyone who used to live in town with the last name of MacDonald?"

"Why?" she asked.

Mary put her hands on her hips. "Mom, are we going or not?"

"It's for a school project," I said.

Mom shook her head. "The name doesn't sound familiar."

"Did Dad know anyone named MacDonald?" I tried.

Mom frowned. "I'm sure I don't know. Sorry. We'll be back in a bit."

After they left, I figured I'd call Dad's old engineer company armory, since he'd given me so many soldiers' names. If that didn't work out, I'd start asking around town about this MacDonald guy. Maybe Ed Hughes or even Mrs. Potter would know about him. I looked up the number for my dad's old National Guard unit in the Iowa City phone book. It was a Sunday, so who knew if anyone would be there. I knew the National Guard had training one weekend a month, but it might not be this weekend. It didn't matter. Now that I had all these names, I would keep trying until I found someone who knew how I could get in touch with one of them.

I dialed all but the final digit in the phone number and took a deep breath. Then I quickly tapped the last button before I could chicken out. The phone rang forever. I'd nearly given up when I heard a rattle on the other end of the line.

"Charlie Company, this is Sergeant Ballard. How may I help you?"

I took a breath. "I'm . . . Can I talk to Staff Sergeant Pratt, Specialist Fredrickson, PFC Gardner, Corporal Andrews, Sergeant Sweet, or, um, MacDonald?"

There were lots of voices in the background. "Whoa, that's a lot of soldiers," Ballard said. "Some of them don't drill here anymore. Who did you say you want to talk to? Can you give me the names slower, please?"

I put the phone to my other ear. "Um, Staff Sergeant Pratt —"

"He's a first sergeant in Alpha Company now. I don't think they're even drilling this weekend. Who else?"

This was the right unit. They'd heard of him. This Ballard guy knew someone my father had known.

"Specialist Fredrickson?"

"Fast Freddy? Yeah, he's been out of the Guard for a while. What's this all about?"

I didn't want to go into the whole thing except with someone who might actually have the answers I needed. Maybe I should have started with the guy from Riverside. "Um, is there a guy named MacDonald there? I don't know his rank."

"First name?

"Sorry," I said. "Don't know that either."

"Hold on a second." I could hear Sergeant Ballard talking to someone else, but I couldn't make out the words. "We have no MacDonald on record."

What was going on here? Why wouldn't the company have records on a guy who'd served with them in the war? Maybe the records didn't go that far back?

"Wait, did you say Corporal Andrews earlier? You mean Christopher Andrews?"

"Yes, sir."

"Whoa, no need to call me 'sir.' I work for a living. Corporal Andrews got promoted. He's a staff sergeant now. You want to talk to him?"

"Yes, s — yes, I would, please."

"Can I ask who is calling?"

I twisted the long rubber coil of the cord on this ancient phone in my fingers. "This is Mike Wilson."

"Okay, hold on." There was a long pause on the line. Finally, I heard someone pick up. "Sorry, Mike, but Sergeant Andrews is in a class conducting some training. You've caught us on our drill weekend. Can I tell him why you're calling?"

"I just . . ." I was so close to real answers about my dad, to talking to someone who had known him and served with him.

"My dad, Sergeant Mark Wilson, used to . . ." I bit my lip. "Used to serve in Charlie Company. He was killed in Afghanistan. Corporal — I mean, Staff Sergeant Andrews was in his squad. I just need to ask . . ."

"Oh. Hey, no problem, buddy. I'll have someone get him out of his class. Can you hold the line again?"

I waited for a long time. I was starting to think they'd forgotten about me when a deep voice came on the line. "This is Sergeant Andrews."

It had taken so long to figure out how to get in touch with anyone from Dad's letters that I hadn't thought about what to say. "Um, hello. I'm Mike Wilson. I think you served with my dad. In Afghanistan, I mean. You were a corporal?"

He didn't answer right away. Finally, he sighed. "Yes, I served with Sergeant Wilson. He was my team leader. That was a long time ago."

"Yes," I said. "Yes, it was. I'm sorry to bother you, but —"

"You could never bother me, Michael. Your dad used to talk about you all the time."

"He did?"

"Of course he did. He always talked about how he looked forward to taking the family on a big vacation when he got home, how he couldn't wait to teach you and your sister to ride bikes, how he would throw the football around with you. He loved you and your mom and sister."

Holding the phone, I pressed my back to the wall and slid to the floor. "I was wondering —"

"I know why you're calling," said Sergeant Andrews.

He did? I smiled.

"You want to know who's been mailing your father's letters to you."

"Yes!" I said. "Was it you? Thank you so much for —"

"It wasn't me."

"Then who —"

"I'm really sorry, Mike, but I can't tell you."

I felt the tension rising in me again. "But they're my letters —"

"Your father trusted Sergeant Ortiz to deliver the letters to you at the right time. Ortiz didn't make it, so someone else agreed to do this for your father. The sender doesn't want to be identified."

I leaned my head back and pressed it against the wall. "Can you tell me anything? Like what you remember about my dad? How he . . . How he died?" There was another long pause. "Hello?"

"I'm here," Andrews said. "Your father wanted you to know what you needed to know when you were old enough to handle it. He wanted you to get to know him on his terms before any of us talked to you."

"But he told me to talk to Sergeant Ortiz."

"He meant after you'd read the letters. And Ortiz didn't make it."

"I know he didn't make it," I said. "So now I have no idea who is sending me the letters or how many more are coming or how and why my father died, and *nobody* will tell me anything! It's not fair!" I felt like a whiny little kid saying it, but it was the truth.

"I know it's not fair. Believe me, I know. But we all promised your father it would be like this, the way he wanted. I'll tell you this. I wouldn't be alive if not for your dad. He was a great man. Best team leader I ever had. As for the rest, you'll have to figure that out when your father and the man sending the letters want you to figure it out."

"Is there anyone else who could . . ." My throat caught.

"Everyone who knows what you want to know promised your father that we'd let you get through all his messages first, and we promised to let the man sending the letters do this his own way. In the Army, we keep promises. We just have to."

He sounded so final. I would have to wait and hope Dad would explain everything. Hope the sender or someone else would answer my questions someday. "Thanks." I sort of choked the word out. "Thanks for your time."

"Tell you what, buddy. After you get the last message from your father, if you still have questions, feel free to contact me. I'd be happy to talk to you then, okay?"

I nodded like an idiot until I remembered I was on the phone. "Sure," I said. "Thanks."

I hung up the phone, closer to answers than I'd ever been before and yet totally shut down. I could forget tracking down any other soldiers Dad served with, and asking around town about MacDonald wouldn't do any good either. Even if they knew him and he was the one I was looking for, I couldn't just ambush him and demand answers. I was stuck waiting, and as frustrating as that might be, that's the way it was. I went to my attic, reread Dad's letters, and wondered.

TWENTY-ONE

Mom had complained a little about the Falcon when she noticed it Sunday afternoon, saying the truck looked unsafe, it cost too much money, I should have asked her about such a big purchase, I was too inexperienced, blah blah blah. I pointed out that I always wore my seat belt, and I would be much safer driving to work in my truck instead of riding my bike, especially at night. Mary weaseled her way in, saying I could drive her to school and to the upcoming junior high skating party. I promised I'd work more hours to pay for the extra insurance, gas, and maintenance, and I threw in the offer to take the truck to Arnath Auto for a full safety inspection.

Mom rubbed her eyes with the heels of her hands. "It'll be another expense, but if you get it checked out and can handle the responsibility and the costs, you can keep it."

So on Monday, I grinned as I sat behind the wheel on my very first drive to school. Even Mary riding along couldn't ruin the morning. I'd tucked Dad's Army bag and hard drive safely into my backpack, so that in fifth-hour study hall, I could at last watch the video letters.

"I'm sorry I didn't bring my computer today," Isma said when we met in our usual corner in the library, after I told her what was going on. "Why don't you ask Mrs. Potter if you can hook that thing up to one of the school computers?"

"I don't want to watch them right out in the middle of the library," I said.

She squeezed my hand. "She has a computer in her office. Maybe she'd let you use that."

"You want to come watch them with me?"

Isma smiled and leaned against me. "Oh, no. These are between you and your father. I don't want to intrude."

I looked into her dark eyes. "You could never be an intrusion."

"Maybe some other time," she said. "For now, go ask Mrs. Potter. You're wasting viewing time."

"Is there something I can help you with?" Mrs. Potter said with a smile as I approached the circulation desk.

I pulled the hard drive from my backpack. "I need to use a computer to watch some videos I have on here."

"What kind of videos?" she asked.

I could have made up some story, but Mrs. Potter was one of the coolest teachers in the school. Besides, I had the feeling that the truth would work a lot better to get what I wanted. "I think these are videos my father made for me while he was in the war," I said. Then I added (idiotically), "Before he died."

"Oh." Mrs. Potter became quite serious. "Well, you can use the computer in my office." She pointed to a door behind her circulation desk. "The computer should be on. If the catalog program is up, just minimize it. Do you know how to hook that thing up?" I nodded. "Okay," she said. "Let me know if you need anything."

Stacks of old books crowded Mrs. Potter's office, and READ posters showing old athletes, authors, and movie stars reading or holding books covered the walls. On her cluttered desk sat a white plastic teardrop-shaped eMac, old but still functional, like most of the computers at Riverside High.

Once I'd set the hard drive up, I booted it, and in a few seconds an icon labeled *Mark Wilson's Videos for Michael Wilson* popped up on-screen. I double-clicked the icon and a folder opened up, showing four files, labeled *Video 1*, *Video 2*, and so on. Only four videos. Why couldn't Dad have made more? I had hoped for a video clip or at least a text file from the Mystery Mailer, but I should have known better. I knew how lucky I was to have any letters or videos at all.

I double-clicked *Video 1* and a QuickTime player popped up with an image frozen in it.

"Oh," I whispered. "Hi, Dad."

Although my father sat in a dark room, I could see him there in the little video window, just like I remembered him. He was wearing his tan desert-camouflage army uniform. He looked right at me, waiting to talk to me as if he were alive again.

I found the play button at the bottom of the window. All I had to do was click that little triangle, and I could hear my father's voice.

I moved the cursor over the play button and stopped.

In the file window, this first video had a "date modified" date of December 25, 2004. Date modified? Did that mean Dad changed the video file on that date, or was that when he filmed it? The second video was modified on May 1, 2005. The one after that was dated July 22. The date of the last video was August 28, 2005, the day my father died. This was it, then. There would be no more videos or letters.

Could I just watch all of these in a row and learn everything? The answers to all the questions I would have liked to ask my father? Would these videos give me any clues about how he died, or why he had to die?

No. That was stupid. How could he make a video after he died to explain how it happened? Unless maybe he'd been wounded and made the final video on his deathbed. But would I want to see him like that, all shot up, or cut from blast shrapnel?

I clenched my fists, breathing out through my nose. The one person who might have the answers I needed, the guy who had sent all this stuff, refused to come forward and talk to me.

There on-screen, Dad stared at me with this pleading look in his eyes, almost like the ghost of Hamlet's father calling to his son. It was as if he wanted to be heard, as if he had been waiting for this moment for the last seven years.

I clicked the play button.

Dad leaned forward out of the shadows so that I could see him more clearly in what must have been moonlight shining in through the windows. He flashed a quick nervous grin. "Merry Christmas, Michael," he said. "It's Christmas Eve night." He pressed a button on his watch and brought it up so he could see it, casting his face in a dim, sickly green light. "Zero one forty-five hours. I guess that makes it Christmas Day. Hey, one less day to be stuck in the war. I have a hundred and fifty-five days left in this place. One fifty-five sounds better than one fifty-six, doesn't it?"

He ran his hand back over his buzzed short hair. "Sorry. I know I already wrote about this in a letter, but it is so weird for me to talk to my son in his future, knowing it means I don't have a future. It's not like I intend to die. But obviously I did, or I will, if you are watching this video now."

Dad unbuttoned a pocket on his chest and pulled out a small, narrow cigar. Then he flicked a lighter and puffed the cigar to life. "Son," he said as he exhaled a blue-white plume, "don't smoke. It's stupid." He coughed and laughed. "And if you do smoke, choose something better than these horrible cheap cigars. A guy in my team, PFC Gardner, wrote to the company to order more of these rotten things through the mail. He told them he needed the smokes to stay awake on guard duty. Instead of selling him a few packs, the company sent six dozen. He said he would die if he smoked all of them, so now we have plenty." He stopped and took a drag on the cigar.

I couldn't believe Dad was smoking. I'd never even tried it because Mom lectured me against it so much. She said some of the people at the nursing home where she worked would spend the rest of their lives hooked up to oxygen machines because of emphysema. The cigar company supported the troops by sending them a product that could kill them. If they survived the war, that is.

"Sorry," Dad continued. "Smoking is the last thing that's on your mind right now, I hope. I don't have a lot of practice at making death videos, I guess."

When he leaned back in his chair, he melted into the shadows, and I could see him even less. He was quiet so long that I had to move the pointer on the screen over the bottom of the video window to make sure it was still playing.

"We had church service tonight. Chaplain Carmichael, our task-force chaplain, was supposed to fly out to spend Christmas here in Farah, but his flight got scrubbed. First squad was out by the landing pad for hours in Humvees, providing security for a flight that didn't show up. Worse, our mail was supposed to be on that Chinook. We haven't had mail in several weeks. A lot of guys were expecting a few Christmas presents in that shipment."

The sound of a sigh came out of the dark. "So we had worship like we usually do, by ourselves on the nice Afghan furniture in the CMOC. Our interpreter, Shiaraqa, joined us. His father had invited us to supper one night during Ramadan, so we thought we'd show him a little bit of Christmas. Turns out the birth of Jesus is in the Koran. Some of their ideas are different, like there's no manger or bright star or anything, and it's just Mary without her Joseph in their version, but we just set all that aside and worshipped God. The same

God. I wish the world could stop fighting and we could all get along as easily."

He leaned forward, back into the light. "I want you to know that's why I'm over here in this war. We're going to beat the Taliban and al-Qaeda so that kids like you and Mary can grow up in a country where you won't have to live in fear of terrorist attacks. I mentioned PFC Gardner. He's a soldier, but he's as young as an American can be and still be in the war. He's like eighteen or nineteen, I can't remember. My point is he's a kid, just two or three years older than you are right now. He wants to be in college learning to be a writer or a reporter or something. Instead he's stuck in this war.

"I'm over here, Michael, because I want you and Mary to live in an America that's at peace. No more kids like Gardner spending Christmas away from their families. No more kids back home missing parents and siblings who are in the war."

There was a blur in the viewer window. I looked closer. The screen showed the desert at night, lit up by the moon and stars.

"The last letter I wrote you was months ago. I think I talked then about the Army giving you time to notice nature. Beauty. I don't know if this camera is picking it up right, but out there tonight is a bright full moon and more stars than I've ever seen back home."

There was a very long pause, and the view flipped back to him in the dark. "I used my satellite phone time to talk to your mom and you and Mary tonight. We normally get five minutes per week, but they gave us each ten for Christmas. Do you remember talking to me? You were so excited about Santa Claus. I had to explain to you that Santa couldn't bring me home for Christmas." He sighed. "Your mom was upset. Crying. Sad about me being gone for the holiday. Mad at me for reenlisting in the first place to get stuck in this war. I don't know. I thought it was the right thing to do at the time. I guess I was wrong. If you're watching this video, that means the last

Christmas I ever had with you was last year. You were just seven years old." He didn't say anything for a long time. There was a sniffle, and when he spoke again, his voice was shaky. "Guess this is my last Christmas."

A pop and static sound came from somewhere, then I heard a different voice sounding just a bit flat — probably coming over a radio. *"All towers, all towers, this is your corporal of the guard. I'd like to wish all you guys a merry Christmas. I know everybody'd rather be back home now, and I know it gets lonely on the overnight guard shift, but I figure that thousands of years ago, and not nearly as far away as it usually is, Jesus Christ was born in a place a lot like this, maybe on a night just like tonight."*

"That's Corporal Andrews," my dad said. "He's not supposed to be on the radio that long. The radios are supposed to be business only." He shook his head. "Staff Sergeant Pratt will probably throw a fit about this. I should make Andrews do push-ups or something as punishment, but I figure it's Christmas, and I'm kind of tired of being a team leader right now."

Corporal Andrews went on. *"So, here's a present for you all."* He began to sing in a low, beautiful voice.

Silent night, holy night
All is calm, all is bright
Round yon virgin mother and child
Holy infant, so tender and mild
Sleep in heavenly peace
Sleep in heavenly peace

"There you go, boys," said the corporal. *"Merry Christmas."*
The radio squawked. *"C-O-G, this is position two. That's a good copy, position two out."*

"*Roger that, C-O-G,*" another voice said. "*Position nine out.*"

"Merry Christmas, Michael." Dad's voice was a wavering whisper from off camera.

The video stopped. I bit my lip and blinked to clear my eyes. The bell would ring soon. I guess that was enough videos for today.

TWENTY-TWO

That day at lunch, Hamilton and Cody joined Gabe, Ethan, and me at our table. They used to sit with Rhodes, and I enjoyed his angry look as he walked past my full table to sit at a much emptier one with Clint and Adam.

The guys were still talking about Friday's game against Traer. "I thought there was no way I could catch up with him," Hamilton said. "But I couldn't just let him score, so I found some way to run faster, and I took him down."

"Seriously, though. Stopping that touchdown was so important," Ethan said with his corn dog in one hand.

Monty snatched the food from him as he sat down. "You going to eat this or play with it?" He tossed it back on Ethan's tray while everyone laughed.

"The best was Wilson, though," Cody said. "Jumping up in the air. *Bam!* Catching it like an NFL star or something."

I shook my head. I'd never realized how much time the football guys dedicated to talking over the games. They all said similar things about how great some play had been, how they worried that we wouldn't have pulled off the win if we'd gone to overtime. Usually, I loved being part of it all. But today my thoughts kept being pulled back to Dad and how sad he'd been in his video.

After lunch, the composition class had come to the library to use all the computers in the main lab, with one extra student being forced to use Mrs. Potter's office computer. When Isma and I went to our corner, we found Denny Dinsler there, facing the back wall with note cards in his hand, speaking quietly.

"Denny?" Isma said.

He looked surprised when he spun around. "Sorry," he said. "I — I know this is kind of y-your spot, but I couldn't . . . find a better place to p-practice."

"What are you working on?" I asked.

"I know it s-sounds crazy." The guy was clearly fighting against his stutter. "But I'm practicing for . . . speech contest."

"That's great," Isma said.

"What's your speech about?" I asked.

Denny shrugged. "About how I'm g-going to beat my stutter." He smiled. "Believe it or . . . not, I'm getting better. But I'll get out of your way."

"No, don't worry about it," I said. "We'll go somewhere else. Good luck, man."

The next day, Mrs. Potter needed to use her computer, so I couldn't watch the rest of the videos then either. Instead, I headed back to the library after football practice. About a dozen women were holding their book club meeting in the padded chairs near the magazines.

Mrs. Potter spotted me and joined me by the doors. She frowned and whispered, "Is there anything I can help you with?"

I pulled the hard drive from my backpack. "I was wondering if I could watch more of my father's videos."

"Oh," she said. "Of course." She motioned toward her office.

I hooked up the hard drive and clicked play on the next video.

Dad sat in a blue plastic chair in front of a white wall — in the guard tower again, but this time bright sunlight filled the room. He slowly ran his hands down over his face. "Hey, buddy," he said. "It's May first, 2005. I'm sorry it's been so long since I've written a letter or made a video, but I've been really busy with missions and with keeping the guys in my team in line. I swear I never stop playing the 'what stupid thing will Fast Freddy do today' game."

He pulled a cigar from his pocket, flicked a lighter, held the flame to the end, and puffed the cigar to life. "So, we're supposed to have twenty-eight days left in Afghanistan. 'One year, boots on the ground,' they told us. Okay. I can do that. I've been counting down the days even way back in the months of training in Texas. Every morning, the first thing I do is cross one day off the little homemade calendar I keep in a notebook in my pocket."

He took a drag on his cigar again. "This tastes terrible," he said. "Like ashes." He laughed sadly and flicked his finger against the cigar to knock the ashes off the end. "Twenty-eight days. Less than a month, and then . . . finally out of Afghanistan." His eyes were red and filled with tears. "Finally starting our way home.

"Then this morning they told us that we are being" — he made air quotes with his fingers — " 'involuntarily extended.' " He spat right on the floor. "They were smart to tell us this while we were standing at attention in formation so the guys couldn't go crazy when they heard the news. When we were released from formation, Staff Sergeant Pratt told our squad to shut their mouths and come to his room in the barracks so we could talk about it. When we got there, Corporal Andrews didn't say anything. PFC Gardner complained about how his college plans would be pushed back even further. Mac cussed up a storm. But Fast Freddy went crazy, like a caged animal. He kept shouting, 'This is messed up! This is seriously messed up!' " Dad sighed. "What could I tell them? We were screwed, stuck in the war in Afghanistan six months longer than we thought we would be."

He smoked some more.

"I tell you, Mikey, I feel more like Freddy than he'll ever know. For a whole year, all I've thought about is getting back home to you,

Mary, and your mom. Now I'm stuck here longer, a whole half a year." He wiped his eyes. "I know!" he shouted. "I know that the only way you'll be watching this video is if I never made it home at all, but right now, while I'm filming this, I still feel like I'm going to make it. And who knows, but maybe I WOULD have lived if the Army would have let me go home in a year like they first said!"

He was silent and still for a long time.

"Your mom wants a divorce. She sent me a letter telling me all her reasons. I got the letter yesterday." He steepled his fingers with his thumbs pressed to either side of the bridge of his nose, the cigar held between his right index and middle finger. "The Army pays me a lot more if I'm married. Your mom and you kids get certain benefits if your mom and I are married. As soon as I read your mom's letter, I asked the commander for special permission to use the satellite phone, and I called her. I've convinced her not to divorce me until after I get home."

He pointed the cigar straight at the camera. "But when I get home, I'm going to work this out. I'll make things better so that we stay together as a family," he said. "Of course, if I don't make it home, well, then she'll just collect a little bit of life insurance money and she'll have saved herself a lot of paperwork and divorce-lawyer fees."

He laughed bitterly. I couldn't move, couldn't think.

"I wanted these letters and videos to be something that would help you. Something you could turn to, especially when you were confused or upset and needed some advice. I wanted to use them to try to be a real dad to you. I can tell you this, though. One thing I've learned from the difficulties with your mother and with a few of the guys I serve with. Stop arguing with people. Let go of your anger. It doesn't matter who wins arguments, who was right or wrong. Nobody really wins, especially in stupid political disputes. Arguing and anger are just another kind of war, and trust me, war is terrible. Be at peace."

He looked straight into the camera. "So your mission this time, Michael, is to forgive someone. I don't mean for you to stir up an argument with someone and figure out whose fault it was. I mean to drop it. Let it go. Find that way to forgiveness."

A tear trailed down his cheek and he wiped it away. "This has mostly been a downer of a video, and I'm sorry about that. I want to tell you . . ." He stopped and looked off camera, then he slumped in his chair. "Great. I can hear someone coming. Probably Sergeant Pratt, with some notes I'll have to tell my guys." He looked at the camera again. "More soon. I love you, Michael."

He moved forward and reached out toward the camera. The video stopped.

I sat in the chair, as still as my father's image in the window. Had I just seen what I thought I'd seen? I backed up the clip a little and played it again. Yes, I'd heard it right.

"A divorce?" I whispered. Mom always sat there and cried every D-Day, talking about how perfect our family had been before Dad was stolen away from us. She acted like the poor wounded widow whose adored husband was killed in the war, leaving her all alone and oh-so-sad, bearing the burden of raising us fatherless kids. She made me feel *sorry* for her. But she'd been lying to us all this time! How could she do it? How could she ask my father for a divorce while he served in such a dangerous place? Why did she wait until what was supposed to be so close to the end of the tour? Why did she do it at all!?

I stood up and yanked the hard drive's cables out of the computer, ignoring the stupid pop-up warnings as I shoved the drive into my bag.

Mom started to ruin our family long before the war killed Dad. Who knows, maybe he'd died because of Mom. He seemed really sad, pretty distracted in the video. Maybe one day on patrol, worrying about how his beloved wife wanted to leave him and tear his family apart, he stepped on a mine or something.

Mrs. Potter tried talking to me as I left the library, but I ran out of there, down the hall, and out to the Falcon as fast as I could. I never liked going to the nursing home where Mom worked, but nothing would keep me from having a few words with my mother today.

By the time I'd screeched into the lot at the Sunshine Care Facility and parked the Falcon, there was no sunshine, no light of any kind, left inside me. I had no idea what I would say when I caught up to Mom, but I knew it would not be pleasant.

"Hey, Mike," Darla the receptionist said when I pushed in through the main doors. "I haven't seen you around here in so long! I can't believe how much you've —"

"Where is my mother?" I said.

"Oh. I think she's on break. Probably back in the kitchen having a snack. Do you want me to get her for you?"

I marched past her. "I know where the kitchen is."

To get to the kitchen, I had to pass through the dining hall and the so-called recreation area, where the staff at the home sometimes screened old movies or the residents played cards. A woman in a wheelchair rolled in front of me, shaking her head slowly. "Ninety-six. Ninety-six years old. I have outlived my husband, both of my children. Lord, let me out of this place."

I had to come to a halt to avoid running into her. Then I was distracted by a groan. An old gray-haired man sat at a table, hunched over at the shoulders. His head angled down and to the right over his chest, and a string of drool ran from his mouth to his bib. His eyes rolled to the side as he stared at nothing. Another woman sitting near the table pulled off her own blue wool sock and held it up in front of her face for a moment, frowning in confusion. "Is this your sock?" she said to me.

A man at a different table wore a red flannel shirt and gray pants held up way too high by suspenders. He looked up at me from his game of solitaire. "I survived Iwo Jima. For what?" He placed a two of hearts on a three of spades. "To end up in this place. Won't let me have my cigars anymore. Say they're bad for my health. I'm ninety years old!"

Not everybody in the recreation area looked so miserable. A group of residents in one corner laughed when one of them finished a story. A woman seemed content sitting in a recliner reading a paperback romance novel.

But when I looked around that room, I saw a lot of lonely sadness. The mournful tone, the defeat in the voices of so many people there, reminded me of the way my father sounded in the video I'd just watched.

In one way my father had been fortunate, I realized. He would never grow old or feeble, never be stored in a place like this, waiting for death and wondering why life went on. And yet despite Dad's sadness, he still held on to his hope of returning home alive, of making things right with my mother.

Would Mom really have divorced him if he had lived? Maybe it was a misunderstanding, an angry letter sent before she'd had a chance to reconsider. My goal in coming in here tonight had been to yell at my mother, to confront her for threatening to break up our family, especially at a time when Dad deserved our support. But being in this sad place somehow extinguished that angry fire in me. Like Dad had said, it was better to put aside arguments and be at peace.

I had memories from when Dad was alive and home with us. One fall he buried me in a huge pile of leaves, and when Mom came outside, he asked her, "Have you seen Mikey?" She said something like, "No. You don't think he disappeared, do you?" Now I know they were both playing the whole time, but back then I laughed and laughed when I jumped out of that leaf pile and Mom acted startled. And when I was six or seven, Mom and Dad built this great fort in front of the TV out of blankets hung over the backs of chairs. We had a little picnic in there and watched some cartoon movie, *Toy Story* or something. Mary and I kept messing around, wanting to bring more and more toys into the fort, but eventually we settled down, and our whole family slept snuggled in the fort that night.

Memories like these, along with things Mom had said, had always led me to believe that we had been a happy family before the war. But Dad's video also brought back vague memories of Mom crying while she talked on the phone and tore up a letter. Had all that happy-family stuff been a lie?

The only one who had any answers, the only person who could tell me about the relationship between my mom and dad, was my mother, who hated discussing Dad. It might be hard, maybe impossible, to learn anything, but I had to try. As I went to the kitchen, I could almost feel Dad with me, like a more positive version of the way the ghost of Hamlet's father had been with him when he confronted his mother. I breathed deeply and reminded myself to calm down and be kind.

In the kitchen, Mom sat at a table reading a magazine. "Michael?" She bumped the table as she stood up. "What are you doing here? Is everything all right?"

I opened my mouth to speak, but Mom gasped. "You're hurt!"

"What?"

She grabbed my wrist and held my arm up to examine a new bruise I'd earned yesterday at practice. With everything on my mind,

I had forgotten to make sure I'd covered it up. "Does it hurt? How did this happen?"

"Oh, another little problem at the farm." I was thinking up some semi-credible story about a work-related mishap when I saw the look of disbelief on Mom's face. She wouldn't be fooled twice.

I'd come in here hoping for honesty and the truth, and I'd brought only a lie. Wasn't that at the core of what had been bothering me? People holding back information? It drove me nuts when Mom wouldn't tell me anything about Dad. I was furious when the Mystery Mailer wouldn't reveal himself and when Sergeant Andrews refused to answer my questions. Derek had encouraged me to talk with Mom. Maybe the time had come for me to put the truth out there myself.

"Okay, fine," I said. "Will you just please promise not to flip out?"

She took a step back. "Why?" Her sharp voice cut into my resolve. "What is this all about?"

"See, that's kind of flipping out right there," I said.

"Michael Mark Wilson, where did you get that bruise?"

"At football practice."

A hard quiet fell on the room. A clock in another room chimed the hour.

"What are you talking about?" She narrowed her eyes. "You don't play football."

"I've been playing all season."

"I never gave you permission to join the football —"

"I paid for the physical myself. I wrote your name on the parental consent form."

"You lied to me. You've been sneaking around behind my back for weeks."

"Mom, you have to understand. I only wanted —"

"I'm your *mother*! I didn't even know you were on the team. I'm probably the *only* person in town who didn't know it! Someone was paying at the Gas & Sip the other day and said 'Your boy's doing a great job.' I didn't know what he meant, but I thanked him and guessed that he knew you from work or school somehow. Boy, what an idiot I've been!"

"I've been doing really well in football, Mom. I'm starting —"

"Not anymore you're not."

"Mom, come on. I wasn't even going to tell you, but I thought that you and I needed to be more —"

"Oh." She held both hands flat over her heart. "I'm supposed to pat you on the back because you were going to lie to me. *Again.* And then you chose to actually tell the truth for once. Well, here's the truth. You will quit that football team tomorrow, or I will call the coach, call the school, call the state athletic association, whoever I have to talk to, to let them know you forged my signature. And that if they have my boy on the field ever again, I'll sue them until they're broke."

"Mom, you can't do that! Just listen to me for once!"

"I just did. I listened to your lies, and then I listened to the horrible truth. You're off the team." The smug confidence in her voice made me want to vomit. She looked at her watch. "My break's over. I need to go back to work so I can make money to support my family. I don't get to waste time playing games. Now go home."

"Mom —"

"Go!" she yelled. "One more word out of you tonight, and I'll take away your driver's license too."

I ran out of the nursing home and into the cold night.

TWENTY-THREE

"How's the truck?" Derek asked that night at work.

"Oh, it's great," I said. "If I still get to drive it."

"That doesn't sound so great." He frowned, looking at the Falcon. "Is there a problem with it?"

"What? No," I said. "The truck is fine. Mom found out about football. Well, I told her about it."

"It didn't go well?"

"I told you she wouldn't be able to handle it. She's making me quit the team! It's the only" — I threw a square hay bale from the flat wagon up into the hayloft, where Derek waited to stack it — "thing I get to do besides work and school." I picked up the next bale and hurled it up. "I should have known better than to try to talk to her."

"Whoa, easy there, buddy," Derek said. "We'll get this worked out somehow."

"It's not just that," I said. "I mean, that's enough. But also . . . It's kind of complicated, but I've been thinking about my dad a lot lately."

"Oh yeah?" He watched me silently for a moment. "I know you're mad. I mean, about a lot of things." I swung a bale up in front of my face, then, with a grunt, I heaved it straight up at him. "Nice toss." He grabbed it. "But this anger, guilt . . . It kind of has a way of eating you up inside. Then, sometimes, the people you're mad at . . . Well, you might not know the whole story."

What was he talking about? I stared at him. He saw me waiting for him to explain.

"It's got to be tough on your mom raising two kids by herself. It's expensive. There's a lot of responsibility. I just think she could use some help."

"Help!? She just ruined my life! Why do you always take her side?"

"I'm not taking anyone's side. Or maybe I'm taking everyone's side."

"She won't let me grow up," I said.

"All mothers are a little like that."

"Are you serious?"

"Okay, maybe she's a little overprotective, but can you blame her?"

"What do you mean?"

"She's lost a lot, Mike."

I sat down on some hay. "You mean my dad?"

He didn't answer right away. He climbed down out of the hayloft to join me on the wagon. When he spoke again, he was quieter. "One day a chaplain shows up at her door, says, 'We regret to inform you . . .'" He grabbed a bale and threw it up into the loft. "Because some idiot didn't do his job."

What did that mean? "You okay?"

"Yeah," he said. "Worried about you. And I think I just hurt my back throwing that last bale." He winced and held a hand to his lower back. "You want to throw these and then stack them yourself?" He grunted as he slowly climbed down off the wagon. "Work as long as you want. Let me know how many hours." I watched him walk into the dark.

"Yeah. Sure thing, man," I said. I went back to work.

On the next morning's drive to school, I came to the stop sign at the end of our block and turned on the radio, twisting the knob until I found classic rock on KRRP.

"Mike?" Mary said.

"I know. I know. My old music is lame." I cranked up the volume a little. "My truck. My music. If you don't like it, you can get out and —"

"No, no, I don't care about the music," she said. She added under her breath, "Though it is kind of loser stuff." She spoke up louder. "I just want to ask you, are you okay?"

"I'm fine," I said. I hadn't told her about Mom's decree, partly because I didn't see the need to tell my bratty sister anything, and partly because I desperately held out hope for some kind of miracle to keep me from having to quit football. I didn't want to stir up more trouble.

"You and Mom have been arguing a lot lately. You never used to. Lately you just seem so mad all the time."

"I have a lot on my mind," I said. "And Mom and I have had arguments before."

"You know what I mean." She tossed a lock of hair back over her shoulder. "Not fights like this." I didn't answer. "And the lies."

"I don't need a lecture in honesty from you," I said. "You were always the one saying I should get a life. For once, you and Dad are in total agreement."

"Oh, don't start in on the Dad stuff again."

I slapped the steering wheel. "He may not be important to you, but —"

"You didn't *know* him! We were babies when —"

"— he was our father and he has a lot of smart things —"

"— he died. I'm so sick of you saying —"

"— to say. *No, I'm sick of it!*" I hammered on the dashboard. "I'm sick of all of this! I can't go on just doing homework and school and farmwork and nothing else. What use is a constant focus on the future if there's nothing good in the present? When I live that way, I have to listen to my spoiled sister, who gets *everything* she wants, who goes out with friends to Piggly's or shopping with *my* money half the time — listen to *you* tell me that I'm not cool enough. Just shut up!" I pointed at her. "Just shut your mouth and enjoy your ride in the truck that I bought with the money I worked for, and do not say one word!"

Mary barely made a sound the rest of the way to school, except for a few sniffles as she wiped her eyes. I knew I should apologize. In her own way, she was trying to help.

"Listen," I said when we pulled into a parking space. But she threw off her seat belt, jumped out, and was running toward the junior high wing of the building before I'd even put the truck in park.

Mrs. Potter was home with a sick child that day, and I didn't feel like trying to explain to the sub why I needed to use her office to watch the videos. By the end of the day, I had calmed down a little bit, but I was still grateful for eighth-hour Woods II. Something about ripping into lumber with a saw and smashing nails with a hammer eased me down from a rage to more of a dull fury.

Cody tapped me on the elbow. "Dude, can you hand me the three-quarter-inch chisel?" I gave him the tool. "You okay, man?"

"Fine." I wasn't okay. After this class, I had to go to Coach and quit football. Would someone like Cody even talk to me after that? The guys would be furious with me for letting them down. I could be heading back to the way things were in junior high, with everyone picking on me all the time. I hammered a finishing nail into my stupid wooden-box project.

"Just that you seem mad. You know Coach always says the team has to stick together. That we should try to help if —"

I dropped my hammer to the table. "I don't want to talk about it!"

Cody frowned. "You know, when I'm mad —"

The fire alarm sounded. Mr. Ferguson looked up from where he'd been helping someone with a project. "Okay, people, scheduled fire drill. Out to the parking lot."

We put our tools down and marched outside, careful to pass the first row of cars according to Ferguson's repeated instructions. We'd be protected behind the vehicles in case the school exploded or something, I guess.

Cody elbowed me when we were outside. "So, like I was saying, when I'm mad, I either lift weights until my muscles are totally fried, or I go to my old man's garage, where he keeps a punching bag. I beat on that thing for a while, and I usually feel better."

"I know what you mean." I showed him my swollen, red knuckles, surprised that Cody and I had this violence-therapy thing in common.

Ethan, Dozer, and Sullivan approached. "What's up?" Ethan asked.

"You okay, Mike?" said Sullivan. "You look a little ticked."

"It's stupid. Just . . ." These guys only liked me because I played football. They were worried about me now, but after I quit the team, at best they'd ignore me, and at worst they'd hate me. "Nothing."

"It doesn't sound like nothing," Ethan said.

"Trouble with Isma?" said Dozer with an edge of teasing.

"Yeah, how's it going with her, anyway?" Sullivan asked sincerely.

"It's . . ." It was great, but I didn't want to talk about it here in the parking lot surrounded by dozens of people. "You know."

Clint Stewart and Maria Vasquez had joined the group. "That's not what I heard," Maria said. Dozer put his arm over her shoulder, and she leaned her head on his. "Hailey Green lives across the street and one house down from Isma. She said she saw you and Isma making out on her doorstep before you went inside, and her parents weren't home."

"Wilson, getting some of that exotic desert loving," Dozer said.

Maria laughed. "Like that girl from *Aladdin*."

Clint grinned. "I hear those Arab girls are really hairy, like their religion won't let them shave anything. What was it like seeing her all hairy and —"

"What!?" I said. Why did these people have to be so cruel? "Exotic desert loving"? And the hug Hailey had seen was hardly making out. "People should stop spreading lies. It's not what you think. Everyone should mind their own business and not make up a bunch of crap about —"

"Ooooh, are you in trouble now!" Maria said. Dozer shook his head like he pitied me.

"Oh, why?" I said. "Because Hailey's gonna be mad at me?"

"No, dude," said Sullivan. "Because she is." He pointed over my shoulder, and I turned to see Isma walking away, pausing long enough to look back and glare at me. "She was right behind you when you were talking about her."

"Isma, wait up!" I shouted, and ran to catch up with her, but just then the teachers gave the all clear. As everyone started moving back inside, I lost her in the crowd.

"Can I talk to you?" I said to Isma after school as she slammed her locker and marched away. She'd misunderstood the situation. I was trying to make people stop spreading lies about us. "Isma, come on." I reached out and caught her elbow just before she reached the door to leave the building.

"Let me go!" She yanked her arm away and shoved the door open.

I followed her outside. "Come on. Let's talk a second."

She was about twenty yards from the school when she finally stopped. "I heard everything they said! Everything *you* said!"

"Just listen a second. I can explain." I reached for her but she drew back.

"Explain what? That you let them say horrible things about me and didn't even *try* to defend me?"

"I did try!" I said. She rolled her eyes and walked away. I jogged around to stop her again. "You're the one who told me not to fight."

She threw her hands up. "Yeah! What a concept! Don't punch people! That doesn't mean you can't tell people off. Don't know how?" She pointed at me and then at herself and then back again. "Pay attention to this right here then."

"I was telling them the rumor wasn't true. What's wrong with that?"

"What's wrong is that you should have silenced that racist crap they said. What's wrong is that you were all, 'It's not what you think,' like kissing me was the sickest idea you could come up with. You're so concerned about impressing your popular sports-worshipping buddies, you act like our relationship is nonexistent. You could have fooled me when we actually *were* making out." She looked down. "I guess you did."

"Isma, listen. It's not —"

"My father likes you!" Tears welled up in her eyes. "Even Mom was coming around. She always said I shouldn't trust boys, but I'd almost convinced her to invite you over for dinner." A tear ran down her cheek. She didn't wipe it. "I hate you for making her right. I hate you for making me cry in front of you!" She walked away.

I called out to her, but she only started running.

If I was still going to be on the football team, I would have run to practice. Instead, I took my time, trying to figure out how my life had fallen apart so quickly. Just this last weekend I'd been living life the way Dad hoped I would, knocking down one mission after another. I was getting along with my mother. I'd hung out with the guys from the team as friends.

Most of all, I finally had a girlfriend. And not just a girlfriend, like a girl to make out with just for the fun of it or a girl to be with just for the sake of being able to say I had a girlfriend. I had Isma, this brilliant, beautiful, funny artist of a girl who really liked me. She'd liked me even before I'd shown the school that I was any good at football.

Now I'd lost her. And why? Because of guys like Clint Stewart and Robby Dozer. Because of Maria Vasquez, Hailey Green, Nick Rhodes, and that whole crowd. They always talked crap about Isma, and she was right. I never had the guts to stand up to them. I'd been so afraid of losing those people I called friends, when they'd never bothered with friendship until I'd scored touchdowns for them.

For a moment I thought about waiting until after practice or even until tomorrow morning to tell Coach I wanted to quit the team, but no. It was best to face the Volcano while my anger gave me something like courage.

"You're late, Wilson!" Coach Carter shouted when I finally made it to the practice field. The team was running its warm-up lap. Most of them were way down past the softball diamond. "Why aren't you suited up? What's the matter?"

"Coach," I said, "I'm quitting the team."

The words were out there, and I couldn't take them back. I waited for the Volcano to explode, but he didn't. "This doesn't make sense," he said instead. "You're doing very well. You seem to be having fun. Why are you quitting now?"

"I have to quit, Coach."

Sullivan was jogging by and came to a stop. "Why would you quit, Mike?" he asked.

"I don't have a choice," I said to him and Coach.

Carter folded his big arms over his chest. "Of course you have a choice."

"No, I . . ."

"I think I'm entitled to some explanation here, Wilson."

I finally looked up and met his intense gaze. I knew he wouldn't like the explanation I had to offer, but I told him the truth about how I'd lied to be on the team, speaking quietly so nobody else would hear. By the time I'd finished, most of the guys were returning from their lap.

"Walk with me, Wilson," Coach said in a far calmer voice than I had expected. He motioned to Coach Brown to take over the practice and led me along our warm-up-lap path. He didn't say anything for a long time. "What have I told you about why we wear that jersey on game days?" he finally said. "What do those colors stand for?"

At first I thought these were rhetorical questions, the opening to his speech, but when he said nothing else, I knew he expected an answer. "They stand for Hard Work," I said quietly. I remembered all the painful hours of practice. "They stand for . . ." My throat caught. ". . . Integrity," I said, knowing I had failed Coach and the team because I had none.

"What else does that jersey represent?"

"The jersey represents Team," I said.

Coach nodded. "We talk a lot about how Team means fulfilling your responsibilities on a play, holding your block to open a path for the running back, running your route as fast as you can to get open so the quarterback can pass to you. We also say Team means things like helping your teammate with homework, making sure he isn't doing something he's going to regret, and looking out for him. But it's more than that. I say that one of the Big Three is Team, not just *teamwork*, because *Team* also means belonging. If you're on this football team, you are part of our group, one of us."

Until the guys had bashed on Isma this afternoon, I had believed that. I wanted to believe it still. But I guess it didn't matter now.

"Wilson, I know your mother. She was a few years behind me in school growing up here in Riverside. I know your situation. You were unfairly faced with the reality of having to choose between integrity — that is, doing what's right — and belonging to a team. You couldn't have them both at the same time, so you sacrificed some of your integrity for the sake of joining the team."

"I know," I said. "I'm sorry, Coach."

Carter held up his hand to silence me. "I understand why you did what you did. If I had been in your situation, I might have done the same thing."

We started our way around the back of the softball field.

"This is my tenth year of coaching Roughriders football. I always have our team photo taken shortly after the last game, not at the beginning of the season the way a lot of schools do. I want the photograph taken at the end of the season because every year some guys quit. Others might do something stupid and become ineligible. I want the picture to represent those young men who toughed it out through the whole season."

That wasn't me. I'd become one of the losers, one of the failures who had quit.

"Do you like playing football, Mike?"

I'd never heard him call anyone by his first name. "What?"

"Do you want to be in that team picture at the end of the season?"

I couldn't speak. I only shrugged.

"Do you want to be in that team photo, Wilson?" he repeated more sharply.

There went "Mike." "Yes, Coach," I said.

"Then we have a problem." He tilted his head to the right and then the left to stretch his thick neck. "Nobody knows about the forgery except you, your mother, and me. I've had you on my team all this time with no permission. That's a potentially serious legal liability. If people find out about it, there could be major trouble. But . . . if you were able to get your mother to change her mind and sign the permission form — I mean really sign it this time — we could get you back in that uniform and forget this whole mess ever happened."

"But isn't that a violation of integrity?" I said. "I mean —"

"I honestly don't know," Carter said. "In a dilemma like this, it's hard to say what's the ultimate right thing to do. I just want you to know that if you can get permission from your mother, you have permission from me. You can go for now, but understand that this doesn't have to be the end."

"Thank you, Coach," I said. I watched as he jogged back to the practice field, leaving me behind.

TWENTY-FOUR

I spent Wednesday night driving around in the Falcon for a while before going home to tear loose on the punching bag in the attic. I didn't even bother going to work. Derek could join the list of people already mad at me.

Mom let me keep driving after I told her I quit the team. I guess she liked the idea of me serving as a shuttle service for Mary.

Thursday somehow sunk even lower than Wednesday. It made the days when I got beat up back in junior high seem like fun times. At least I had learned how to defend against physical attacks since then. But word had somehow gotten out that I was quitting the team, and now, at various times throughout the morning, Adam, Clint, or Rhodes would whisper (not too quietly) about how I was a wimp or a coward. Sullivan completely ignored me. Robby Dozer complained loudly that I'd let the team down.

At lunchtime, I sat down at a table in the back. The greasy beef burger and soggy tots didn't do much for my appetite, so I picked up my book, *Nevermore: Poems of Edgar Allan Poe*. I figured if I had to be miserable, I might as well read poems that let me know others were too.

"Mind if I sit here?" Ethan put his tray on my table and sat down across from me. "You going to tell me what happened?" He ate a tot.

I closed my book and put it down. "I quit the team."

"I know you quit the team. Everybody knows you quit the team. Nobody knows why."

"Does it matter?"

"Yeah, it matters! You're good, Mike. We need you. More than that, I'm kind of worried about you. First what happened between you and Isma, then you just quit the team. Some of the guys are saying you quit because of her. It's no secret she hates sports."

"Leave her out of it. She's not why I had to quit."

"Then why?"

"I can't tell you." If I told him the truth, and anyone found out, it wouldn't be long before the whole school knew, and then the "mama's boy" jokes would never stop.

Ethan didn't say anything for a while. Finally, he rose and picked up his tray. "I'll be over with the guys. You should come with me."

"Yeah, right," I said.

"Dude, don't do this," he said. "Don't totally disappear again."

He said that as he walked away, leaving me alone so he could join the others. I thought about following him, but I couldn't handle all their questions today.

I tried to get Isma to talk to me on the whole walk from seventh-hour history. The shop and the art room were both located at the end of the school's back hallway, and we usually talked at least a little bit while waiting for Mrs. Kamp, the part-time art teacher, to arrive from the elementary and unlock her classroom. Today Isma wouldn't even look at me. "Come on. I'm sorry," I said. "What else do you want me to say? What do you want me to do?"

"Sorry I'm late." Mrs. Kamp hurried down the hall, jingling her keys in her hands. She unlocked and opened the door. "Mike, shouldn't you be in shop class?"

"I'm going, Mrs. Kamp," I said. Seeing that Isma hadn't gone straight into the art room, I held out hope that she might talk to me.

After Mrs. Kamp went inside, Isma turned to face me. She closed her eyes and took a deep breath. Then she opened her eyes again.

"I want you to leave me alone," she said.

I watched her walk away.

"Where were you yesterday?" Derek said when I showed up at the farm after school. He had the deck off his rider mower and was scraping the bottom of it with a putty knife. He must have noticed something in my look, because he put the tool down and stood up. "What's wrong?"

I told him everything that had happened in the last few days, even about what I'd learned in Dad's video. "So, even though Mom's a huge liar and always acted like we were a big happy family, even though she'd planned to divorce my dad, I still took your advice and Dad's advice and calmed myself down so I wouldn't be too hard on her. What does she do? Ruins my life!"

"Wow, buddy. I'm sorry all this happened. But . . . maybe she'll change her mind about football at least. Have you tried talking to her?"

"This all went wrong because I tried to talk to her in the first place! I've barely said two words to her since she made me quit the team."

"Have your dad's videos helped?"

"I can't even watch them! I don't have a computer, and Mrs. Potter's been home sick. I haven't been able to use her office computer."

"Maybe I could talk to your mom," Derek said.

I rolled my eyes.

"Okay, maybe not," he said. "But hang in there, buddy." We went back to cleaning and reassembling the lawn mower.

* * *

That night after work, I stopped at the Gas & Sip to fuel up the Falcon. She ate a lot of gas, but not enough to make me miss riding Scrappy everywhere.

Just as I finished filling the tank, Sullivan came out of the station. He offered his trademark cool reverse nod and joined me at the pump.

"What's up?" he said.

"Um . . . nothing. Just getting off work." I hadn't expected him to want to talk to me.

He jerked his thumb toward the parking spots in front of the station. "Park the truck. Let's go for a walk." He actually smiled when I hesitated. "Trust me, man. It's cool."

I moved the Falcon and paid for my gas, and the two of us set out on foot, walking the streets of this town where we'd both grown up. It was a warm night for late September, and a lot of people our age were out on the square, some cruising, a few skateboarding around the fountain in the center green. At first Sullivan's route seemed random, but after a few blocks, I figured he had a destination in mind.

"How did team supper go?" I asked after a while to break the silence.

"It was cool. Mr. Pineeda was crazy like always. Dozer ate a whole Big Porker."

"Wow." The Big Porker sandwich overflowed with a full pound of barbecue pork.

We reached the abandoned railroad tracks and headed south. When we were out of town, we stopped on the Runaway Bridge, the gurgling waters of the English River fifty feet below.

Sullivan picked up a rock and threw it over the side into the water. "So it's like this," he said. "I was pissed when I found out you quit. So mad, I couldn't talk to you all day, because I didn't want to be a jerk."

"I didn't have a choice," I said.

"Hang on." He held up a hand. "I'd like to know why you quit, but Ethan says you're not talking. You must have your reasons. Just . . . I want to know if I can convince you to come back. I think Coach will take you back."

"I can't."

"You're really letting your friends down, Mike."

"You mean my friends who give me crap in the halls all the time, who ruined things for me with Isma?" I said. "Friends who spread rumors about me, about Isma, who attack me just for showing up at Nature Spot? Those guys only acknowledge the existence of the guys on the football team, and they can't stand anyone who isn't. Somehow letting them down doesn't feel so bad." I kind of lied about that last part.

"Don't even try to lump us all in together!" Sullivan said. "You criticize people for assuming that anyone who isn't on the football team is crap, but what does it say about you when you assume that everyone on the team is exactly the same?"

He had a point, but I wouldn't admit it. "Still, all those guys were —"

"They didn't know you, man. *We* didn't know you. How were we supposed to? You never talked to anyone. You never participated in any activities. You went to school and went to work, and that was about it. Anyway, do *you* hang out with everybody in the whole school? Do you go far out of your way to talk to that kid — what's his name? The kid with the stuttering problem. Nicky Dinsler's little brother?"

"Denny," I said.

"Yeah. You best buddies with him?" I'd talked to him a few times, but not very much. Sullivan waited a moment for me to say something, but my silence answered for me. "That's what I thought.

Yeah, Nick Rhodes, and that idiot in your class, Clint Stewart. Their pal Adam What's-His-Name — those guys are jerks. Nobody likes them. But this isn't like the movies or comic books. No supervillains here, man. Just normal people. And people can be mean and they can be cool on the same day. Dozer, Moore, Bracken? Yeah, they say a lot of stupid things sometimes, but they're good guys. Loyal friends. We all came up together."

"Yeah, you're all real close," I said. "I noticed that."

He shook his head. "Rhodes isn't as good a tight end as you are, Mike. Worse, he gets all upset and loses his mind out there, then we wind up getting knocked back fifteen yards for a penalty. Why you quit is your business, but if it's because of what happened out there at the fire drill, if you're mad at the guys . . . you also gotta know, you still have friends. At least, I'm still your friend."

"Just coincidentally a friend who might help you win more games?"

"Yeah!" Now Sullivan sounded mad. "Yes, fine. We need your help. Okay? I need us to make the playoffs. I need a scholarship. The way our district is shaping up this season, we can lose only one more game and expect to make it to postseason. So, yeah, I'm your friend no matter what, but I'm also asking you to get back on the team and help us."

I didn't know if I should believe him or if he was telling me what I wanted to hear just so I would help him get what he wanted. More and more, that's what it all came down to, the lies versus the truth. What was real. What really counted.

Sullivan clapped me on the shoulder. "So, sorry to get all weird and emotional on you, but I wanted you to know that."

Neither one of us spoke for a while after that. The river valley began to melt into darkness, and we spent some time chucking rocks into the river. "Good luck tomorrow," I finally said. "I hope you guys win."

"I hope *we* win too," he said.

That talk with Sullivan helped me survive Friday. Seeing the guys again and again around school in their game jerseys constantly reminded me of my failure.

Mrs. Potter hadn't returned yet, so I couldn't get access to that old computer back in her office. I told myself that was why I had to delay watching the rest of Dad's videos, but there was another reason. With these letters and videos, my father cheated himself into the future. He lived again and communicated with me in ways that challenged me to be a better person, while at the same time offering that sense of approval from a father that I'd never had before. These last two videos would almost certainly be the last I ever heard from my father, and I felt a sense of dread at that knowledge.

These thoughts bounced around in my head as I finished reading *Hamlet* Friday night by the lonely light of my desk lamp in my quiet attic. *We exist as the words of our thoughts or our mouths,* I thought. If I played out the rest of Dad's videos, his existence in the present would diminish. "The rest," Hamlet says as he dies, "is silence."

A knock came from the bottom of the attic stairs. It was too early for Mom to be back from work. Mary had sneaked out to the game, and that was probably over by now. "Go away!" I yelled.

"Mike, I need to talk to you," Mary said as her head popped out of the stairwell.

"No. I'm serious. Go away." I got up and went to block her way up the stairs. She pushed past me and came into the attic. "You're not staying," I said. "Get out of here!"

She pulled out the metal folding chair at my desk and sat down. "Don't you even want to hear how the game ended?"

"No, I don't."

Mary leaned back in my chair. "North English beat us twenty to fifteen."

"Great," I said. "Now leave." Not only did I not need a reminder that I wasn't on the football team anymore, I *really* didn't want to hear about how the team had lost.

"I talked to Isma," she said. "I told her you missed her."

"You what?" How did Mary know Isma wouldn't talk to me? "Why would you talk to her? What do you mean, I miss her?"

She rolled her eyes. "Mike, seriously. Everybody's heard about what happened. How you kind of screwed up during that fire drill —"

"Yeah, I know I screwed up. I don't want to talk about it. Would you just leave?"

"Isma's cool, Mike. You found yourself a really pretty, really great girlfriend."

"She's not my girlfriend."

"She still likes you."

"No, she doesn't," I said. "Why? Did she say something?"

Mary laughed. "You're such a dork. No, she didn't flat out say 'I still like your brother,' but she mentioned you quit football and . . ."

"And what?"

"And I can just tell she still likes you! Women can tell these things."

My sister was hardly a woman, but I didn't want to argue about that. Anyway, if all she had was some kind of mysterious feeling that Isma still liked me, I'd rather just be left alone. "Gee, thanks for telling me all that," I said. "That's so useful."

"Would you knock it off?"

"Knock what off?"

"This attitude! This total loser act." She pressed her hands to her cheeks. "I never thought I'd be saying this, but you've actually been pretty cool this year, Mike. You were good on the football team. A couple dorky girls in my class have crushes on you. Your truck is old and I hate the color, but at least you've got your own ride. Then you also had a girlfriend."

"So what?"

"So don't just give up!"

"I don't need advice from my annoying little sister."

"You do too."

"Get out of my attic."

Mary stomped back down the stairs. A moment later, her bedroom door slammed. I had questions to answer on the study guide for English, but somehow the prince of Denmark's pain didn't seem to matter much right then. I closed my book and flopped back on my bed, thinking of Dad's videos and how lost and miserable he'd been and how I felt the same.

TWENTY-FIVE

Monday brought Homecoming Week. A bunch of people dressed up for Monday's "Blast from the Past" theme, wearing hippie outfits for the sixties or huge hairdos for the eighties. I went as the Great Depression. No costume required.

After school that day, I took Dad's red-bull bag and went to the library. Mrs. Potter had returned, and I couldn't wait any longer. When she let me set up in her office, I sat down to watch my father's last messages to me.

Dad waved at me from where he sat. The white tower room shined brightly as the sun slanted columns of light through the dusty air. "Hello, Michael." He checked his watch. "It's Friday, July twenty-second, 2005." He wiped his hand down his face. "I've . . . um . . . stopped counting the days. Anyway, it's been a couple months since I made my last video for you, so I figured I'd better borrow Gardner's camera and make another.

"To tell the truth, it's been a rough couple of months. It's real depressing to have to stay longer than we thought we would. Your mother has agreed not to divorce me at least until after this deployment, and I'm hoping I can get her to come around and avoid it altogether." He shrugged.

"Listen, I wanted to say that maybe I shouldn't have told you about that. It's just that the whole thing had surprised me, and I was upset. I had this idea that you should know the whole truth about life and your parents. Now, though . . . I don't want you to be upset with your mother about this divorce thing. She deserves better than that, and anyway, if you're watching this video, the situation hardly matters because it means I died, or I will die, before any of that happens."

I paused the video and dropped my gaze to the floor. Then I looked at the image of my father. I'd sure let him down on all that he'd just asked of me. "I'm sorry, Dad," I said out loud. I resumed the video.

Dad leaned forward, put his elbows on his knees, and rested his chin on his folded hands, looking directly into the camera. "One night," he said quietly, "right before we came on our guard shift at zero one, PFC Gardner walked into his tower to find the soldier he was supposed to relieve had brought a live grenade to the tower with him. He told Gardner to leave. Said he was going to blow himself up.

"Gardner was smart. He keyed up his radio during the conversation so I would hear. I joined the two of them on the guard tower. The guy was just huddled in the corner, tears running down his face, his hands shaking and his finger on the pin. He kept talking about missing his kids, wanting to go home. It took a while, but eventually me and Gardner talked him into handing over the grenade. They sent that soldier back to the main base at Bagram to get some help. I hear he's doing okay."

Dad was quiet for a moment, but then he smiled. "We've been doing a lot of toy-and-candy missions for the kids in villages all over Farah province. You should see the look on those kids' faces when they get a brand-new toy, maybe their only toy. The boys get together and make little wars with their new plastic army men. The girls will hold a Barbie doll or a fuzzy stuffed animal like it's their own baby." Dad folded his arms and rocked them back and forth in a cradling motion. "Yeah, maybe handing out toys and candy doesn't win the war, but these kids have had it rough, and it's good to see them have some fun."

He grabbed a cigar from off camera and lit up, coughing a little. Then he cleared his throat and smiled. "Another thing that has really cheered people up has to do with this young Afghan girl named Zulaikha who we came across in a village called An Daral. We were on a mission there to see about building them a new school, driving down this narrow lane on our way to the river. All of a sudden, Corporal Andrews shouted down into the Humvee, telling us to look at this girl who was standing near the wall."

Dad frowned. "She was ugly, I have to say — disturbing to look at, with her upper lip not joined in the middle, and her top teeth so crooked that they stuck straight out from under her messed-up nose. I guess they call this cleft lip. She was born that way. I felt so sad, seeing her like that, knowing that doctors could fix that, but she's had no access to medical help."

He rose from his chair and reached his arms up, stretching. Then he crossed the room and leaned on the big cement ledge at the base of the window, looking out in silence for a moment. "Helping this girl was not one of our official missions from the Army." Dad turned back to the camera. "But Andrews wouldn't give it up. He bothered every officer on base. He offered to pay any costs himself. He even wrote to Congressmen about it. I asked him why it was so important to him to help this girl, and I'll never forget what he said. He was even more serious than he usually is, and he just stared at me and said, 'Please, Sergeant. I don't know if I can make it if we don't do this. I've seen too many bad things in this war. Too much goes wrong over here. I need something to go right.'"

Dad stood up straight. "Finally, our physician's assistant was able to get the girl to one of our doctors in Kandahar for the surgery she needed. You should have seen her when she came back, Michael. It was a miracle of a difference. There was just one tiny scar. Otherwise you'd never know the girl had ever had a cleft lip.

"Corporal Andrews was right. We needed to help Zulaikha. She needed the surgery so she could talk, eat, and drink right, but we needed to help her. We needed to win one. She's helped me find more joy and purpose through the difficult period of this involuntary extension. She's reminded us all of the importance of dedication to our mission of helping the Afghan people build a better country. Zulaikha is an inspiration, a brave little girl in a tiny village in Afghanistan, who has no idea that I owe her more than I can ever repay."

Dad puffed his cigar, then sat back down in his chair. "I was talking to Ortiz and the guys in the Gentlemen's Smoking Club the other night. MacDonald has even joined us now. You remember how I talked about the Cowboy Way, about not knowing the best way to do something, and having no guarantees that anything would work out right, but trying anyway?" He flicked some ash. "I've just realized it's more than that. It's like those old Western movies from the fifties and sixties where the good cowboy wore the white hat. While the cowboy didn't always know how to handle a certain problem, he knew what was right, and he'd ride into town and do his best to stop the bad guys. I should have figured that out a long time ago. The Cowboy Way isn't just about making things up as you go along. It's about making things better for everyone.

"Try to help people, Michael." He shook his head. "When we were in Texas training for the war, some of my fellow soldiers and I went into Austin for fun. A homeless man on the street asked if I had any change. All I had in cash was a dollar and a quarter, but I figured the Army was paying me pretty well, so I gave the man my money. One of my buddies said that was a stupid waste and the bum should get a job. I thought of that part of the Bible where Jesus says something like, 'I was hungry and you didn't feed me. I was thirsty and you didn't give me a drink.' I had to try to help that man at least a little bit. You'll make zillions more five- or ten-dollar bills in your lifetime, Michael. And sometimes just listening and understanding someone, letting him know he's not alone, can make all the difference.

"That's your mission with this one, Michael. I've asked you to do something nice for Mary and your mom. Now I want you to find a way to help others. It's a mission I hope you'll stay involved with for the rest of your life."

Dad looked down and didn't say anything for a long time. He didn't look up when he spoke again. "I wish I had figured this stuff out a long time ago, before they sent me to the war. When I left home, you were only seven years old, and you looked at me like I had the answers to everything in life. Truth is, I don't know how much these letters and videos have taught you about what it means to be a man. That's because I don't have many real answers. I've been tripping through life, mostly clueless. If I ever make it home, I'll live the Cowboy Way and start changing some things. I'll take a risk and put in for some better jobs. Your mom talked about wanting to go to college, but neither of us really knows how to get all that stuff started. If I make it home, I'll make sure she uses the G.I. Bill benefits I've earned in the Army. I owe her that. I owe you all so much."

He took a long drag on the cigar and blew out smoke a moment later. Then he stood up and walked toward the camera. "I *miss* you all so much." The video froze.

My father talked about not knowing much about life, but so much of what he'd said throughout his letters and videos made perfect sense to me. All my life people had called him a hero, and in recent years, I'd wondered more and more what that meant. But if persistence and never giving up was one requirement for being a hero, then my dad surely qualified. There he was, miserable, and stuck in the war even longer than he thought he would be, and what did he do? He kept soldiering on. He didn't give up. And right then I knew that I couldn't either.

I moved the cursor over the remaining video file and took a deep breath. My finger shook on the mouse. There was only one final video to watch now.

TWENTY-SIX

In the video window, Dad leaned forward, reaching out toward me. He didn't seem to be in the guard tower. Instead his M16 leaned against a desk behind him, and a small American flag and a calendar with the days crossed off in red marker hung on the wall. I clicked the play button.

Dad smiled at me as he sat down in a plastic chair. "Hello, Michael. Today is August twenty-eighth, 2005."

I paused the video and sat staring at him frozen on the screen. My heart hammered so heavy in my chest that I could hear and feel it up through my neck and ears. This video had been made on the very last day of my father's life. I knew this and he didn't. How could I watch this, knowing he was destined to die right after filming it? How could I not watch it?

I reached out to the mouse and moved the cursor over the play button again. Even as I thought it, I felt stupid, but somehow it seemed to me that if I clicked the mouse and let the video play, it would be like letting Dad use up the last few moments of his life. Like if I could keep the image still like this, he would be okay. He still had more to say. He was alive. Playing the video would be letting events take their course, events that led to his death.

But that was dumb. Illogical. I clicked the mouse.

"I stopped counting when our tour here was extended, so I don't know how many days I have left." He looked around him. "This is my room in the barracks. Not much to look at, really. I'm sorry it's taken me so long to make another video. It's been a rough month. The Afghan National Army soldiers who train near our base got hit pretty bad when they were on patrol up near Bala Boluk.

"We provided security for the presidential election back in October. Now we're busy getting ready for Afghanistan's vote for parliament. It's pretty great helping these people get back on their feet after they've been at war for so long. Now they'll get to vote for whoever they want to represent them in their government."

He shook his head. "Of course, the Taliban hate voting and especially the idea of women voting. Basically, they want to destroy everything that is good, and they're threatening to cause all kinds of trouble. There have already been a few bombings near the polling places. New death threats seem to come all the time." He shrugged. "We just stay alert and do our best."

Dad reached down off camera. "I have something for you." He sat up, holding the faded tan bag with the two red-bull patches sewn on the flap. "I've been using this bag throughout my time here in Afghanistan. It's great for carrying maps and notebooks and pens and things like that. I went ahead and sewed on these two patches. This is the patch for the mighty Red Bull of the Thirty-fourth Infantry Division. See?" He showed me the brown-and-tan version of the patch on his desert uniform. "This is my insignia, except the ones on the bag belong on the dress green uniform that we only put on about once a year for inspection.

"There's also this." He held up his hand, showing a big silver ring with a square red stone in the center. He slipped the ring off his finger. "I've been thinking a lot, and I want you to have this." He turned the Army bag around and opened the flap. "I'm going to put it in this small pocket." He slid the ring inside and then reached off camera for a moment, returning with a threaded needle. "Then I'll sew the pocket shut with real loose stitching." He was quiet for a long time while he poked the needle through the fabric of the bag and then pulled the thread through. "I never thought I'd sew this much, but the Army has had me sewing on all sorts of name tapes and patches on my hats and things." He produced a jackknife from offscreen and cut the thread. "There. Done."

He put the needle and thread aside, flicked his knife closed, and then placed it off camera. He held the bag up so I could see where he'd just been sewing. "So if you're watching this, and my plan for you to get this bag and ring on your birthday has worked out, then you should find this last present from me inside this pouch."

I paused the video and opened the bag in my lap. Sure enough, the loosely sewn pouch was there. I grabbed the fabric and ripped hard at the stitches until I'd broken through. The metal inside felt cool in my fingers. I pulled the ring out and slipped it onto my finger. It fit perfectly.

My father was truly the last person to touch this ring. Now I wore it. Under the center of the red stone was an emblem of a golden castle, and on each side of the ring were the Red Bull insignia, just like the patches on the bag. Arched over the top of the stone was the word *Essayons*, and in a curve around the bottom was the phrase *Let Us Try.*

I resumed the video.

"The castle under the red stone is the emblem of the Army Engineers. That word, *Essayons*, is the engineer motto, meaning 'Let Us Try.' When I've been scared or when I didn't know what to do here in the war, I've looked at this ring. It kind of reminds me of the Cowboy Way, you know. Don't know how to do it? Not sure if it will work? Scared to get started? Well, let us try!

"That's a motto I hope you'll take to heart as you're getting more into high school, this amazing time when you get to choose who you want to be and what you want to do with your life. I hope you'll remember this. High school may be the best or the worst time of your life, but you will never completely leave it behind. You can have a lifetime of regrets, or good memories that go with you through the years. You write your own story. It's up to you to make it a good one."

Dad sat back in his chair. "There's a big painting on the wall in the airport at our main airbase in Bagram. It's the silhouettes of three soldiers with a quote underneath that I wrote down." He flipped through some pages in a small tan notebook and then read, " 'This is a tribute to all who have fallen during Operation Enduring Freedom. Live a life worthy of their sacrifice.' "

Dad smiled and looked out of the screen at me. "I guess that says it all, Michael. If you're watching this, then it's too late to do anything for me, but there's still time for you to do all those great things I always hoped you'd do. That's your next mission from me, maybe the biggest mission of all. Take your chances, be bold, live a good life, and help others to do the same. I hope —"

There was a loud clanging sound. Dad rolled his eyes and sighed. "Hang on," he said. "Someone's at the door. Come in!" he called and looked to the left. "What is it, Mac?"

There were sounds off camera and then someone else walked into the shot. "Sorry, Sergeant, but I'm supposed to come get you. They just called for QRF. We have to roll out."

I stood up and paused to freeze the image. The other guy. Mac. MacDonald. At first I didn't recognize him. He looked so much younger. But after playing the video through again, listening to the guy's voice and looking at him closely, I couldn't deny it.

The guy in the background, the soldier with my father on my father's very last day, was Derek Harris.

This was impossible. Derek had never served. He'd mentioned knowing my dad when they were in high school, but he had conveniently left out the fact that he had been with Dad in Afghanistan. What was going on here?

I played the video.

Dad pulled on his armored vest and helmet. "What do we got?" He grabbed his M16 with the big grenade launcher under the rifle barrel.

Derek threw his hands up. "Something about Taliban messing with the UN guys at a polling place they're trying to set up."

Dad snapped his helmet's chin strap into place. "Let's go." He headed for the door but stopped. Then he ducked down to look into the camera. "My turn for a mission," he said. "I love you, son. Good-bye, Michael."

"Good-bye, Dad," I whispered.

A few minutes later, as I packed the hard drive into the bag my father had given me, I bit my lip and took deep breaths through my nose, trying to get control of myself. It was Derek all along. He had the answers to all my questions this whole time. I had to go see him.

Outside the library, I took the senior hallway as a shortcut out of the school. I didn't want anyone to see my red eyes. Nick Rhodes came out of the bathroom with his hair wet from practice. "Hey, loser," he said as soon as he saw me. "Oh, what's the matter? Trouble with your raghead girlfriend?"

I stopped, my hands on the door. Dad had warned me to avoid fights — well, to avoid starting fights — unless I could find no way out of it without losing my honor. He'd also talked about and shown through his example the importance of sticking up for people. To fight or not to fight? That was the question. Right now every part of me wanted to crush this guy.

I could shove open the door and walk out, leaving that moron behind. That's what Isma would want me to do. But could I do that and keep any honor at all?

"Hey, Mikey," Rhodes said. "Thanks for wimping out and quitting the team."

I remembered how that guy in Afghanistan had wanted to fight Dad and how Dad refused to get violent that day. Sullivan was one of the coolest guys I knew, and he thought Rhodes was a joke. Laura didn't like him either. Why did I have to fight this loser to prove anything? What difference did his stupid words make?

I turned and faced him. "I feel sorry for you, Rhodes."

He might have said something back, but I wasn't paying attention. I rushed out the door and hurried to the Falcon. I had more important things to deal with.

TWENTY-SEVEN

As I drove up the hill toward the farm, my feelings veered among shock, excitement, and anger. Derek had served with Dad? That meant I might finally get some answers. But how could he have kept so much from me, especially when he knew how desperately I wanted to learn more about my father? That anger built into fury as I got closer and closer.

I rolled into the driveway just as Derek drove the tractor around the corner of the barn, Annie trotting alongside. He waved when he saw me. I hit the brakes and skidded to a stop right in the middle of his gravel drive, throwing open the door and jumping down as soon as I killed the engine.

Derek climbed down from the tractor. "Whoa, buddy. You're going to get in an accident driving like —"

I held up my right hand to show him the ring. "Recognize this?"

He frowned. "You get a class ring or something?"

"It's an Army Engineer ring. It belonged to my father."

Derek froze right where he stood. Except for a few wrinkles at the corners of his eyes, a few flecks of gray at his temples, he looked exactly as he had in the video. "Where . . ." He seemed to choke on the word. He cleared his throat. "Where did you get that?"

"It came in a package with my dad's Army bag and a hard drive with videos. You should know. You sent me the box. Why didn't you tell me?"

"Tell you what?" He pulled his cross necklace out from under his shirt and rubbed it. "I don't know what you're talking about."

"You were with him on the day he died!" I shouted so loud that my voice echoed around the farm. "You were there! It's on video. I saw it."

"Mike, this isn't . . ." He stepped back, holding out trembling hands. "I can't —"

"I want to — I *need* to know what happened to my father. You were there. Tell me what happened."

He seemed to be having trouble breathing. He bent over and rested his hand on a front tractor tire. "I don't know what you've been told, but you have to understand —"

I took a few steps closer to him. "Nobody's told me anything. Nobody will talk about it. Why won't you tell me?"

"Mike, you have to —"

"Tell me how my father died!"

"I killed him! He's dead because of me!" Tears welled at the bottom of Derek's wide, wild eyes as he staggered back a few steps. "I messed up and it got your father killed! I killed him! It was my fault! My fault! My fault!"

I thought maybe I should stop right then. This was obviously very hard for him to talk about. Maybe I could ask again later. But that's how it always was about Dad. The topic would get shut down before I ever learned anything. It had to be different this time. "Derek," I said, "I have to know."

He looked at me in horror as the tears rolled down his red face. He wiped his nose with the back of his hand and took a deep breath. "Okay. Okay. We were on Quick Reaction Force, QRF. They called us out. When they scrambled us like that, they didn't waste time telling us the mission until we were rolling out in our Humvees." He breathed so heavy that his shoulders heaved. "I was reassigned to your dad's squad after one of their guys had to go get his appendix taken out. I was the driver for B-team's Humvee. Your dad was alpha team leader, with his team and the lieutenant in their Humvee. We had reports that there was some kind of trouble at a polling place in this village halfway to An Daral. I don't even remember the name of the stupid town.

"They got" — he held his hands about a foot apart — "thick walls, you know, everywhere in Afghanistan. So the streets are lined with walls on both sides. I drove the lead vehicle down a dirt street that was actually wide enough for two lanes. There was this wet spot in the road ahead, and this Afghan guy at the side of the road pointed at what looked like the muddier side, like he wanted me to drive through the muddiest part. Someone said something like, 'We should probably drive where the local guy says it's best. He must know the road,' but I thought I knew better. I drove on the opposite side. In three seconds we were stuck up to the axles."

"What happened?" I asked.

"The Afghan guy threw his hands up in the air and said something that must have meant, 'You idiot! I told you to drive on the other side of the street.' We were there for hours trying to dig out, some of us digging while others formed a security perimeter around the vehicles. And then . . ." Derek wiped his eyes. I felt bad for making him relive all this, but I had to know. I watched helplessly as he went on, "We were stuck next to this broken-down wall in front of a little poppy field. Behind the poppies was a high mud-brick wall. That's where they started shooting from. Andrews and PFC Weebly had been pulling security over in that field, and the first shot nailed Weebly in the leg. He hit the dirt. Andrews took cover behind a big rock. We ducked behind our vehicles and tried to return fire, but there were dozens of Taliban. It was raining bullets." He put his hands to his ears like he was back there again. "So loud. A rocket-propelled grenade flew over and blew up somewhere in town. If the aim had been a little lower, a bunch more of us would have been dead right there."

He stood up and paced the grass. Annie followed him, her tail hung low. "Your dad . . . Your dad got things together. He shouted to everybody to abandon the stuck vehicle. We'd be crowding into alpha team's Humvee.

"Still, we couldn't move. The Taliban had us pinned down. Your dad yelled that we had to get Weebly. Then he ran out into that field, launching a grenade out of his 203. That hit the wall and stopped the firing for a little while. But he took a round to the arm." Derek winced as though he himself had been shot. "He fired off so many rounds to keep the enemy down. He ducked behind a boulder and threw a grenade over their wall. That stopped them long enough for us to destroy the stuck vehicle and remove all the weapons from it. Andrews and Ortiz ran to Weebly, firing the whole time. Gardner rushed out there too, and while your dad kept firing, the three of them carried Weebly back to the vehicle.

"They started shooting full force at us again pretty soon, though. Ortiz got hit in the arm and the upper thigh. I don't know how he kept moving. Your father took another round in the shoulder, kind of by his neck. There's not a lot of armor protection there and he was bleeding pretty bad by the time he got to the Humvee. When we were finally loaded and Freddy took off, we were stuffed on top of each other, us guys who weren't hurt scrambling to get field dressings on the wounded guys."

Derek sobbed and pressed his fists to the side of his head. I reached out and gently put my hand on his shoulder. After all this time, I had the truth, and it was tearing Derek up to tell me.

"So much blood everywhere! When we . . . When we . . . got away from the village, we stopped and called for a medevac helicopter. We'd got Weebly's wounds under control, but . . ." He cried. "Ortiz went first. He just kind of looked off into space with these wide eyes. I'll never forget that look. Then he was gone. Your father.

He kind of . . . went to sleep . . . right out there in the empty desert . . . before the . . . before the medevac bird reached us. The other guys made it. Thanks to your dad."

Derek sobbed with his face in his hands. "If I had just listened to that Afghan guy, instead of thinking I knew better. If I hadn't got us stuck like that . . . It was my fault." He fell to his knees. Annie licked his cheek, and he looked at me with red, tear-filled eyes. "I'm sorry, Michael. I'm so, so sorry."

I shook my head. I'd come here harboring so much anger over the way Derek had hidden the truth and my father's messages to me. But how could I hold on to that anger? For all these years, he'd not only carried my dad's letters, but all that guilt. That's why he paid me so much for working out here, why he always somehow found some work for me, even if all he had were simple chores he could have easily done himself. Why he worked so hard fixing up the Falcon only to sell it to me so cheap.

What a horrible, painful secret to have to live with for so long. No wonder he didn't want to be identified. No wonder he never told me about any of it.

"You have nothing to apologize for," I said. "You did what you thought was best. For all you knew, that Afghan was pointing you to the muddiest part because he wanted to make sure you got stuck in an ambush zone."

He wiped his nose. "Your dad had told the whole Gentlemen's Smoking Club about the letters. With Sergeant Ortiz gone, we all agreed that I should carry out his promise to your father, since I lived here in town and all. Over the years, I thought about coming clean on everything. But how could I tell you about any of this? First you were too young to know about it. Then as you got older and we worked together out here, I was afraid you'd hate me if you ever found out. I kept telling myself that I could maybe tell you later. Then your sixteenth birthday was coming and I knew I couldn't put it off any longer. I had to send you the letters and videos so you'd read them in order. I wanted to send my own note with the letters, to at least tell you how many more to expect, but after you'd told me you wanted a note like that, slipping it in with the letters would have given me away. I'm so sorry."

Derek had been hiding this secret, agonizing over it, for seven years. What could I possibly say to this man to make things all right? I twisted Dad's engineer ring, my ring, on my finger.

"All these years, you've grown up without a father," Derek said. He had begun to catch his breath again, regaining some control in his voice. "All my fault."

"Don't blame yourself," I said. "Blame the Taliban. Don't let them ruin your life too. Dad died trying to save people's lives." I thought about what Dad had said about that painting. "He'd want you to move on, to live a life worthy of his sacrifice. He told me that in one of the videos he left me."

Derek nodded.

"Come on," I said. "Let's get a soda or something."

We went up to the house and sat at the kitchen table, where Derek poured us each a glass of Coke. "The thing about your dad — well, about him and Andrews really — near the end there, he really believed in the mission. I think he saw how rough it was for so many little Afghan kids, especially for the girls, and he knew we had to help. He was totally committed to the mission to help the Afghans rebuild their country, to all of us in his unit, and to his family back home. I never met anyone so selfless." Derek stared at his untouched drink, the condensation gathering in little drops, running down the glass.

"There's one thing I still don't understand," I said. "Dad never mentioned you in his letters or videos. He called you MacDonald?"

Derek actually smiled. "Right. MacDonald. I was a weird guy back then. When I was first switched over to your father's squad, I kept talking about what I knew the best outside of the Army. Farming."

I frowned. "Then . . . MacDonald —"

" 'Old MacDonald had a farm,' " Derek sang. "MacDonald was the nickname they gave me. A bunch of the guys had nicknames. That little guy, PFC Weebly, was really named Weebler. A fat soldier in a different squad was known as 'Pork Chop.' Everybody called Specialist Fredrickson 'Fast Freddy.' "

He went on to tell me how he'd joined the Guard shortly after 9/11 because he wanted to fight for freedom against the terrorists.

"You really think this long war in Afghanistan has protected our freedom in America?" I asked.

Derek shook his head. "Eventually I figured out that it was like your dad said one night over there. Maybe our job wasn't to fight directly for American freedom, but to help the people of Afghanistan reclaim theirs." He took a drink. "I know you've had trouble understanding the point of what we were doing over there, but if you could have seen those boys and girls going to school after being denied an education for so long, Afghan men and women finally getting the chance to vote, all the new construction going up, you'd know that what we did helped a lot of people. It was important. Your father believed that."

"I know he did," I said.

"It's just . . ." Tears welled in his eyes all over again. "I've been home for seven years. *Seven years*, Mike. I still have nightmares sometimes. If I allow myself to think about it, to really focus on it and remember it . . . I can't hold myself together. I don't know. I feel like maybe I breathed in so much Afghan dust that the place stayed with me. All of it. The music, the little kids calling out for candy and soccer balls, and . . ." His voice shook. He swallowed. ". . . and the bad stuff too. How am I gonna . . . ever get past this?"

I fidgeted with the ring on my finger, reading the *Essayons* inscription around the red stone. I drank the last of my soda and set the glass down. "I don't know," I said. "But we will. Somehow. We need to find a way to let go of the war, of what we've lost, and of the past. We need to stop trying to hide from the truth of all that so we can start living for today and tomorrow. We have to. All of us."

"You're thinking of your mom," he said. "I know she and your dad were having problems, but some of those problems were just the basic deployment stress we were all under. She took your father's death unbelievably hard. It's not going to be easy to get her to talk about this."

"I know," I said. "But we have to start somewhere."

"That reminds me," Derek said. "I have something else for you." He left the room, and I petted Annie until he returned with a large manila envelope. "Your father wasn't going to write letters for Mary. He said he didn't know the first thing about what advice to give a daughter. Said your mother would take care of it. But Ortiz told him he had to write something, and after he got started, he found plenty to say." Derek looked down. "It's my responsibility to pass them along. I don't know if he wanted them kept secret until she was almost sixteen or not, but . . ." He handed me the envelope. "I'll leave that all up to you." He sat down and sighed. "What are you going to do about your mom?"

I stood up from the kitchen table. "There's been enough silence. Enough lies. We need to get the truth out in the open so we can start to move forward. I have no idea what I'm going to do. But Dad was always talking about the Cowboy Way."

Derek nodded and smiled.

"I'm going to saddle up and try," I said.

TWENTY-EIGHT

Coach had talked about Hard Work, Integrity, and Team. I had been working hard for years, but I hadn't had integrity with the team of my own family. Every time Mom and I had to talk about anything that was in any way difficult, we'd somehow push it aside. Either she'd become too upset and I'd let the issue drop, or one of us would find a way to dodge the conversation entirely. In order to have integrity, I had to be honest with Mom about what I needed. About what we all needed.

That night I paced the dining room, waiting for her to get home from work, thinking about what had gone wrong in my family. I figured Mom was a lot like Derek in the way she was so torn up over Dad's death, except instead of being super generous like Derek, Mom was super protective. Maybe she was trying to keep our family exactly as it used to be because she felt guilty for having told Dad that she wanted a divorce. I couldn't know for sure because we never talked about any of this. That was going to change, starting tonight.

The loud, gravelly thunder that could only be the muffler on Mom's ancient Ford Escort grew louder and louder. I looked out the window to see her pull into the driveway. I reminded myself to stay focused on getting Mom to talk about Dad and making some changes around here. Hamlet had said about confronting his own mother that he had to be "cruel only to be kind." Bringing up this old, painful subject might seem cruel, but it was a lot more kind than letting us all go on like this.

When Mom came in through the front door, she dropped her purse and keys on the dining room table and smiled at me. "Hey, Michael. How was your day?"

"It was . . . fine," I said. In a way, I almost wished she had come in grumpy and exhausted. It was a shame to have to ruin her good mood.

"You okay? You don't look so good. You're not getting sick, are you?"

"No, I'm not getting sick." I said. "I was wondering if we could talk."

"Oh?"

"I wanted to say that I'm sorry for having lied and gone behind your back to play football. I'm sorry I didn't tell you about a major purchase when I bought my truck." I held the back of the chair tightly. "I should have been more open and honest with you."

She looked surprised. "Thank you, Michael. I appreciate that. But let's just forget about it now. That's all in the past."

Agreeing with her would be the easiest thing to do. That's how we usually handled problems around here. We just forgot it in order to avoid talking about anything that might upset anyone.

Time to take my chances. "Mom, I think we need to talk about Dad. And what he would have wanted. For all of us."

Mom's eyes widened. "We'll never know —"

"I know." I held up my hand to show Dad's combat engineer ring. "Derek Harris has been fulfilling a sort of promise he made to Dad, mailing me letters and videos that Dad made for me. I know that Dad wanted more for all of us."

"What? Michael, please don't start up about this right now."

"I'm sorry," I said, "but I need to talk about —"

"What?" Mom said. "What possible good can come from bringing all of this stuff up again? Derek shouldn't have sent you those letters and things. You're not old enough."

"Dad thought I was old enough."

"He was wrong."

Mary had left her chair in front of the TV and stood in the archway between the dining room and living room. "Please don't start fighting again," she said.

I held up my hands. "I don't want to fight at all. But Mom, I can't go on living like this. I need more than just schoolwork and farmwork and helping out here at home. Dad wanted more than that for me. He told me so in his letters."

"Derek had letters from your father all these years, and he never told me? Why didn't he say something? It's not right for him to keep them secret. You shouldn't have been reading them." Tears ran down Mom's cheeks. "You're not ready."

"Mom, listen to me. I already read the letters. I'm ready. We're all ready. We're all desperate for something new."

"New like going behind my back to play football?"

"I'm sorry about that, Mom, but if I had asked you ahead of time, what would you have said?"

"I would have told the truth, unlike you! I don't want you playing football, Michael. There's better things to be doing with your time. You need to focus on your studies."

"Mom," I said calmly.

"Then you rush out and buy that truck!"

"What does the Falcon have to do with this?"

"I know you don't understand now, but as your mother, it's my job to protect you."

It was happening again, just like always, the dodging of the issue, talking around the truth. "What about what Dad wanted for us?"

Mom threw her hands up. "All of a sudden, it's all about your dad? I'm not good enough for you?" Tears welled up in her eyes. "Don't I work hard enough? Don't I slave away at two jobs every day? And you want to ambush me with all this?"

"Mom, no, it's not like that."

"You're great, Mom," Mary said.

"You've worked so hard for us," I said. "I know it's been tough, and I want to thank you for all you've done."

"This is how you thank me?" Mom shouted. "By yelling at me?"

"I'm not yelling."

"Just give him a chance to talk, Mom," said Mary.

I tried again. "You've helped us so much. You've sacrificed a lot. Dad talked about helping others, about how a real hero —"

"Oh, here it comes again!" Mom said. "All that hero stuff. Seven years I've been hearing that, how my husband was a hero when he died."

"I know it's painful to talk about him," I said. I put my hand on her arm. "You were crushed. Sad. Anybody would be."

"No!" She yanked her arm away from me. "I was angry! I was mad at him, all right! I'm a terrible person! It was my duty to be the sad widow of the fallen soldier, and I was sad, yeah, but I was also mad!" She flicked her finger against the ring on my hand. "You got his ring? His precious letters! Probably a bunch of advice from the big war hero?" She slapped the table so hard that a stack of papers fell off the end. "What did I get? A folded flag and a couple thousand dollars that barely paid for a funeral." She glared at me. "You don't think you're getting the chance to live your life? What about my life? I work as hard as I can in two jobs that I hate, and in this economy I'm lucky to have the jobs, and they're still not enough to pay the bills!" She stepped around the table toward me. "You think I don't *know* that my own son spends his money helping to fix the furnace or my junk car's stupid fuel pump?" She hit the wall. "I'm not stupid! I wanted to go to college! I could have done something with my life!"

"You still can, Mama," Mary cried.

She looked at Mary in anguish. "Baby, we don't have the money. We have a measly ten thousand in the bank from your dad's life insurance that he made me promise I'd save for your educations. How am *I* going to afford college when I can barely afford basics around the house?"

"Somehow, Mom," I said. "I don't know. I don't have all the answers, but we have to do something. If you want to go to college, we can find a way to use Dad's G.I. Bill, and maybe the ten thousand. I can borrow the money when my time comes, and then we'll figure out what to do about Mary."

Mom pulled a tissue from her purse and blew her nose. She lowered her hand but didn't face us. "I've messed up everything in my life, but I've kept telling myself that the one thing I've done right is made sure you two would have it better." She stepped away from me. "When you were little and in junior high, Mike, I saw you playing football, and that's all your dad ever seemed to care about. I hear about you in the same wood shop classes that he used to take. You were with that, that girl" — she noticed Mary and I scowling — "who *happens* to be Muslim, and near the end he was so wrapped up in helping those people. You are so much like him, Michael, and I wanted . . . I still want so much more for you."

I put my hand on her back. "You've done that, Mom. Mary and I are going to make it just fine. But we can't be so focused on the future, or on the past, that we ignore our lives in the present."

Mom hugged me, resting her cheek on my shoulder so that I could feel the wetness on her face. "I'm sorry," she sobbed. "I'm so sorry." Mary took a few timid steps closer to us, tears on her cheeks as well. Mom and I both reached out to her until she joined our circle.

"It's okay, Mom," I said. "I'm sorry too. For a lot of things. But we need to let go of what's gone wrong, and start working on making things right."

Mom, Mary, and I stayed up talking late into the night. The conversation became tense or sad at times, but we actually had an honest and respectful discussion about everything from finances to curfews, and from dating to household responsibilities. We even started talking about long-term future plans. Mom agreed to at least check into the costs for programs for registered nursing.

It hadn't been easy for any of us, but by the time I went to bed that night, I felt like I'd accomplished the mission Dad had given me to do something good for Mom and Mary. And it felt good to me too.

Tuesday morning came ridiculously early. I drove the Falcon to school with Mary, who was dressed in a leopard-print shirt with a cat-eared headband and whiskers drawn on her face. Today's Homecoming Week theme was "Zoo Day," and everyone was supposed to come to school dressed as their favorite animal.

She frowned when she saw me looking over at her. "What are you looking at?" She tried to sound annoyed, but she wasn't very convincing. Mom had laid down heavier restrictions for her than for me the night before, such as an earlier curfew and more frequent check-ins when she went out with friends. At first she tried to argue about this, but I think she finally figured out that if this deal opened things up for me a little at sixteen, life could only get better for her.

"Mike?" she said. "You know how you're always telling me what Dad would have said about stuff?"

"Yeah." I sighed. "I'm sorry if I was overbearing and —"

"Do you think he wrote any letters for me?" She looked out the window. "I'd like to read them."

Maybe my little sister wasn't completely terrible. I'd only read the very beginning of Dad's first letter to Mary, enough to know he had the same plan for her letters as he'd had for mine. "He wanted you to have his letters when you were a little older." I could tell she was about to complain, so I hurried to continue. "But I'll see what I can do."

"Mike?" Mary laughed. "You're still a dork."

Coach Carter was in a teacher meeting all morning, so the first chance I had to talk to him was in seventh-hour American History II. I didn't even put my books down at my desk but went straight to his. Coach let me stand there while he finished checking a test. Finally, he looked up. "Yes, Wilson?"

I unfolded the football permission slip and handed it over, with my mother's signature — her real signature — in big swooping letters on the blank near the bottom. Coach examined the paper for a moment and then looked up at me. "Integrity." He waved the signed permission slip. "Can you deliver Hard Work?"

"Yes, Coach."

"Then welcome back to the team."

I couldn't hide my grin. "Thank you, Coach."

Carter said nothing, but I could swear that the slightest smile began to crack through his usual tough expression.

I went back to my desk, catching nods and encouraging waves from Ethan and Gabe. "Hey," I said quietly as I passed Isma's desk. She stared straight ahead as if I didn't exist.

I still didn't have a date to the homecoming dance, though I would go alone if I had to. Laura had apparently forgotten about me as soon as I was off the football team last week. She was going to the dance with the guitar man, Hunter Thorson.

All week long, I tried everything I could think of to fix things with Isma. She wouldn't talk to me face-to-face, so I slipped apologetic notes into her locker through the vent. I didn't know if she found them. It would take more than saying sorry or writing her a few notes to make this up to her.

So I came to school on Thursday with a new plan. I knew it might not work. In fact, it might make things worse, and make a fool out of me in front of the whole school in the process. But at lunchtime, instead of going straight to the cafeteria, I took my full Army bag to the bathroom and changed inside a stall. "Okay, Dad," I whispered, remembering how he'd finally taken a chance with that girl at the dance. "Let's try that Cowboy Way now."

Even though today's homecoming dress-up theme was "Superhero Day," I still caught a lot of stares and laughs as I entered the cafeteria. The costume had cost a fortune in Iowa City last night, and I'd had to paint a metal garbage-can lid to serve as my shield, but I thought I made a pretty convincing Captain America.

"Good one, Cap!" Dozer yelled out.

"Yeah, look out for Red Skull," said Ethan from our table.

I gave a salute and the guys all laughed, but I continued my march straight toward Isma's table. I stopped only to talk to Mrs. Potter, who was on lunch-monitor duty.

"Mrs. Potter?" I said.

She laughed. "Yes, Captain America?"

After adjusting the itchy blue mask over my nose, I put my hands on my hips and stood like the characters always did on the covers of the comic books. "I'm going to have to ask you to take a phone call in the office," I said in a bold superhero voice. Now a lot of people pointed and laughed. Out of the corner of my eye, I noticed Isma staring at me, holding her sandwich halfway to her mouth.

Mrs. Potter frowned. "I have a phone call?"

"Not really, but I'd rather you weren't around to stop me from the superhero deed I must do next." I let her see the half dozen roses I had hidden behind my shield. "It's kind of important."

Mrs. Potter looked from me to Isma and back again. "Right. I have that phone call. And then, you know . . . the books in the library . . . should all be reorganized or something." She laughed as she walked out of the lunchroom.

This was it. This was the moment. *"Essayons,"* I whispered to myself, marching to Isma's table in all my red, white, and blue spandex glory. Isma watched me approach, her cheeks turning red. When I saw her put her sandwich down and get ready to leave, I ran to her, planting one foot on the bench seat to leap up on top of the table.

Everyone in the cafeteria roared with laughter and shouts of encouragement for Captain America.

"What do you think you're *doing*?" Isma shouted over the noise.

"Isma Rafee!" I said in my deep superhero voice. "I am on an important mission! I think you are amazing! You're brilliant and beautiful and so very talented!"

I jumped off the table to the floor, taking a knee in front of Isma, who turned in her seat to face me. Tears welled up in her eyes.

I whipped the flowers from behind my shield and held them out to her. "Isma, I may be Captain America with incredible super-powers, but I'm powerless without you. Will you go to the homecoming dance with me?"

She smiled, took the roses, and nodded as a tear ran down her cheek. "You know I will," she said, standing and pulling me up.

I let my shield clang to the floor when I threw my arms around her, squeezing her close and swinging her around. All around us, people sprang to their feet, clapping, cheering, and whistling. In that moment, it had nothing to do with my costume, but I felt like a hero.

TWENTY-NINE

Friday night after the game, the cafetorium had been transformed into a celebration with music and swirling lights. I'd cleaned up and put on my dress pants and a new shirt, actually excited for the homecoming dance.

"Hey, Captain!" Mrs. Potter said. She was one of the chaperones. I nodded to her.

Cody jumped up on stage with the DJ. He said something to the guy, who handed him a microphone. Arnath had this big stupid grin, and I knew what he was going to say. "Roughriderrrrrrrrrrrs!" Cody shouted.

"Mount up!" a hundred of us yelled at once. The music kicked up again, and people went back to dancing.

Matt Karn walked by and slapped me a high five. "Nice game, Wilson. Good to have you back."

"Thanks, man," I said. It was great that he had put on clean clothes for the night instead of his lucky game shirt.

"Yeah, nice game." Sullivan gave me a little punch to the shoulder before he went off to find his date.

It had been an awesome game. We'd beaten the Sigourney Sailors thirty-five to six. I hadn't scored, but I picked up a lot of pass yardage, and I had a few key blocks. The whole team had been on fire with enthusiasm, and Sigourney never really had a chance. Best of all, Derek, Mary, and even Mom had come out to watch us play. Things were going to be okay.

A slow song started, and right away I looked for Isma, who had been on the other side of the cafetorium talking with some of the people from the musical. Ethan and Raelyn danced close together only a few yards away, and Ethan gave me a big smile and thumbs-up. I started heading toward Isma, only to run into Denny, who was moving to the side of the room. He looked a little lost without a date.

One of the missions Dad had given me was to do something nice for someone else. On Monday, I'd invite Denny to join us at lunch. I admired his courage. In the meantime, maybe I could help him out a bit here. "Where you going, man?" I said.

"I was g-going to get some punch," he said. "I'm . . . really thirsty."

I put my arm around his shoulders and guided him back the other way. "Naw, get some punch later. Kendra Hanson, man. She's over there off to the side, and nobody has asked her to dance. Check out how awkward she looks, trying to act like she's not embarrassed that everybody has a partner but her. You have to help her. Go ask her to dance."

"She's embarrassed?" Denny asked. "What if she turns me down? What if I don't d-dance right?"

"Denny, you have a stutter, but you're still doing that speech contest, right? You don't know how that's going to work out either. That's okay. Just Cowboy it. Go ask her."

He nodded and went to talk to Kendra. A few seconds later, she smiled and joined him on the dance floor. He was pretty awkward, but they'd work it out.

I stopped worrying about it because right then, Isma made her way to me through the crowd. She wore this great black dress with a mid-thigh-length skirt and a V-neck front with wide shoulder straps. She smiled as she pushed back a lock of her dark, lightly curled hair. She looked perfect.

"Hey, Captain," she said. "Would you like to dance?"

"More than anything," I said.

We stepped close together and moved with the music. In that moment all our friends, the memory of the game, the school, and everything we'd ever known faded away until only Isma and I remained. She rested her head on my chest, and I pulled her closer. We danced like that, slowly, together, as a field of tiny bright lights spun around us into the night.

*   *   *

Dear Dad,

In one of your letters, you said you hoped I would find a way to pray and find my place in a church. I'm looking into that. In the meantime, I don't know about Heaven or any kind of afterlife. I have this idea that if I pray really hard, maybe God will let you read this letter. But even if you never get these words of mine, that's all right. I still need to write them.

I know you think you haven't been much of a father to me, being gone for so long. You've apologized about that a lot, but I know you would have been around if you could have. And the truth is, the war didn't end quickly like you hoped it would, and many kids — too many — have grown up missing parents that they lost in Iraq or Afghanistan. I'm very lucky. When I was a little kid, you were a great dad, and through your letters, you'll always remain that way.

You said you thought you'd done a bad job telling me what it means to be a man, but the truth is that you gave me something far more valuable. Because, you see, I think what our family was always missing — what you helped me find — was not just an end to the lies, but the desire to start exploring the truth. Not just my relentless pursuit of a bright, far-off future, but a more careful focus on the present. For a long time, I spent nearly all my time reading books about other people's lives. You helped me start making stories of my own.

You tried to tell me about one truth, the idea of living the "glory days" of high school to their fullest. But while I'm glad to be more actively involved in activities and friendship, I realize that all that "wonder years" stuff is only part of the picture.

What's more important is like what Polonius from Hamlet *said, "To thine own self be true." I'm not playing football to try to impress people or for popularity, but because I enjoy the game. I've learned the difference between high school stature and true friendship, and I choose the latter. I've learned you were right when you said that true friendship takes work, takes effort, but that it's worth it. You gave me that gift.*

And you introduced me to the Cowboy Way. I do my best to live by that philosophy all the time. I've even made a deliberate effort to be more friendly to guys like Denny Dinsler, so maybe they don't feel so alone. I don't know what I'm doing half the time, but that's okay. That's the point. Essayons, *right?*

For years, people have called you a hero, saying you fought for freedom. For a long time, that bothered me because I just couldn't understand what our soldiers were doing over there. I understand now. You really were a hero, but not, I think, for the reasons a lot of people believe. You went to Afghanistan to try to help, because somebody had to, because that girl Zulaikha and so many Afghans like her deserved better. You gave it all not only for them, but also for your own soldiers.

You will always be a hero to me, Dad. You did it. Your plan worked. You came back to help me when I needed you the most, and I'll always be grateful for the extra time we had.

I dream about you sometimes. In the dreams, it's like you never died, or you died but somehow came back to life, or you're dead but somehow visiting. In some of the dreams, we're riding around in the Falcon together. I wish you could visit, Dad. I wish you could come see the Roughriders now that we're in the playoffs, or that you could be there when I graduate in a couple years. I wish you could someday meet my wife, my kids. I wish . . .

I'm finishing this letter standing on the Runaway Bridge with a lighter in my hand. I'm going to burn this paper, and let the red-white sparks and gray ashes carry my words, floating down through the night, out over the water, borne by the breeze and current toward you.

Thanks for giving me my life, and for the strength to chase my dreams.

Good-bye, Dad.

Always your loving son,

Michael Mark Wilson

ACKNOWLEDGMENTS

Dear Reader,

Thank you for investing your valuable time with If You're Reading This. *Your support means a lot to me, and I promise to continue to work hard to bring you the best stories I can.*

If you've enjoyed If You're Reading This, *then you and I both owe thanks to a small army of good people. Since this novel was inspired so much by events and experiences from my life, a thousand times a thousand thanks goes to those who helped shape that life in such a way that enabled me to write this book. I offer heartfelt gratitude:*

To my family, with special thanks to my sister, Tiffany, who taught me about younger sisters, and for her hospitality on my many trips to New York.

To my fellow soldiers, the men of the good old 834th Engineer Company, later reorganized as Alpha Company, 224th Engineer Battalion, in Davenport, Iowa. Thank you for your patience with me and for teaching me to be a combat engineer. Thank you for your service.

To the brave men of Delta Company, Second Battalion, 135th Infantry Regiment in Albert Lea, Minnesota, with whom I served in Afghanistan, and especially to those soldiers in the Gentlemen's Smoking Club. Thank you for helping me get through our time in the desert, for saving my life, and for preserving my spirit. I could not have asked for better comrades. For the rest of my life, I am in your debt.

To Staff Sergeant Matthew Peterson and Staff Sergeant Ryan Jackson for answering hundreds of questions about the Army, and for teaching me what it means to be a soldier. Thank you for your patience with me. Sorry I didn't take more notes back when I was serving.

To my advisors and fellow writers in the Vermont College of Fine Arts family, too many to name here, but with special thanks to Jill Santopolo, Erin Robinson, Rebecca Van Slyke, and Monica Roe, who helped me through several moments of doubt with this novel, and with double special thanks to Clete Smith, Marianna Baer, Carol Brendler, and John Bladek for their thoughtful feedback on early stages of this manuscript.

To my most excellent agent Ammi-Joan Paquette, for giving me my first Yes *and for making my* Dream *a reality. Thank you for all your support.*

Because If You're Reading This *represented a significant emotional and technical challenge for me, I must offer thanks:*

To Al Ling, for answering questions about Iowa high school football rules, Joe Osweiler for useful information about Iowa farming, and Georgianna Heitshusen for advice about my characters' fashion.

To Carsten Parmenter for making sure my small-town Iowa football scenes worked right.

To Kris and Andy Dinnison and the team at Atticus Coffee Shop in Spokane, Washington, for allowing me to move in on Fridays, where I made a number of breakthroughs on this novel.

To Charles Young, Terribeth Smith, Chris Satterlund, and the rest of the fantastic Scholastic sales team.

To Antonio Gonzalez, Emma Brockway, Candace Greene, Emily Clement, Emily Heddleson, John Mason, Elizabeth Parisi, Chris Stengel, Lizette Serrano, Tracy van Straaten, and Annette Hughes.

To Paul Gagne and Bob Deyan for their hard work, professionalism, and fun in making quality audiobooks.

To Rachel Griffiths for the foundational idea behind this book, and for David Levithan's support, with special thanks to Arlene Robillard and Ann Marie Wong of Scholastic Book Fairs and Book Clubs for their support of this idea, and for the wonder of Scholastic Book Fairs and Clubs.

To Charisse Meloto, the ultimate superhero of publicists.

To Arthur Levine for a wonderful imprint.

To all the wonderful people at Arthur A. Levine Books and Scholastic. Thank you all so very much for always bringing your absolute best to everything you do. It is a joy to work with you.

To Cheryl Klein, my editor and dear friend. Your editorial genius is second to none. More important, you kept the hope alive through all my doubts through the long revision process behind If You're Reading This. For that, and for so much more, I will be forever grateful.

To my wife and best friend, Amanda, most of all, without whose patience and support this book and everything else would not be possible. Amanda, you are my life.

Finally, you should know that I owe a great deal of gratitude to my late father, Dan Reedy. He taught me about fathers and sons, and with his sudden and untimely death in my youth, he taught me about loss and grief. I could not have written this novel without his inspiration. Years ago, when I told him I wanted to be a writer, he told me, just as Michael's father tells him, to always hold on to that dream. I did it, Old Man.

Thank you once again, dear reader, for spending time with If You're Reading This.

Sincerely yours,

Trent Reedy
www.trentreedy.com